THE PAPER THIN SKY

JAS SINGH

The Paper Thin Sky

First Edition (Paperback)

Copyright © 2013 by Jas Singh

Published in the United Kingdom by Jas Singh

All Cover Photographs © Jas Singh

Distributed by www.lulu.com

This is a work of fiction. Autumn Lane school and the
characters appearing in this work are entirely fictitious. Any
resemblance to any real school or persons, living or dead,
is purely coincidental.

ISBN: 978-1-291-41433-2

PREFACE

Time is a slippery thing, and I find it hard to believe that the first draft of The Paper Thin Sky, my first novel, was completed over a decade ago in 2002 when I was still in my early twenties.

It has gone through various edits and revisions since then, and I am indebted to the very helpful insights and notes on the text which I have received from many of my friends over the years. Their invaluable assistance has greatly helped me to improve my work.

Of course, the choice any author makes on whether to accept a note or not is a very personal one, arising as it does from a combination of technical awareness, poetic intuition, artistic risk appetite and the author's own personal style and sense of aesthetics. The responses of any early readers are, however, always invaluable, whatever they may be, even if at times they are difficult to hear. To all of my readers thus far, I offer my deepest thanks.

Indeed, it is the encouragement and support I have received from such readers which has finally inspired me to self-publish my book. In the spirit of the self-publishing endeavour, however, I hope you will forgive any remaining typos or formatting errors which may remain in this edition. Any such mistakes are purely my own.

As will become clear, this book is about many things, but it is dedicated both to my parents and all of the wonderful mentors I have had the pleasure of meeting and learning from in my life, without whom I never would have reached my full potential in anything.

They have all, in their own ways, inspired me to write this book, and I hope it inspires you in turn.

Jas Singh, May 2013

London, England

for my parents

and for all of my mentors

I. FADING LIGHT

Chapter 1

There is a hill I know, from which you can get a view of the city, its roads and avenues, its streets, the roof tops, the glass office buildings, the busyness of it all, the melee of vehicles, the canals with their floating barges, and the rails. And the rails. There is a small station of four platforms at the base of the hill, and the trains shoot through or come to a halt, one after the other, and the P.A. announces arrivals, departures, delays and inconveniences and the people shuffle their feet uncomfortably as they stand on a clear day, waiting impatiently. And I am on the hill, resting against the bonnet of my car, arms folded, waiting, waiting. I glance about into the sky and the sun blinds me and I am dazed, for the time of a single breath. I look down and see the train approaching at speed. A freight-train, a lumbering juggernaut of a train heading straight for the station at high speed, undoubtedly passing through to somewhere - and I see it coming in from the left, still quite a distance from the station - and on the right, there's the train I await. It approaches and begins to slow, and I smile - soon I'll be with them. The people on the platform crowd the edge, preparing to board the passenger train, which is tardy. Normality. Yet in my mind I know something here is wrong, wrong, very, very wrong, and then it hits me. There's the sound of a train horn and the sound of brakes applied at high speed and as my arrival slows it's halted not by its own machinery but by the juggernaut itself which hurtles head-on into it and both front carriages are lifted directly off the tracks and head up into the air together and there are screams as the two machines come crashing down onto the platform and pin the group of passengers waiting there and there are the sounds - the sounds of the trains continuing their movement, their grind, their collision into one another, the juggernaut ripping up the smaller passenger train like paper tearing through the carriages and soon there is blood mixing with fuel seeping out through the twisted cages and there is fire and pain and agony and screaming. I shake uncontrollably. I am unable to move and the words in my mouth fall silent as I ask Him for some hope that this is not it, that this is not the end for them. I fall on the hill side in shock, shivering, sweating, and watch as the collision continues in slow motion now with the trains coming to a halt slowly and the screeching ear-piercing whine of the tearing machines lowers in pitch until it's gone and all I am left with is the idea that she speaks no more-!

I shake my head to come out of it. I breathe deeply as I recover, and push my waking dream deep, deep down below, and, with Autumn approaching, I slowly wind my way through the streets to join the morning traffic. I notice the sun doing its best to stay with us, to lighten our mood, lingering for one last lazy day. I put away the dream and focus on other things of importance. First day of the '02-03 school year, a new term, a new time, beginning anew. A fresh start, fresh challenge.

Oh God - the trains, the trains.

Deep breath. Don't think about the past. It never happened, they never were. Think about work. Yes. I've led English at Autumn Lane for a few years now, but never has the promise of a fresh term seemed as important. Been busy this last week, with the year's development plan to put together, I'd asked some of my staff - the more conscientious ones - to come in early to help get things moving, setting up schedules, going over curriculum changes and teaching schemes, pouring over the latest GCSE results, trying to work out which texts our older pupils as a whole would perform best with this year. It's a fine balancing act. Rarely, you'll encounter a pupil who's more keen a learner than his teacher is a master and it can be difficult keep up. But I still believe in leading from the fore. Being in the thick of it. Influencing not only my pupils but also some of my less enthusiastic colleagues. Some teachers can be so set in their ways, it's hard to alter their behaviours, but on the whole my staff are pleasant enough, and decent teachers. I should be grateful. I've heard horror stories.

Regardless of this, carrying all the administrative burdens of being department head, coupled with a tight teaching schedule and supervising a form group, is not easy - but I do get it done. I don't fear hard work. In fact, just now, it's exactly what I need. The energetic promise of fulfilment through my work, entering some new mental state besides silent mute despondency, and the thought of watching youngsters' horseplay, fill me with euphoria. After so much struggle of late, to have something positive to meditate on feels good, I'm bathing in warmth, feeling strangely weightless. Like I'm nothing. No thing. I'm not sure if I'm driving. If I am actually here.

I shiver. Turn Left. I've just remembered. It seems a certainty that this year is inspection year. Will be hectic, but at least we have a chance to show what considerable improvements we've made since our last Ofsted visit. Christ, I'm looking forward to an *inspection*? I smile, wryly. Things must be desperate.

And our pupils don't make life easy for us. They're good enough in class, but on the corridors? Out there amongst themselves? Animals. Sometimes I give in. Resign myself to saying that it takes a miracle to float a sinking ship. But that may be too harsh. Since an inspection has to happen, this is the best year for it I guess. We have some good kids. The last lot received their GCSE grades last week, and there was much improvement on last year, with my English department proudly marching far ahead as the vanguard.

Through my rear view mirror I spy in the car behind me a dog being slapped by its owner with a large plastic bottle. What on earth is she *doing* to the poor brute? I turn right.

There's a new member of staff on my team, but she couldn't make it in for our pre-term meetings. Not sure why, but then I can't force people to give up the beach for me. I just thought it would be good for her to get familiar with the place. Oddly, I can't remember her name. Henry knows the girl from somewhere, and he speaks highly of her, so he can reintroduce me. Besides, as our pastoral Deputy he'll be mentoring her for a while as she segues into her new job. I can't remember her name. That's no good. It escapes me, yet I helped interview her only a few months ago.

Then again, I have been otherwise occupied, since then.

I do remember something about her. She had grey eyes. I suddenly catch an eyeshot of my school, Autumn Lane High, and from here, from this road, you get a wonderful view of the entire campus, a small cramped building of red and blue bricks, steep grey tiled roofs and assorted modern-designed annexes feeding into the main building. I'm strangely warmed by the sight, and as I turn into our main drive a wholesome wash of feeling seeps through me.

Eyes. Her eyes. Serena's eyes. Gorgeous, huge, round and brown and they simply dissolve me if I hold my gaze too long.

Sometimes we'll be talking and she'll lean forward across the dinner table - like you would if it was just your first date and you want them to know you're interested. She'll look me slowly right in the eyes without blinking and I'll see her pupils dilate and then I'm hers and we're waking up together the next morning, husband and wife. That's us, that's what we are, who we are, the two we want to be, a keen light in her eyes, always.

I brake sharply. A kid darts past. Fool with a death-wish.

Or, rather, there *was* always something. Something in us, so strong, powerful, inside, which burned with ferocity, something in her eyes, a wonderful opalescence, perplexingly deep. Fading. These last few months - since - my heart dips as my mind digresses. Damn you Dean, bury it and don't think or speak of it again. Start afresh today. Focus. Be still inside. Let go of the past. She will speak to you again.

I put the gear in reverse, complete my parking manoeuvre, and as I lock my door a football lightly bounces off the back of my legs and a uniformed child apologises without stopping his run. Just as I'm about to call after the boy, there's a bespectacled gentleman by my side.

"Dean!"

I turn and beam, "Mister Lewis. How are you Henry?"

"Fine, fine. You missed morning briefing, but then you heard it all last week. How are you feeling?"

"Eager." I reply, dry.

"Yes," he smiles. "You look rested. How are… things?" he asks.

"I'm alive. You know how it is. You?"

"Fine! Elizabeth nagging. Constantly. Ok otherwise. Well, come with me Dean, Ms Dunley is waiting."

I frown and open my lips to respond but he's off in the opposite direction. Sounds familiar, my new teacher? I shrug, follow. Henry Lewis' hair looks greyer than ever. Of course, I won't tell him. We are friends after all. At least his wife's picked out a nice tie today. I smile at the memory of a horrific yellow strand he once wore that had attracted huge, bulbous wasps one Summer past.

The school is besieged by pupils, their bags flying loosely beside their shoulders as they rush about like flies with their friends. Occasionally, a new arrival, some uncertain year seven child, looks around and turns a pasty white colour as he realises he is lost, and then he strides confidently along as soon as another of his own kind is sighted. Their numbers swell around the sides of the building, their playground shouts echo against the walls. Set back from our main building on either side are the gym, the science labs, the technology workshops, and a block of temporary classrooms which impede onto the school lawns, a pleasant view of which is ever available to me from my classroom window. The children gather around a quad, where in the centre of the grass there rests a rather elegant fountain, out of place and unsure of its purpose, a feeling mirrored in the myriad pupils gathering to begin their yearly academic toil. Some crazy child in an attempt to get to the main entrance has cut across the quad and encountered the skin-headed behemoth Mr Marshall Jones, who is busy pointing and shouting "Fool! You can't read son? There's a sign that says no walking on the grass! Stupid!"

I roll my eyes at his screams, then the entrance of the school swallows us whole as we fold into its morning shadows and disappear from view. Henry stops at his office, turning to look me in the eye. He notices something in my expression. "Problem, Dean?" he asks.

"Um... Well – I'm afraid don't remember much about this woman."

"You will, she's very pretty."

I chuckle at this, and he points at me "Nice suit. New?"

"Yes. Nice tie. Wife?"

He smiles knowingly and nods, then opens the door with a flourish.

We go in and I make out a blonde young woman sitting by his desk, wearing a black trouser suit, peering through small reading specs at a teaching timetable. We stand there for a minute, and she keeps reading until eventually she notices us.

"Oh! I do apologise, I was trying to memorise this." She stands and smiles at us both, peering from Henry to me and then back again.

"No worries. Ms Dunley, this is Mr Dean Sekar, our head of English – you might remember him from the interview - I know he remembers *you*." Henry laughs. Ms Dunley smiles, a little confused.

I flounder. "He's poking fun at me, Ms Dunley. It's been a stressful Summer break, and I have to apologise, but - I don't remember your first name...?"

"Should I take this personally? It's Jennifer." She laughs and shakes my hand and I notice how short she is – some of the kids will tower over her – but she's obviously very self-confident. I stand, staring. "Something wrong?" she asks.

"No. No."

"Right," says Henry. "We've all got a lot to get through today. The Head – well, he's away, so I'm taking introductory assembly for our new arrivals-" he checks it off on his schedule "-and I can't really spend as much time as I promised with you, Jen. So, Dean, she's all yours. Jen, I'm still your mentor as we discussed, but, Dean, you'll have to deal with all the paperwork induction – I'm afraid something just came up. I can't do it, sorry."

I frown. "You want *me* to go over everything? I'm kind of pressed for time, Henry." I assert, a little annoyed.

"Well, Dean, you know how it is. Head's not here, so I'm in charge. Sorry."

"But there's not enough non-contact time on my schedule, Henry."

"You may have to stay back a few evenings then, I guess."

"Henry – you know I've made plans this week."

"My hands are tied, Dean."

"Well," I breathe deeply. "The whole point of last week was – to avoid – oh, never mind." I sigh, and something occurs to me. "So where is the Head anyway?" I ask, off hand.

He shrugs. But I catch a quick look. He's uptight. There's something he's holding back. Silence. He stares at me through his glasses and I know he's expecting me to just get on with it – he's the boss, even if we are friends, and I can do it, but I'm not taking on his duties tonight. I accept. "Ok, Henry, Jen. But we'll have to skip it tonight, I have to be somewhere. We'll make a start tomorrow evening, ok?"

Ms Dunley shrugs, and Henry nods. "Yup! Fine! Good man. Now if you'll both excuse me-"

"Are we still ok for lunch?" Ms Dunley asks as I'm half way out, and I think it's meant for me, but –

"Yes of course, I'll see you then." Henry replies, locks his door behind us, and then shoots off, briefcase in hand. I head off in the opposite direction, stopping to pick up my new form group's register on the way, and as we walk to her classroom she speaks quickly at my side. "Well, look, I hope I won't be too much trouble. I'm sure Henry-"

"What? Oh – don't worry. I'm used to it. Henry enjoys pulling things on me, I think. Keeps me on my toes. He likes it. It'll be no trouble, I just have things to deal with right now. Nothing major. It's fine. No big deal." I smile.

"Still. Sorry. For not making it in, pre-term. I wanted to but had some family business to attend to. I'll have to make it up to you."

I miss what she says. "What? That's ok. Don't worry. Let's just get you into your room before the kids rumble in, you're not on timetable for an hour or so, and it's a year seven group so today will be ok. Give them some introductory spiel, go over what you'll be doing this year with them, stretch it out if you need to, or use a basic textbook exercise. Just so long as you make sure they know who's boss." We reach her room and I hand her the key. She wanders in, her small curved figure dwarfed by the high-ceilinged class, her black suit a silhouette against the white daylight emanating from the windows. I remain in the corridor, far away on the other side of the door.

"Feel free to organise the tables however you want them." I gesture round the room. "I better go, my form will be coming in any minute now." I explain, just as the school bell sounds.

Seconds later I sense the mass of pupils entering the corridor from either side, as running kids move into my peripheral vision. My voice is suddenly beaten down by the noise. "Oh, and a tip. The kids at this school will respect you in class only if you lay down the law to them. A nice bunch of kids for one teacher can be a truckload of terrors in another's class. I'm up the corridor if you need anything, but try to be cold and hard today, Jen, they'll sum you up in the first three minutes. Don't smile at them! If you do you're finished."

"The pupils on my practices didn't mind me smiling!" She laughs.

"I'm serious."

"Oh. Ok." She says, happy, as I head off against the stream to get to my room, deftly dodging swinging backpacks and pupils' heads along the way.

Chapter 2

Several hours later I'm sitting at my desk during lunch break, marking some holiday work I'd set for my year ten – now year eleven – GCSE class. I'd set something to try and keep them involved, interested and in the game over the long Summer break, and most of what I've had back is encouraging, promising. The window's half open and they're all out there, running, shouting, screaming, swearing. There is a comfort in these sounds. Familiarity. I lower my lids for a moment and all I can see are Serena's eyes, deep, brown. Lifeless.

I turn my mind to a lesson plan. My new year ten group, first thing tomorrow, so potentially interesting. Well, relatively so, anyway. I wonder how they'll respond to the exam texts. This, of course, presumes any response on their part, but then I do have a handful of good kids coming through, I certainly do. I really shouldn't be so negative.

Ms Dunley popped in earlier, asked me where to find Henry. I recall she has a lunch date with Henry and I make a mental note to remind him that he has a wife and two sons. I took a moment out of my non-teaching time in the morning to go and check on her class. She had them sitting, bolt upright, listening, paying attention, following her every word. I was impressed - quite a classroom presence for someone her age and size.

I mark another exercise book and then give up. I lean back in my creaky chair. For some unknown reason I find myself wondering how or why I arrived at where I am now. Tiredness slowing my thoughts, I wonder back through my time as a younger man, and I remember.

I was lost.

Years ago, as an undergraduate, I had my head inserted in my books, pages upon pages of twentieth century literature and critique, and I was getting tired. Settled at my usual spot, studying for finals in an ancient university library, I had no idea what I would do after I finished, but I had thought about a PhD.

Slowly, awareness came, slowly, as is the way of certain but unwelcome realisations, I began to know what the academic world would do to me, know who I would become, and the answer saddened me. I had the unshakeable, intense notion that it would soon twist my form into that of a book-buried, boredom-inducing, brain-numbingly boffin-like, boring, boring baboon, with books for bananas.

I lacked direction. I found myself re-living old moments and their inherent joy and pain. I couldn't study any further. I felt the need to impart knowledge, not hoard it.

I remember now, and I smile. I was tired. So very tired. One night, when I'd finished reading for my 'existentialist literature' exam, I switched my shoes for trainers and ran, bathing myself in sweat, vowing not to study any longer than I had to, forcing myself to consider other options, avenues, roads, and with each sprinting step I came no nearer to my future. All I knew was that I could no longer dwell in the blank-firing world of academia.

There was a post at the university and one of my tutors wanted me to stay and work very closely with her on some detailed examination of some obscure author's texts. I explained I was tired of it all, and that I needed a new challenge. But she wouldn't stop, she just went on and on about it until I finally saw red and got out of there, slamming the door behind me. I then realised I'd left my jacket in her office, went back in and had to slam the door all over again.

Frustrated, lost, directionless, I was looking back to times gone by for an answer, craving direction, meaning, reason to my being. Lonely and upset at things which lingered from the past in which I searched for myself, one night I walked across Cambridge to see a friend. I arrived at her house, soaked to the bone by the rain, and she laughed at my stupidity in forgetting my umbrella and at the same time welcomed me in, embracing me despite the film of water clinging to me. I warmed myself by her fire and then, over dinner, I discussed my crisis of self-faith with her. I told her how I felt, how I suddenly had this urge to speak of the things I'd learned. She listened, enthralled, and raised her eyebrow and challenged my eyes, looking into my soul with those spherical mirrors, her eyes, projecting a deep light of their own through my darker core. She made me feel so calm. Content. Like I wasn't there. Like I was nothing.

Then she made the suggestion that I should teach.

Her voice when she spoke, soothed my fragmenting mind, and as we talked it out, the idea began to solidify, and seem right, and her words made so much more sense to me than anything had ever done. I made up my mind with her, that night, and then something more remarkable happened. I remember it so clearly. As I finished my wine and made for the door her hand on my shoulder told me not to go that night. Her eyes called me back. That night I fell and she was the reason.

I'm startled by the sound of kids running past the class, shouting obscenities. There's something I have to do just now but I've forgotten. For a moment I close my eyes and Serena meets my gaze again, silent, mute, uncommunicative. Deep breath. I sigh, place my finger on my desk and trace the path of the oak's grain from one side to the other, and consider the grain, the crevices, the cracks, the dips, on the surface. Were I minuscule, would these be mountains, valleys, gorges and cliffs? Dry lakes and flat plains? Would I find my refuge down amongst them from the things unresolved which stand watching over me? Could I find a hiding place.

I glance at my phone as it buzzes lightly on the desk, a reminder of something. Phone my father. Yes. That's what I have to do. The signal's weak on my mobile, I move around my classroom for a boost.

"Hello?" Dad answers.

"Um, Hi Dad, it's me – De" – rubbish – I move to the window. "Dad, it's Dean, can you - " it cuts out. I curse.

I pop out of my room and turn left to the exit, step outside and hit redial.

"Son?" Clear now.

"Hi Dad, sorry about the line it's temperamental - you know."

He chuckles "Yes, yes. Technology! Troublesome. How is everything Dean?"

"Quiet - first day back – everyone's tired already! Busy term ahead. Psyching up for things.

Inspection looks likely, so we're busy, you know how life is."

"Yes, I do. So can you still make it tonight?"

"Oh yes, of course, I just wanted to check the time-" I spy something unpleasant. "Oh, God, can I call you again in ten minutes Dad? Sorry – trouble." I end the call.

I just saw the tail end of a little boy being dragged around the corner of the temporary block. He didn't seem to appreciate it. I walk briskly over, and I hear shouting and prepare myself, and turn the corner and –

There she is, Miss Layla Larter, with her many facial piercings and blonde dread-locks, tie ripped to shreds but at least it's around her neck. Beside this white witchesque beast of a fifteen year old lumbers the massive Carter, a dark-skinned boy who always dresses smartly and wears sharp-looking spectacles. He looks quite the intellectual. He's currently twisting a chubby boy's arm so far up his back that the hapless youngster can scratch his head from behind.

"Fuck." Mutters Carter.

"Let go of him now." I boom, projecting my voice through Carter's head. He sheepishly looses him. Carter's grown. He's gained a few inches on me. Dangerous.

"Wha's wrong Sir?!" spits Layla.

"What the hell are you doing?" I shout more than ask.

Carter is about to speak but Layla pinches his behind and he mutes, an odd private language if ever there was one, but why am I not surprised? The little boy appears confused, and scratches his head, looking from teacher to tormentors and back again. I sniff. It smells of piss back here.

Layla looks me in the eye. "Wasn't doing nothing, Sir. What's it look like Sir?"

"Like you should both be arrested."

"Well, Sir, I dunno what your talkin' about, we just showing him some self-defence moves, he might need them, a kid his size. Isn't that right Ed-wad?" she addresses the chubby little one. I realise I know him, he's actually in my new year eight form, and I remember his old teacher saying he's quite intelligent for twelve.

"Um... y-yeah, Sir... em... yeah. Yeah, they were helping me." Edward confirms, looking down, and I know somehow that he's not going to tell me the truth, he's far too timid, fearful for his life. I bore into the two criminals with steely eyes. They look back at me with the usual looks of blank innocence. Moments pass, the only sound the little boy scratching his head.

"Sir, we was just-" Carter Mumbles.

"Shut up Carter!" Layla shouts.

"Both of you shut the hell up and get out of my sight. If either of you come near this young man again, I won't be pleased at all. Get it, sweetheart?"

"Where's the Headmaster, Sir?" she asks.

"He's busy." I reply, bemused.

"That's not what I heard-"

"Layla, get a move on."

She displays her pierced tongue, wags it up and down in the air, a sickeningly adult, erotic gesture, and then blows me a kiss, and takes Carter's arm and pulls the giant away. As the odd couple move off, I'm left with little Edward.

"Edward?"

"Yes Sir?"

"What was that about, really?" I ask, trying to tease out some small part of the truth.

"Um... nothing Sir, they were helping me... um... what she said... they're my friends."

I give up. I don't have the time just now. "Do yourself a favour and find some *other* friends."

"Yes s-Sir." He says, with a vacant expression. Does he even have any friends, I wonder? "Now disappear - and make sure you tell me, Edward, if they pick on you again, you hear?"

"Yes Sir." He looks at his shoes. "Can I g-g-go Sir. I need some d-dinner."

"Yes. Go on." He turns to walk away, and then something occurs to me.

"Edward!" I call. He looks back, and I continue. "Did you by any chance 'drop' your dinner money recently?"

"Um… Y-y-yes Sir…"

"Have this." I hand him a few weighty coins.

"Um…" he hesitates. Goes red.

"Edward, just go, forget about it, and never tell anyone, ok?"

He smiles, appreciatively. "Yes s-Sir."

Poor boy. He wanders off, a cloak of my sympathy enveloping him. I make my call and tell Dad that I'll see him around four-thirty. Then I head for my room hoping to God that those two keep low profiles this year.

Chapter 3

Well. I'm home. Sitting in the car at the steering wheel and holding it so tight my knuckles ache, but I can't let go. Mild outside but I'm freezing and I don't know why. Just holding on to the wheel, with my cold, aching hands. There's a pain that started up on my way home. Just between my shoulder blades. Someone is holding a gun against my back and pressing incredibly hard, and I'm just staring at the house, frightened to move for this illusory gunman might just fire, and all the while I'm shivering in my own cold blanket. What's happening? Why can't I move?

I went to see Dad. He lives in a small time-forgotten village not too far from here – a very peaceful place, where villagers drop by and chat aimlessly at odd hours of the day. Tonight, his neighbour called in. Margaret. A lovely old lady. She'd had a visit from her grandchildren and had baked for them dozens (dozens!) of cakes. She offered the leftovers to my father and I, and we'd sat there in the living room talking about nothing, sipping tea. Her cakes! Delicious. I asked about village news. The cricket club was in the grip of indecision. Should it serve tea or forsake English tradition and move on to coffee. Margaret favoured tradition, whilst Dad supported coffee, arguing that if the players were more alert they might just hit the ball for once. I didn't care either way.

This evening, I was just happy to be there, resting in an arm chair in his little cottage with a real fire dancing and warming me. We used to do this regularly, Serena and I. We would go over and listen to all the village gossip, and play chess against my father, and then the radio went on and sometimes earth-shaking political debates took place, and we all laughed at our toothless nonsense way into the evening as we played charades, fuelled by alcohol. But the last few months I had been visiting Dad alone, and I felt her absence deeply.

Occasionally, in the past, we would have watched films together and Serena and I would have fallen asleep on the floor as the credits rolled, totally exhausted in each other's arms and Dad would have crept out and gone to bed. It was warm in that home of my father's, where he lived alone, Margaret bringing him a constant supply of cakes, Serena and I telling him off for eating too many. But then we would bite into her cakes ourselves and as the crumbling surface gave way we would succumb to the lemon and ginger and carrots, cream and icing.

All I knew at that moment, this evening, was happiness. I was so happy to be there. To listen to my father's voice, which had cracked years ago and was finally moving into a sort of harsh but soft tone that would have befit an elderly teacher.

An elderly teacher. I was trying desperately not to think about school. With the arrival of Ms Dunley I had, of course, anticipated spending time working with her, and I'd planned for that, expecting Henry to shoulder half the burden, and then, on our first day back, he was forced to go back on his word, and imposed a few more evenings' workload on me. Like I didn't work enough. Well, at least it would be a good term. With good kids in our strongest subjects and an inspection forthcoming, we could really prove we'd achieved something. I felt so good about this. Positive. Proud.

But then Margaret started to talk about her grandchildren and how sweet the youngest one, Allen, could be, and his terror-inspiring older brother, Sean, and how lively but unlike they seemed when playing. She went on and on about it, and I wish I could have just listened, but I couldn't. Suddenly I felt as though I were in another room looking into all of us and my scars inside were itching, bleeding, burning. I wanted to go home, right away. I wanted to be near Serena and to hold her and sleep beside her again. Dad sensed my upset. He 'ahemed' rather loudly and displayed his annoyance at Margaret by choking on some cake. Somehow, she realised her folly, silenced herself, then got up and left politely. I appreciated that.

And on my way home, I felt good again.

The dip over, I felt happy about coming home. I just wanted to be near Serena and to hold her and sleep beside her again. But then the pain began – a man holding a gun in my back. And by the time I reached my drive I was frozen. Freezing cold and unable to let go of the goddamn steering wheel.

So now I'm holding. Tight. Tight.

And it passes. I take a deep breath and pause a moment, taking in the sight of the house before me. So quiet. Yet I know Serena will be in there, lying on the couch, resting. And suddenly my being is filled with love and it melts away the cold. When I step out of the car I notice the trees. Calm. And it's a warm evening, and yes the sun is there small and low on the horizon, fading to a fluorescent orange at its peak. So quiet and utterly peaceful. An abandoned football is rolling forlornly down the street emitting reflections of the fading light of day.

I head for the house with renewed purpose. Next time I go to see Dad she'll come with me. She will speak again and she'll be with me, always. My mobile phone starts buzzing in my pocket.

Cursing, I drop the keys, and take the call.

"Hello?" I mutter.

"Dean, it's Henry."

"Henry? What's wrong." I'd rather he left me alone tonight.

"Well. Um…"

I sense his hesitation.

"It's about the Head…" he continues.

"And? When's he coming in?"

He clears his throat. A pause.

"Dean – um… he's not going to be coming back."

"What? Is he ok? Is he ill?"

"No Dean, he's not ill, he's fine I think. It's not like that. Look, there's been a serious problem, and well, he won't be returning, it was confirmed today."

"What was?"

He evades the question. "I'll need to see you first thing tomorrow morning. No. Wait. Not first thing. Come to my office for lunch - I'll be out 'til then. We need to see how we're going to handle this. But this - oh, this could be very bad for the school, unless we get a handle on it quick smart." The phone shook with his apprehension.

"Why do you need me, Henry? What's going on? Where's the Head?"

He takes a deep breath, I lean against the front door, determined to take no business into the house with me tonight. "Well, Dean," he said. "That's just it. I'm on my own. As of today neither the Head nor the other Deputy are on duty. They've both resigned."

"What on earth? Why?"

"Well, they were both been caught in a… compromising situation."

"Go on." "No. We'll have to talk more tomorrow. I've had enough of this for one day."

The call ends. I stand for a moment. Then I turn the key and open the front door, my mind racing, trying to unravel Henry's cryptic call. And for an instant, the pain hits me in the back again, and I stop in my tracks, wince. Then it's gone. I shake my head and determine that I am not going to think about work anymore. I want Serena.

I wander over to our living room, and there she is, lying on the sofa. She's semi-conscious. There's a scented candle burning on the table, the only other light source a reading lamp in the corner. The music system is humming some classical music to her. She notices me and swallows. No smile. We don't speak anymore. Funny. I'm sure we used to. I wonder what she sounds like when she speaks. I'm losing her voice in my memory.

There is a deep solitude in this now dark place.

I go to her, and kneel down by the sofa, and – nothing. She's just lying here, as she has been for months now, silent. Her eyes. Leaving me. I wish I could reach her. I go to kiss her forehead, but she just turns to face the wall and I don't know if she's sleeping but I don't think she wants me here, so I leave her. Go and wash my face in the bathroom and look into the mirror and see myself and feel refreshed by the water on my pale brown skin. My complexion is so odd, a peculiar mix half-Indian and half-Caucasian in origin, a pale but definite brown, more Mediterranean in appearance than Asian. I look tired, but satisfied, no grey hairs yet. Good! I smile, and as I dry myself off, my mind takes me to the time when I was a boy.

Chapter 4

Twenty years earlier, the boy was washing his face in a basin full of hot water. Slowly the make-up broke off and floated on the surface.

An hour ago the young man had been on stage, breathing hard with his arms outstretched, perspiration seeping through his black hair and streaming down his face, mixing the paint. The young man stood alone, looking from side to side, into the distance before him, his mouth partly open, having just spoken the closing words of the closing speech of this silly play, having spoken words from the beginning of the comedy to its very end, having held on with concentration and focus within each scene bar one of the farce, he now stood poised ready to bow, receiving his applause in the makeshift theatre that was the school hall.

He bowed once and was then joined by his friends. They placed their arms around one another and swung as a Christmas song was played out over the speakers, and they felt alive, and young, their smiles spotlight beams on their faces. Then the director joined them on stage, a senior gentleman with an uncontrollable large white mane floating above and behind him. His head darted from side to side like a startled animal's, yet he looked upon his troupe proudly and then took a bow with them. And so the audience left, and as the school hall fell silent the players retired for the night.

The young man reached out to grab a towel and once his face was rubbed down he spotted three grinning figures to his left. One, a tall thin Sikh boy sporting a blue turban, was sucking on an inhaler intermittently. Another young man, a short but wide, broad, pasty-white boy came forward and shook the washer's hand. "Well done, Dean! Me and Aj loved it. You were great. Really funny. They all loved you out there! Especially the bit where your trou-"

"Yes... that bit was extremely droll... Richard was hysterical," muttered Ajeet.

"Oh God, I hated that part! But thanks guys, really." Dean laughed. "Did you like it, Yasmine?"

The third member of the party, an Asian girl, peered out from behind her specs. "Yeah, Dean. Loved it. How'd you do it?" she smiled, making eye contact.

"I just did as the Prof told me to!" The boy called Dean shot a pleased look at his reflection in the mirror. Average height and build for a *thirteen year old, his wet hair clung for dear life to his head. "Thanks guys," he said. "I really appreciate it. I'm glad you liked it."*

"You know all the girls were asking about you? Wondered which class you were in..." Richard giggled inanely.

Dean smiled.

"You're blushing, Dean." Yasmine said.

"No I'm not!" Dean chuckled and threw his towel at Yasmine, who then chased him round the small wash area, with the boys smiling as they looked on. Then, Richard, anxious at being excluded from horseplay of any kind, turned on the taps and jammed them with his hands, causing the water to squirt out in a thousand directions to cover his running friends, whilst Ajeet stood, silently, enjoying the spectacle.

There was a noise at the door.

"Mum! Dad!" Dean was startled, and all motion in the room ceased.

"Come on son. We have to go home. Hello everyone. You all ok?" asked the mother.

"Yes, Mrs Sekar." Replied Richard, quietly.

"We were just congratulating Dean on his performance." Ajeet said.

A pale Mrs Sekar beamed from the distant doorway, whilst Mr Sekar senior, his bronze Northern Indian skin glistening in the low light, spoke in far more serious a tone. "Ok son. We have to go now, ok? Come on."

The three youngsters, Ajeet, Richard and Yasmine, all said their goodbyes and shuffled out politely. Dean remained behind in the room, his parents looking at him from the other, darker, side of the doorway. Silence. Then Dean spoke. "Did you like the play? Did you? Is everything ok?"

Both parents smiled. "Yes we liked it," his mother said. Her hands shook slightly. "Now we have to go, so change and let's go. Your father has work tomorrow and-"

"Ok, Mum." Dean replied, smiling. He felt so light. He was floating. Joyful.

Minutes later he headed for the front of the school, his parents having gone on ahead of him. He dragged his school bag behind him, full of his home-made play costume, props, and school books, and as he passed the double doors to the hall he noticed a spotlight still on. He wandered in and paced up and down by the front of the hall, in and out of the pure white ray before the stage, taking in the set one last time.

It had been closing night and all had gone well. Even a collapsing portion of the set had been rescued by Dean and his very amateur stage group and the accident made to look like an integral part of the performance. The structures which had been so carefully placed in position by them suddenly, for no reason whatsoever, came crashing down, yet with adrenaline pumping, Dean stepped back onto stage, muttered a quick one liner to the crowd which had them in stitches and then proceeded to pull the set back together whilst the others looked on and somehow built it in to the play. It was a skilled improvisation. Dean was very proud. He smiled.

And then jumped.

Someone had called out his name. Turning, his eyes strained as the spotlight beam narrowed and came to rest solely upon him, and he could make out the shadow of a man standing on a balcony, aiming the light his way.

"Professor Lloyd? That you?" Dean asked.

"Who else Dean?" He shouted down. He often spoke with an un-menacing, manic sort of excitement, and even in the dark, Dean could make out his distinctive jerky head movements and wild hair following behind them.

"Did you like it then Sir? I didn't get to ask you when I was backstage – you were busy with-"

"Did I like it? I loved it! You were smashing out there Dean, my boy."

"Thanks Sir, but it's all down to you."

"Nonsense. I especially liked your improvisation." He pointed at the boy from seventy feet away. "Keeping a cool head whilst all falls apart around you. A great life-skill, Dean. Remember how to do it."

Dean shrugged. From outside the school a car horn could be heard.

"You'd better go." Professor Lloyd shouted.

"Yes. Um... I was just - looking, one last time? You know..."

"Understood, but go now, or else the caretaker will lock you in, and make sure you're in science on Monday. I'm going to blow something up! Safely, I hope."

"Where else would I be?" Dean laughed.

The professor's silhouette shrugged, and then he suddenly switched off the spotlight and Dean stepped back a few feet as the hall and all around him were plunged into a complete darkness. And *for a moment, the only thing he could see was a blinding negative image, a retina-burning imprint hurting him from the strength of the spotlight, two piercing somethings in his eyes.*

The light lingered momentarily, and then it faded.

II. COLD BLUE

Chapter 5

When day breaks, I prepare breakfast for my absent Serena, away in her own place, and as I step out the sky passes at an unnoticed pace from pink to amber and blue, and there are small shreds of drifting white, grey. I notice the trees slipping in the wind, and the soft bronze light behind them, and the leaves, browning, waiting, to fall. I stay for a moment willing the world to pause.

I walk peacefully and lightly into my class this morning, take the register, quietly have a word with Edward, who has arrived a little too late, even for the second day of term, and send them all on their way to their lessons as the bell goes. First period for me is silent, free of pupils, no teaching. I have nothing to do.

I take a walk along the English corridor, and as I step out of my room I'm immediately hit by the high-pitched sound of pupils' generic chatter, emanating from behind closed doors, echoing up against the ceilings of the corridors, and bouncing off the windows, before reaching the dead floor, silent. It is not the riotous sound of classes in disarray, more the measured banter of kids who have been set work, yet can't help but talk as they complete it, which fills the air and my mind. And yet, as I walk slowly past each class - each different, unique group - my presence seems to be felt, signified by a lowering of tones. I catch a sight of each group for only a second at a time. Some children watch the board, blank, as a member of my staff instructs them. Others fidget at the backs of full rooms, as a Shakespeare DVD plays and a teacher maintains a keen watch on the watchers. Whiteboards, blackboards, display boards. Kids reading out from books, straight-backed, trying hard to pronounce something hitherto unpronounceable, answers being teased out of reluctant, defensive, youngsters. Someone is shouted at for chewing gum in class. In another room a mobile phone goes off and is confiscated.

In the distance, Ms Dunley carries a pile of books into a room, backwards, but does not see me approaching. A flurry of activity occurs in the room behind her, as the teenagers awaiting her fall into a hush. And through the double doors at the end of the corridor two small, red-cheeked pupils, come running, and I raise my voice and tell them to get to their lessons *now*, and they apologise and wander past, looking down. I walk through the doors, cutting all sound from the classrooms behind me, and marvel at the sudden peaceful silence brought to this noise-filled world. Take a deep breath. It feels better to be here than home.

Better to be somewhere I count. Somewhere I have an impact. Make a difference.

I turn on my heel, and repeat the experience of walking down the corridor, reversed in space and time, and at peace.

Chapter 6

"Dean this could look *so* bad for us!" Henry bangs a fist on the table and looks down.

I'm leaning on the inside of his office door. This is really very unsettling. I've known this man for over ten years and in all that time I have never seen him so – agitated. His arm keeps twitching and he's playing with a pen and now staring at me.

"Dean – we-" he cuts off, then "have you had lunch?"

"Nevermind. I'm not hungry. Really." I fold my arms. "Henry. You know me very well. You know I can be trusted, so... I'll do everything I can to help-"

"You will? Everything?" Henry asks.

I frown. "Yes of course! But look, you have to just come out with it – whatever it is. I have no idea what you're on about."

"Sorry. I'm just annoyed. A little... frayed. It's taken me by surprise is all. No one saw it coming. But some of it was *so*..." he makes and indistinguishable sound, and then shouts "-it's a complete farce!"

Looking like a blind man who's just been hit by a truck full of guide dogs, he pauses to compose himself, takes a deep breath, and begins. "Ok. The Head is a married man. Yes?"

I nod.

"Well. He's a married man who's been having an affair-"

"So what?"

"-with the Deputy, who, as you know, is also a married man."

The idea takes a moment to sink in, but suddenly things are a little clearer, and yet - "so - my God Henry what's the issue? This is the twenty-first century! Who even cares?"

"Dean, Dean. It's not *that*." I bite my tongue as he continues. "A gay affair would be fine. We could deal with that. It's not school business. It's a non-issue in and of itself. It's something for their spouses. But this is… more complicated. Actually, what they did is downright bloody unbelievable. What they did!"

"What?" I ask, puzzled.

"I'm disgusted at their stupidity. Two men having sex is not a problem. I'm a liberal man - it doesn't concern me. But what they did? It's just stupid. About two weeks ago, they set up some kind of rendezvous for their fun and games, and decided they would film the event."

"I'm trying not to think too visually about this, Henry." I joke, and then immediately lose my smile upon seeing his expression.

"It's not at all funny, Dean. You know why? They picked the Headteacher's office as their venue."

"You're joking!" I say, shocked, amused, and fully aware of the proverbial flying through the air and about to hit the other proverbial. "Um, I'm reluctant to ask… but how did anyone find out? They would have pretty much been alone – unless?" I leave it hanging.

"Unless indeed. As if doing it here wasn't stupid enough, they recorded it using some old worn-out school equipment – remember those defunct media studies s-vhs cameras we never seem to get round to throwing out? Anyway, somehow – although you'd think they'd have been more careful for Christ's sake – they managed to leave the tape *in* the camcorder."

I curse, realising the direction the sordid tale is taking.

"Exactly. But you see, a pupil was – with the Head's permission I might add - on campus last week with some friends, working on some final year GCSE Media coursework or something, and just guess what he came across?"

This gets worse by the minute. Suddenly my new acquaintance, the gentleman with the gun, returns and is pushing the barrel of his gun deep into me. "Go on…"

"Well, Dean, the kid in question was Governor Smith's son, and being a dutiful young man, or one up for a laugh at any rate, he takes the thing home to his mother. She's naturally sickened, enraged and after contacting the LEA she calls a meeting with those two. So, after an embarrassing, tense dressing down – no pun intended I assure you – from the Governors, the two were told it would be best for them to go quietly. Apparently they didn't see eye to eye between them on what to do, and stormed out of the meeting. But we had confirmation yesterday. They've both resigned. And did I know anything about any of it? No!" He throws his arms in the air. "Why would they want to tell me? I'm just the one remaining Deputy. Not like I'm important. No! I only have to take charge in their absence, that's all. But do they tell me at the time it all happens? Do they? Do they hell. No, I get to hear about it yesterday morning – which is just *typical* of our bloody Governors - and since the culprits also resigned yesterday, I'm now in charge. For Christ's sake." Henry's risen from his seat and suddenly there's a thud on the wall to my right. His glasses have landed awkwardly and cracked. They lie

49

there. And all I can think is that he's practically blind without them.

"Henry... come on, Henry." I hand him his glasses back. "We can deal with this." Yes, we can really keep news of this nonsensical ridiculous scandalous farce from spreading amongst the kids, staff, parents, and the wider world. Right.

"I'm meeting with Governor Smith this afternoon. She has the tape. I'm going to ask her to hand it over to me, and I'm going to personally dispose of the damn thing. Goddamn it Dean, it can't get out. We need to get rid of the thing. Christ!" He gestures wildly and then lands back in his chair. I've never seen him so unhinged.

"Does anyone else know what you've told me?" I ask.

"No, no. I'll explain it in a briefing once the tape is back in my hands. Dean, don't tell anyone about the tape. Let's keep that quiet, I can do without the truth getting out. It's not exactly the impression I want to give parents who want to send their kids here. Better just to leave it ambiguous - you know - 'they resigned for personal reasons'. We've got enough on our plates for this year Dean, if I can avoid a media circus, I'd rather."

I shrug. "You're the boss, Henry. So what can I do?"

"Hey?"

"What can I do?"

"Oh… Nothing just now, Dean. I'll keep you informed. I think I just needed to vent, you know?" And then he suddenly laughs, hysterically, and momentarily the tension is alleviated. "Would you *believe* it, Dean? They taped it! At School! And lost the tape! Fucking idiots."

I nod, concerned for his sanity. "Goodluck for this afternoon then, Henry. I have to go. Lesson soon."

"Ok, ok…"

I'm about to leave and then I realise something. "You have spares?" I ask, recovering his broken specs for him.

"What? Oh. Yes. Nevermind. Sorry… you get going. Working with Jen tonight?"

"Yeah. Yeah. Don't worry about it. I'll take care of her."

Chapter 7

The end of day bell goes, and my last class bundle out of the room in their own hasty, noisy way. It's late afternoon and the end of teaching time offers me a brief reprieve before Ms Dunley is due to join me. I should be relaxed. And yet - I'm getting an intense tickling anxiety in my gut. The tape. That must be it. I'd forgotten about the whole scandalous affair for the afternoon. Too busy throwing misguided young fools out of my class and into the corridor to be able to imagine the Head filming - oh God - I'd rather not think about it.

Ms Dunley's a little late. I stand and walk across the classroom, switch off the light and notice it's beginning to darken outside. Winter approaches, and yet - a hot fire, warming, dancing, leaping, little flames, in my father's cottage in the village where people come and go as they please, Margaret bringing cakes, and *she's* by my side, staring into the fire, the light in her eyes. The world pauses the smile on her lips as she plays her hair with one finger. You are here, there, home, awaiting my return. But you're not. You're nowhere. Sometimes you can't even lift yourself out of bed for the pain in your legs. You're silent. So -

Silent.

How do I reach you? Can I say these words to you? Can I utter them without you smiling bitterly and turning to face the wall or will I have to once again watch you pause in the garden and stare blankly into the clouds as if you were awaiting life to return with the rain from the frail sky? How do I reach you. You lie, mute, as if speech would shatter you like glass.

I miss you.

"Idiot! I told you not to swear – what's your problem? I said it simply enough!" I can see the *real* idiot from my window dragging some tiny pupil – oh God it's little Edward - by his coat. The man infuriates me. I shake my head in resignation. Jones freezes for a moment and smiles, and I keep watching.

"Marshall! You have your hands full I see!" There's a brief chortle followed by a snorting sound. Oh God. Enter Mr Geoffrey Michaelson. The school's resident, extremely rotund, bald, drama-queen and gossip monger, amongst other things. Well-liked by some, for the quickness of his tongue. Michaelson of Geography and Jones of PE, the odd couple, both hairless, both wickedly, differently yet equally malign, stand there like a pair of Gestapo officers.

They engage in some light-hearted banter with the scrawny child Edward looking about him as if he's just been kidnapped. And then Geoffrey says something mildly interesting. Unashamed, I strain my ears to pick it up.

"You've heard, I take it?" Geoff asks.

"What? Anything interesting?"

"I'd release the detainee first, Mr Jones. Then I'll tell you. It concerns our 'leader'..." Geoff asserts cryptically.

Mr Jones, who has evidently forgotten poor Edward, is now repulsed by the child and pushes him away. "I'm letting you off this time but don't swear again!"

Edward bolts and Jones shares a smug smile with Michaelson, and mutters something, which I read to be 'little wanker'. This man is a nasty creature. I'm not actually that far away from them. I see them, hear them, but they can't see me. I'm in darkness.

"Marshall what I'm about to tell you can go no further because it's quite distressing and in the interests of the school I'm only letting the best of us know - you know - those of us who are really clued in, if you know what I mean." Geoff speaks with a mock seriousness that I find utterly unbearable. It would be refreshing if he actually cared for the school. But he doesn't. Yet from what some of the staff say about him, the way they praise him, I seem to be one of the only people who can see him for what he really is. I have an icy feeling that I know what he's about to say, and –

I whisper a curse. Michaelson has placed his hand on Jones's arm and led him out of earshot. Ah well. If *anyone* was going to find out it would have to have been Michaelson. And the world follows shortly. Crazy, crazy school.

What am I still doing here?

How can I *reach* you?

"You ok Dean?"

I unfreeze with a start. I turn and remember. Ms Dunley.

"Hello Jennifer." I say.

The lights go on. Her blonde hair's tied back in a sweet ponytail. Her specs age her a couple of years, but then that's not what you tell a lady. So short, with a wonderful curved figure, her pretty face cut with the determination of inexperienced youth. A very, very beautiful woman. But I'm not attracted to her.

"Dining on ashes?" she asks.

"No..." I smile. "I'm fine."

"You sure? You seem a little self-absorbed." She smiles, teasingly.

"Oh God, please don't say that." I laugh, as she sits herself down at my desk, I wander over and lean on the surface nearby.

"Mind if I ask you a question Dean? What brought you here? Henry says you were a high flier. Cambridge, wasn't it? What are you doing teaching in a state school? Wouldn't a private school have paid you better?"

I'm taken aback by her forward confidence. "Well." I pause. It's funny she should ask. Only moments before, I was wandering the same thing. What the hell *am* I still doing here?

"I was studying for finals. I hadn't worked out what I was going to do with my life – at one point I wanted to be a career academic, but, I changed. Quite suddenly. One day, I had this intense moment of self-doubt and I went to see... a friend and she suggested teaching, and something about that just seemed *right*. It just felt like the truest thing I could do for myself. I don't know why I lost the desire to study.

"How do I explain? One day you're fine. Happy. Content. Then you begin to doubt. One day. And then you're gone. Out of your old life where you were bored and straight into a new one. I don't know. It's hard to explain. You can hold two completely opposed attitudes in your mind at any one time, not realise they're both there and not see that the line between them is so fine, then one day you cross over, and then maybe you'll wonder again how you got there... Haven't you ever felt that way?"

"Can't say that I have. Sounds like you just changed your mind!"

"But it felt deeper. Maybe it's just me? My own uncertainties. Maybe you're more settled." She's more than ten years younger than me and it shows. She's bemused. I notice the quizzical expression. The sense of curiosity.

"Maybe you just think too much." She smiles. "How long have you been here, Dean?"

"Autumn Lane? Since I started teaching, so about thirteen years I guess. It's a long time to stay at one school, but when I arrived this place was in a far worse position. No one cared, the staff especially, and it rubbed off on the pupils, who just sat back and learnt nothing. It was *very* hard to stay motivated. First few years almost killed me. Well, not literally, but they were tough. I personally worked hard here, put myself out for the kids and they could see I was doing it, and they responded. I enjoyed the challenge.

"Slowly, the old crowd of disaffected teachers moved on, and a new, keener bunch of whipper-snappers arrived. Enthusiastic, full of energy. When Henry Lewis came in as Deputy he spear-headed some major changes in the pastoral care of staff and pupils, and our efforts paid off. Things just started to change. I knew him before he even got here, so he managed to persuade me not to leave, to stick it out – believe me, there were several occasions when I just wanted to go.

"But it can be such a rewarding job, when you have a group of kids who admittedly aren't geniuses, but are at least *interested* in learning. But then sometimes? I don't know. The extra duties, the corridor hassles, playground fights, picking up the slack of one or two choice members of staff that keep sending kids round that they can't control, disruptions to my lessons, late pupils, rebels, taking care of my form group, heading the department, the whole damn thing just wears you down. I think I may be due one of Henry's pep talks soon," I laugh. "Odd though. Sometimes this place reminds me so much of my own school when I was a boy - sorry, I'm rambling -"

"No! Not at all…"

There's a moment. She smiles and I'm tense.

"Jen… the first thing we need to go over is the staff handbook. Let's look at – actually, do you have your checklist?"

She interjects. "I have the checklist. Sorry… Um - yes - er… You're sitting on my papers, Dean." she chuckles.

"What? Oh! Sorry!" I lean forward and her hand brushes my leg. Phantom fingers disturb my insides.

"As I was saying we need to go over-"

The door is pushed open and Henry appears, beaming. "Dean!" he shouts. "Oh, hello Jen."

"What can I do for you Henry?" I suppose if he's smiling he must have good news, yet - why am I so anxious?

"Good news, Dean. What we -" he shoots Jennifer a quick look "-discussed earlier - all sorted. No need to worry. I have the... The records I needed. Meeting went fine. Everyone happily in agreement."

I'm relieved. Even if the tale spreads and becomes a suburban legend, at least we have that tape now. "Ok, Henry. I'm glad."

"Right. Just to let you know, I'll be making an announcement in the morning briefing tomorrow. Ok, I need to go – see you both around." He smiles and heads off in a rush. Over these last two days the pace of his heart and mind has quickened considerably, I'm sure. I'm relieved, yet -

"What was all *that* about? He looked very tired. But happy. What announcement?" asks Jen.

"Oh, it's about the Head. Long story. No need to worry, he'll explain tomorrow."

"I'll call him later."

And I think, yes, I *shall* remind Henry of his family.

"Anyway, so if we turn to page fifteen there's a-" I begin.

Then Henry's back. "Oh, yes, I forgot to ask, is everything going smoothly between you two? First few days are always an immense pain. Again, sorry I couldn't be more help."

I'm about to answer but Ms Dunley jumps in. "Everything is fine."

So, this late afternoon, we went over a few sections of the staff handbook. I spoke to her about the school's history, and our department development plan. Then I briefed her on the groups she would be teaching, and went over a few teaching schemes. We set up times for further, regular meetings between us, to go over the more menial issues, the practicalities of ordering stock, supplies, and books. I mentioned that, later in the year, she would probably have to shadow another tutor to see how a form group is run.

She left a little while ago. It's six-thirty and I'm alone here in the class now. Lights off. I'm relieved that I can go home. I'm relieved that I'll see Serena very soon. I'm relieved that Henry has the tape, although I don't envy his task of checking and disposing of it. And yet. And yet. Within me something is stirring and I can't for the life of me see what the hell is going on. I pack my things and leave. At least the tape is safe.

Chapter 8

A week later, Henry happily announced that he had been appointed as acting head of Autumn Lane High School. The Governors felt that a full recruitment procedure would have taken too long at just this point and in this crucial year it would be better to promote from within, to elevate someone who knew the school inside out. So they did just that.

However, the situation left one or two further gaping holes in our hierarchy, namely the absence of two Deputy Headteachers. The Governors, in their infinite wisdom, decided that the right man for one of the acting Deputy posts was the incredibly undependable Mr Geoffrey Michaelson. Of course, Geoff bolted at the chance to bully more staff, and, for some insane reason, Henry, who had on more than one occasion berated Michaelson, seemed to endorse his application.

Had I the chance, I would have begged him to re-consider, but then I am but a lowly department head, what would I know? Correction. I *was* but a lowly department head. At some point, I don't even recall the day, I found myself in Henry's new office facing him and Governor Smith herself, and for some odd reason I accepted a semi-promotion of my own, as the full extent of the re-structuring was unveiled to me.

"Time's against us, Dean." Henry said. "We don't see the point in going outside the school, and we know you're perfect for this. You can do it."

"What? I've only been heading my own department for a few years, and –"

"We know, Dean." Mrs Smith reassured me, the light reflecting deeply off her brown skin, the timbre of her voice almost as dark and rich. "We know. And we're impressed. And we want you to continue. Your staff are among the best here. We feel they can handle it with a little less involvement from yourself. As you know we're going to try and re-structure things so that there'll no longer be a need for a 'curriculum' Deputy – we're going to spread out duties amongst a number of department heads, including yourself. You'll be a right-hand-man of sorts for Henry and Geoff. A department head with some Deputy duties, as it were, and only for the coming year – you'll actually have to lead the other departments."

Henry leaned forward and took up the sales pitch. "Dean. I know we can make this work. This'll be a tough year for the school. But you and I know each other so well, we've talked time and again about what this school needs – we agree on so much! Geoff has his moments but he's sound enough… We know we're in the cycle for an

Ofsted inspection – I don't know when it will be, we won't get official notice for a while yet. But we know it *has* to happen this year, and we should start to prepare - they won't give us much notice. We think it might be a full scale assessment, so we feel we need a dedicated co-ordinator for the inspection, to get things moving right away and standardise our approach and paperwork.

"Other schools might handle this piecemeal but we both know we need a more disciplined approach here at Autumn Lane. I know that you can do this. Sure there'll be times when you have to do extra, and sometimes you'll be a sort of ambassador for the school - but that won't be too much work. In fact that's more Geoff's responsibility. I suppose you'll be staying back a few more evenings. But we're going to work it out so that it all fits together! You can have some more non-teaching time if you need it. Maybe we could take your form off your hands-?"

"No. My classes are my classes. My form is my form. I don't want to dump any of them." I say, resolute.

"Well then, if you want to. You can teach all your classes, you'll still head your department, but you'll just be taking on a few extra duties. It'll work well, you'll see. You'll be a sort of half-Deputy, leading the field as it were, and there'll be much kudos for your role in a successful inspection. It's a great addition to your CV, Dean, and I really need *you* for this."

I paused and thought. This whole thing made no sense! Geoff? A Deputy? And me? It would never work. Never. I'd be too busy, surely. Money had of course been offered, but I didn't care so much about the raise. I was sure I didn't want to do it, and in my mind I drew a line in front of me and placed their offer on the far side, and promised myself I would not cross it.

But then something inside me, some insane piece of me, hit self-destruct and I began to warm to the suggestion, and the line I'd drawn suddenly took on motion and moved toward me at speed, a slender beam of white light with no origin. Perhaps it was the fleeting fantasy of success that drew the line, the boundary, closer toward me, and although it would be hard work, perhaps this was part of my fate, to do great things for this school. To help make things *better* and to be successful here. As one of Henry's right-hand-men, I'd make waves, I thought, so -

- and Serena would come back to me and be whole again and we'd go and visit my father and sit by the fire and be warm and happy as we told stories of the warm daytime, way into the cold, cold night -

- this was it. An opportunity to make things work again. I crossed the line. It moved off behind me and I moved forward into my new duties.

I broke the news to Ms Dunley on the same day.

"Congratulations!" she said, rising up to kiss my cheek. She was soft, and her scent intensified and vanished like a firefly in the night.

"Thanks," I said.

"You know, I guess this involves a lot more evening work. But I live alone. So I don't need to run off home to cook dinner for anyone," she laughed. I smiled. I had that kind of freedom once.

Something inside me suddenly tried to pull itself back into the past, to a time of no responsibilities and innocence.

"Anyway all I'm trying to say, Dean, is that if you need a right-hand-woman to put in some overtime, I'm your girl."

I laughed, but she was serious, so I replied, "Thank you. I may hold you to that!"

"Please do." She muttered, as we left the building.

Chapter 9

So I wish, when things were once again looking positive, and I was feeling in control, readying myself for my new duties whilst going on with my chalk-against-blackboard, on-my-feet teaching, I wish I knew how it came to this.

I watched from the rear of a makeshift conference room, and Henry was there on his own, sitting at a square, battered school table surrounded by a mass of news-people, dictaphones, notebooks, cameras, microphones, the whole circus, giving a statement about an incident that allegedly took place at the school, and a couple of resignations that had been handed in.

How did all of this happen?

Henry Lewis did his best, fending off finger-pointing questions, giving simple, limited answers handed to him by the Local Education Authority legal team. He waved his hand at questions and muttered something in reply, then turned a very tired head to face his next assailants.

A man stood up and asserted the name of his paper, then paused, chewed on the end of his pencil, seemingly trying to phrase the thing just right, and said "what do you think of the stills we published?" There was laughter all round amongst the gang of hacks. Reporters. Poisonous freaks with daggers for pens.

There was a group of us, the senior staff, cornered at the back of the room watching everything, and for some reason Ms Dunley was also there by my side. She nudged me lightly.

"You ok?" she asked.

I breathed deeply. "No. I can't believe this. What on Earth happened? A couple of weeks ago, he said he'd destroyed the tape."

"You *knew* the truth?" I felt a slow burn rise on my cheeks at her words. I felt like a conspirator.

"Yes Jen, I did, ok. Don't make an issue of it." I snapped.

"I'm not! Just curious. He only told you and no one else?"

"Yes. He didn't want this to blow up unnecessarily. I would have done the same I guess." To be honest, I wasn't sure what I would have done, but I felt I owed him some loyalty. "Anyway he told me because-"

"Because you were friends before you were colleagues. And he trusts you, and you admire him. I know." She nods, not taking her eyes off Henry.

I raised an eyebrow. She'd been talking to Henry, clearly. "He looks so tired," she says. "I wish I could do something for him. One of my world-famous head massages. Learned the technique in India you know..." The sentence trailed off as she realised its un-befitting tone. I wondered whether I really *should* have that chat with Henry about remembering his wife, with this pretty young butterfly around.

I whispered through gritted teeth "Why can't they just leave it now? We know what's happened. The whole country knows, it's been on the BBC. What are they hoping to get from this? They don't care about a thing, they just want to drag us through every last bit of mud."

"You need to relax, Dean. They're just doing their job. He'll be ok. But you need to show some strength for him here. You're one of his first officers now."

She was right. Suddenly my acceptance of this bizarre promotion was put into perspective and I realised I must have been crazy. Merely two weeks ago, Henry had announced that the Head and the Deputy had resigned for personal reasons. Of course, everyone sensed something was being held back, some important piece of information, and although he already knew exactly what that was, who would lead the fight for answers and freedom of information?

Why, the bald Mr Michaelson of course, disseminator of all information not concerning him. Michaelson scuttled around and whimpered on about having heard something *more,* rumours that the two had engaged in homosexual activities at the school, probably only vicious gossip, you see, but what if it were true? He went on and on. The rest of the staff looked around, shocked, sniggered a little at the whole scenario and then left the meeting, satisfied by Henry's rather vague verbiage. That night, they went home, had a drink and a good old laugh about our former bosses and then forgot about it all as they unfolded themselves and made love to their spouses.

A week after that briefing, the promotions came, and our odd little trio was elevated. Henry, Geoff and I tried our best to forget about our over-excitable former Headmaster and his gay lover Deputy, and focussed instead on the future. But it wasn't over. It was about to come back and haunt us, the first challenge of our over-stretched responsibilities.

On my way into school one morning I stopped to pick up the Guardian and on the front page of a gutter rag sitting next to the Times I saw a shot of two men half-clothed, with portions of their bodies and faces blanked out for decency, and the caption "Good Head!" splattered across the top. Next to this, a shot of our school. I had difficulty breathing when I finally reached school and showed Henry the paper.

His response threw me. In a fit of rage, he kicked dents into the Headmaster's desk. Once he'd regained his composure, he knew what he had to do. By the afternoon, the BBC had been and gone and every daily newspaper had phoned in to ask about the matter and on the advice of Governor Smith and the LEA, Henry decided to hold a press conference, which he insisted on fielding alone.

So, today, during this press conference, I saw every ounce of professional pride and passion that he carried for our struggling school bled out of the man. A week ago, he had been fine. Newly promoted, he was relieved at finally having taken charge, despite the circumstances. Today, Henry Lewis looked barely alive.

The conference drew to an end moments ago. One by one the hacks, now tired and bored, decided to leave and phone in their own versions of the scandalous "Good Head" affair.

Fantastic. The best start to a year that a school could ever have! The group of staff I am standing beside dissipates. Ms Dunley walks over to Henry in this now empty room and puts a hand on his shoulder. He looks up, smiles, and lays his hand on hers in return. This bothers me.

Out of the corner of my eye, I see two shadows shoot past the room. And somehow, I know who it is. I walk out and find the troublesome couple whispering sour somethings into one another's ears. Carter, the beast with faux-intellectual eyes, sees me and pinches the girl's behind. Layla Larter turns to face me, purses her lips, and blows me a very adult kiss. Are these two really only fifteen? I wonder sometimes.

"Whassup Sir?" she asks.

"Nothing." I say, quietly and firmly. "What are you two doing here?"

Carter spreads his arms wide and returns a blank expression. "Nothin' Sir. Just chattin' yeah?"

"Yeah Sir. Jus' chattin'." Layla confirms, playing with her torn school tie.

"I see. Well, go home. It's nearly six." I turn on my heel and head off in the other direction. She throws a comment at my back.

"Hey Sir, so what else do you have on those old media studies tapes?"

"What's that supposed to mean?"

"Nothin' Sir. Just wondering. We have a right to know don't we…"

I smile wryly.

"So. Who sent it to the press then, Sir?" she asks. Slowly. Cautiously. Looking me in the eye. I think about it.

"Why don't *you* tell *me*…"

I pause. Silence. She just looks me in the eye.

"I don't know, Sir!" she shrugs, an all too exaggerated gesture.

"I... don't... know... Sir. I bet you bloody well do."

She puts on a look of pain. "Sir! How could you say that! We're just chillin' and you making all these accusations! I'm hurt." She smiles and blows that kiss again, blowing it over her lip ring. God damn it, I *hate* it when she does that.

"Listen you two." I point at each in turn. "Stay out of this, and out of trouble. I've warned you enough times. You've been excluded once already this term and we've only been here a month. You keep screwing up this year and you're finished. Now get out of the school. Go." I turn and walk away, but she can't help having the last word.

"Well, Sir, what can I say? People have a right to know how fucked up this place is!"

I spin quickly to respond, but they're gone.

When I return to Ms Dunley and Henry they're deep in conversation. I join in and we argue the matter out a little. Unimportant as it now seems, we're curious as to how the tape reached the press, especially as it was previously in the hands of a school Governor.

Henry insists he destroyed it, but is shocked at the reaction of some of the staff and Governors, who seem to be pointing the finger his way, as if he would have yielded the weapon used in his own battering. Someone must have given it to the press before returning it to him but Governor Smith certainly wouldn't do that. And why would the press wait? They would have published straight away. The news reports mentioned something about a source inside the school. A teacher? A pupil? Both? We'd never know.

In any case our powerlessness to stop this nonsensical juggernaut is apparent. But I have a thought. Layla and Carter - were *they* the ones who somehow got hold of a copy and sent it on? We discuss it, a little, and I'm intent on grilling them for it, but then I'm told to calm down by Henry - nothing could be done even if they were the ones. Nothing.

Chapter 10

Thanks to the fickle nature of the press, interest in our school had waned by the turn of the month, but the press conference had marked the beginning of a gruelling two weeks for Henry, as he responded to one interested media party or another, and occasionally the odd reporter was caught snooping about on site and asked to leave. They wouldn't give up. They were determined to unearth some other corpse at our school, and seemed dreadfully frustrated at the fact that Autumn Lane was usually a pretty mundane, dull place to be.

On occasion, Henry relied on me for support, as TV people, press people, even politicians became involved and had their say, and I hit on an idea. I suggested to Henry that, since I was about to start co-ordinating efforts for an inspection, I might in due course turn this around by inviting the press back for a feature on our improving standards. Henry beamed at me, seemingly pleased at having me by his side.

He told me to keep the idea on ice, until the 'Good Head' thing had died completely. Instead he pointed at a number of bundles of paper he'd gathered on his desk and told me to get to work, to have a strategy for inspection-preparation ready by the end of the month. I swallowed, realising that my days were about to get longer, and longer, and longer. Why on earth had I agreed to this?

And where was Mr Michaelson? Who knew. He seemed to be burying his head in the sand somewhere, or drowning in his ever-present coffee mug, leaving Henry and I to pick up the slack. I was irritated by his non-presence, but still, Henry defended his appointment as acting Deputy. Why? Even Ms Dunley was more helpful. She'd been steadfastly refusing to go home each evening until she'd done something to help us. It was nice to have an upstart at the school, passionate about all the right things.

I'm driving home now and I'm exhausted. I've been so busy, skipping lunch on so many days and not being able to think of anything except for school work, and staying in 'til almost eight every night to make sure it's all done. Already I'm beginning to see that the rosy picture Henry painted of our Head-Deputy-Co-ordinator team was more than slightly glossed over.

God, there is just too much to be done for this school. All of our paperwork has sat gathering dust for a number of years, and several teachers are quite obviously going to fail to impress the inspectors. A pupil in my form, caught by Henry as he happened to be walking past, had been repeatedly throwing a pencil at his Religious

Studies teacher and the foolish tutor had simply been picking it up and handing it back to him.

I did get through that barrage of paperwork from Henry. But, as I ran my first meeting with the department heads, I found them to be unenthusiastic and unresponsive to me. I ran through the points the inspectors would cover: the type of school we were, the expected and achieved standards, the quality of teaching and management, improvements from six years ago. Their eyes began to glaze over, and I was back before a class of disinterested children. I realised this role was going to take tact and a lot of diplomacy.

I shift uncomfortably in the driver's seat, as something heavy sinks to the bottom of my gut. I'm looking forward to resting tonight when I get home but then I realise what awaits me there is hardly a bundle of joy. For the whole Summer Serena has been lying there, unresponsive to anything. I used to take her with me to places, my father's house, shopping, wherever. But since that day she hasn't wanted to go anywhere. Not that she tells me. I just know it. Speech, her nursing career, housework, cooking - she doesn't care for any of it now.

She shrunk so far into herself that fateful day, I don't know how I'm supposed to reach her, or even if I can. She's oblivious to what's been happening in my life, I've sat and told her about the promotion, the press, everything, but I don't get a single word back.

And as I become busier and unable to spend any time with her, she walks further away towards the horizon, when I'm not there she eats only pieces of fruit from the kitchen – things she need not cook – she's losing weight and becoming frail, light, empty. And as I try to follow her my legs fail me. I wish I could go home, to *something*. Anything. A voice. A word. A moan. A smile. Anything!

But I've only just pulled into the drive and my phone's buzzing. God, why don't you leave me alone, world, I'm tired, hungry and God knows what time it is.

"Yes!" I shout into the mouthpiece.

"Son? Is everything ok?"

"Dad? What? What do you mean?" I snap.

"Well. I was expecting you…"

I'm about to reply and then I stop open-mouthed. Oh my God. He *was* expecting me. I arranged it over a week ago. Oh shit. I've never forgotten before. Shit.

"Oh Christ… Dad look, I'm so sorry… I had to attend this meeting-"

"You should have phoned me."

I swallow. "Look I know, and I'm sorry, I just... things have been so hectic after the promotion. We've got problems at the school and-"

"Dean, maybe I'm not making myself clear. You should have phoned. You think I like sitting here on my own tonight? I could have been doing other stuff this evening but I needed some advance warning... if you can't be *bothered* to see me, I-"

"Oh for God's sake. I've been so busy, Dad. I don't have any time to even think right now, so just-"

"Just what?"

"Just shut the fuck up!"

There's a shocked pause on the other end. Then the phone dies. Oh shit. Shit. I didn't mean to lose it. Not with him. I storm into the house, throw my briefcase down and stride into the lounge only to find the television on, muted, staring blankly at me, and my wife, lying on the couch staring blankly at the floor. I sit opposite.

What the hell kind of insane situation is this? This isn't life.

"How are you?" I ask her. I say it quietly. She looks up at me momentarily, her hair a mess, her face tired, her eyes half closed, her body limp, weak, and I wonder who I am watching. Could this be my wife? Could this really be her, she who took care of me as my friend throughout university and she who inspired me to become a teacher? She who nursed sick little babies at the hospital, a vocation for which she had such passion? She who makes – no, made - love to me? For all I see now is an empty shell, nothing of that past remains, what has happened here? You aren't her. What the fuck is this! What have you done with her!

"Why can't you just respond?"

Her eyes look startled and they gaze up at me. Nothing else moves. Not her lips. Not her head, nothing. God damn it!

"This is crazy! You think it's been easy for me, living with our loss? You think I can take much more of this? Things are happening in my life Serena and where the hell are you, Serena? You're nowhere. For God's sake come back to me! If I mean *anything* to you then please come back."

I can tell by her eyes she's scared, and before I know it I've knocked over a vase and smashed it, scattering a handful of dry dying flowers all over the panelled wood flooring. I kneel down before her, and look into her brown dim eyes.

"Where are you? Come back. Please, just a little at a time. I *need* you…" I leave it lingering. Awaiting some response. But… Nothing. Even her breath is so faint that she may as well not be there at all. Nothing. Is she even real? Is she really here? What happened? Did she die? Did I? Am I crazy? Insane? Please… No… let me be sane. Allow me this peace.

She fixes her eyes on me and when they close they exude tears. So many tears, her body jerks as a body does when crying from the depths. But she makes no sound, not even a whimper, nothing, and I cannot watch.

I cannot watch anymore.

Somewhere, deep, inside, something, a thread, stands up on end, splits, waiting to be pulled, and then the untying begins and I sense it, and I let out a long scream and run from that insane television lounge and out of that house. I slam the door, and I run and run in my shirt and tie with night coming I run and run around the same roads, those houses full of complete people with no pain, past the parked cars and in and out of the shadows between the street lights, existing only a flash of light at a time, no more, again and again I run, my footsteps echo but no one sees me, watches me, or tells me I'm mad, and I run until I am too tired to move, I let out a scream and I stand, panting, by our house.

Then I'm in my motionless car. So tired and so utterly fed up. I grit my teeth and grip the wheel so hard my forearm muscles cry for mercy and suddenly the gun in my back returns and I feel a sharp pain in my eyes as the bastard finally shoots. My head hits the wheel and I dream -

- that I'm in the lounge once more. Looking at my wife. She is absent, staring at the ceiling. And then she looks at me, and smiles one last time and it's gone, the image dissipates. I float away, my whole being lifts and is grounded elsewhere in moments.

I'm cold. Shaking. I'm standing by some trees on the edge of a faceless place and before me the water stretches out for miles and miles and in the distance, yes, I see her, standing on water, a miracle. And then I look down and see what I have mistaken for water is in fact ice. Smooth, blue, translucent ice, beneath which the waves and currents of a vast, deep ocean move ceaselessly, silently fighting one another.

Silently. Fighting.

And I see her there in the middle of that great ocean and for a moment she notices me and smiles as if she knows me and her hand reaches out and she waves weakly and then the ice caves in! Beneath her delicate feet the ice suddenly buckles and without moving her hand - her sweet hand - she sinks in an instant, unable to respond, and my heart ceases to function and I leap onto the ice and run with all my energy screaming silently in agony the ice cracking wherever I place my feet and as I approach the spot I leap into the air to follow her -

Don't leave me!

But I cannot follow for when I land I hit nothing but ice as it has closed behind her and all that remains is a small gap and as I land I realise it is too late, that no amount of pounding or punching at the ice will allow me to follow her down. I look down the hole and she is shrinking exponentially but being rocked side to side like a leaf blown about in the wind her clothing skin-tight her hand outstretched reaching out to me, but she goes down. Down, down, down her eyes looking up, vacant, drowning, sinking - I plunge my head into the ice and it freezes me in place. I manage to puncture the ice with one hand and I feel something slip down my finger and it sinks - something - a ring - our ring... and she has become a tiny tiny speck, indistinguishable, but I'm frozen. And she goes on without me and becomes smaller and smaller and the pain becomes an emptiness, a nothing.

Soon, she vanishes, and I am left there watching, my arm outstretched and frozen in position by the ice, as my tiny memento, my wedding ring, floats down after her, like a final burst of love.

Chapter 11

"Now stand back class! Quick!" shouted the professor as his untamed hair did a summersault, and he threw a handful of dusty powder across the naked flame of a bunsen burner. The pupils held their breaths as a ball of flame appeared, rose up slightly towards the ceiling and then dissipated, and they all laughed.

"Ok class I hope you enjoyed that..." a paper aeroplane flew past him and landed on the bunsen, inflaming instantly. He bounded over to the fire, extinguisher in hand. A short burst of foam later, the crisis had passed. But the master was not at all pleased with his apprentices.

"You young fools. That could have been dangerous! Who threw it? Who threw it?!"

Silence. The professor's head darted from one pupil to another and he repeated the question. Dean, Ajeet and Richard all tried to hide behind one another yet were unable to manage the impossible, as the professor continued to glance around the room in his own unmistakable way. It was too late. He knew.

"Mr Sekar. Remain behind please. Everyone else away you go... I'll be explaining that little explosion in our next lesson, so remember it!"

The bell rang out, calling the pupils home. The room emptied and Dean sat with a guilty expression staring into the end of a gas tap on the lab table before him. As the door slowly closed behind his classmates, Dean's gaze rose and followed his teacher. The professor walked backwards and forwards behind his bench, past an immense copy of the periodic table, a diagram of the internal workings of the body, a 'hazardous liquids' notice, and then over to the other side of his blackboard where he stood before a safety display.

"Dean my boy. Care to explain why I had to rescue the class just then?" The professor asked, wandering over to his table. Dean shrugged.

"Well, Sir... it wasn't that big a fire. I'm sorry. Just thought it would be funny." Dean shrugged. He came over and sat down beside Dean and bore his eyes into him, stern-faced, until Dean shrank.

Then he smiled. "No harm done. But don't do that again... ok?"

Dean relaxed and nodded.

The professor took up a test-tube in his hand and tapped the top with his finger. "So tell me young Mr Sekar, how has life been treating you after the play?"

"Ok, I guess."

"Come now, Dean. The whole school was talking about you well into this New Year, wondering what next from this talented young man!" the professor's hair flowed over to the left momentarily, then back again.

Dean beamed and blushed at once. "Well… I dunno. I dunno. It's nice I guess."

"The girls noticed, I hear." Professor Lloyd chuckled. Dean reddened further.

"One or two, yeah… heheh…"

"Don't worry Dean. These things are important. You'll see. Plenty of time for that though. Just make sure it doesn't go to your head! Make sure you keep your eyes wide open. Always. So much goes on around you at any one time my young friend. Don't be a fool to amusement and enjoyment - but do have your fun, and live in those moments of happiness. They don't last forever young man. They don't last forever."

Dean frowned and swallowed. And then shrugged. As much as he valued the professor as a friend and mentor, often the import of these lectures escaped his grasp.

"Your friends are waiting for you, you know," the professor said, tidying up some equipment. Dean shot a look at the door window. Yasmine peered back at him and gave a small wave. Dean grinned, and her eyes returned the gesture. In the background, Ajeet and Richard stood throwing a tennis ball from one side of the corridor to the other. The ball smacked Richard in the face. Dean chuckled. The professor glanced at the door, then at Dean, and then back to the door. He smiled.

"What is it professor?" Dean asked.

"Nothing! Not for me to say anyway. Yet I do wonder how long it will take for you to see. Tell me Dean are you a happy young man? Everything ok now at home with your parents?"

Dean shrugged once more. "I guess so. They still fight sometimes. They don't talk to me much then. Mum gets tired easily. I don't know, Sir, I don't know. I'm fine. Really. Shouldn't I be?"

"You should be! You should be." He paused and looked sharply at the door to Dean's friends

and then back to Dean, as if he was waiting for someone else to join them. Then he grew distant momentarily, and for a moment his hair rested placidly on his shoulders, and he stopped gesturing and tidying, and his voice became a soft quiet inaudible sound, and his eyes blanked. "You should be happy..." he said, and smiled. "I remember when I was younger, free of all cares. Happy, innocent. you know? Hmm..." He brooded for a moment. "Do you know what the final lesson is Dean?"

Dean shook his head, unclear as to the professor's point.

"Well." The teacher continued. "The last inno-"

A technician suddenly appeared at the doorway, and called the professor over. "Sorry Professor Lloyd, we'll need a signature for these chemicals, and you'll need to check them."

"Ok, no problem!" The professor's voice had raised once more, and as his hair regained animation, he headed for the door at full speed, and shouted over his shoulder. "Good talking to you Dean! But don't you dare throw paper planes in my lab again. Let yourself out..."

Then he was gone. Dean sat there smirking, and then his friends were with him. "Hey Dean, what's he said? Detention?" Richard asked.

"No!"

"Of course not Richard, Dean here could burn down the entire school if he wanted to and they would simply turn a blind eye," Ajeet teased.

Yasmine placed an arm around Dean "You two leave him alone… he's the school hero…"

"Oh yeah Dean, I gave Sarah your phone number." Richard said excitedly.

"What?" Dean asked.

"And I told Aysha that you don't like her."

"What?" Dean's jaw dropped.

"Well I thought you'd had a fight with her-"

"Yeah, but - Oh bloody hell Richard I was trying to fix things up with Aysha not get rid of her. Damn it. Nevermind." Dean shook his head in resignation.

"So which will it be Mr Sekar… Sarah or Aysha? I say Aysha. She can read." Muttered Ajeet.

"Oh you would say that you brain-box!" Richard responded. "I say Sarah – she has big-"

"Guys. Stop." Dean said. "I dunno. I dunno who I like."

Yasmine's arm fell away and Ajeet sucked on his inhaler. Silence.

"Hey," said Richard. "I just had an idea…" his gaze moved to the front of the class.

Ajeet rolled his eyes. "Why oh why do I not like the sound of this?"

Yasmine giggled. "I think I know what you're thinking Richard…"

They looked over to the front bench where Professor Lloyd had given his demonstration. There the burner sat, enticing them. Yasmine and Richard ran over to the bench.

Dean and Ajeet exchanged nervous glances.

Moments later there was a bright flash, the sound of a minor explosion, and the sight of four laughing, fearful school pupils running down the science block corridors.

"He will kill us! He will kill us all!" shouted Ajeet.

"Shit!" Richard panted. "I didn't mean to burn the ceiling! Shit! Shit! Shit!"

They ran, Dean and Yasmine laughing, her hand grabbing at Dean's coat. Then someone stepped out from behind a corner. Dean fell. He'd hit something. A large, immense creature, whose form now clouded Dean's entire vision.

"Watch where you're fucking going!" The larger boy bellowed.

Dean shook his head and realised his mistake. The behemoth before him was unhappy, and before Dean could apologise the child-giant had reached down and lifted him to his feet by the scruff of his jumper. Ajeet took a number of steps back.

Richard came to Dean's side. "Let him go Arnold."

Arnold turned his head slowly, as if there were no other way for a head so large to be moving, and spat down in Richard's direction. "Shut the fuck up. Dick."

Richard remained there. Silent.

Dean found himself being dragged over to the wall, and Arnold's face was all he could see, that great big immense head of pain, shouting jealously into his face, breathing all over him. "You know what your problem is Dean, you got no fuckin' sense you think you're so smart with

91

your acting shit - you're a pussy! A pussy! I'm gonna bust your face for you one of these days - just watch."

Dean breathed quick, and stared over his shoulder at Yasmine, and pleaded with his eyes. She looked torn. She came over, and put her hand on Arnold's arm.

"Hey, Al. Come on, he just made a mistake, that's all. Come on. He's sorry."

The head of Arnold turned over to face the girl and looked her up and down. "I don't like him, Yas. He's a pussy boy and he knows it."

Then she reached her other arm around the monster and placed her lips to his and he responded and as they kissed Dean could not escape either the grip or the view of his best friend Yasmine kissing her brutal boyfriend. Ajeet and Richard shook their heads in disgust and looked away. But Dean saw it all, and as she passed her other arm around the brute he loosened his grip and Dean escaped, and the three boys ran to their freedom whilst the two embraced and kissed, their eyes closed.

Chapter 12

"Dean, I really appreciate this you know - Dean?"

"What?" I ask. It's nearly seven and Ms Dunley is riding home in my car. Her own is in for a service and she needed a lift and I'm sure she's been talking about *something* beside me but I have been a million miles away in another place, somewhere long ago.

I smile. I like it there. It's warmer, full, a pregnant time, more joyful than this place of cold nothing now. I have the curious sensation that I cannot see the thing fully, for what it really is or what it really was.

"You ok, Dean?" she asks. Frowning behind those specs of hers.

"Yeah. Yeah. Just really, really tired. Too much going on all at once. So unexpected, you know?" I glance at her. I'm pushing the speed limit. "This promotion thing, stuff at home. My father's not talked to me in a while – I don't know. Nevermind. I - I've had difficult times before, I've pulled through."

Deep inside, my heart, my thoughts, and my mind have all been taking me there, to that warm time when I was young, where the snags in the thread lie buried.

"Dean. Um - look. Oh hang on, left here - and it's a block of flats right at the bottom of the road," she points, I obey. "Um - yeah, like I was saying - I know you don't really know me so well but, if you ever want to talk, or anything, I'm here."

She takes her hand and places it on my left leg and gives a gentle squeeze. It's a friendly gesture, I know. We will be good friends I'm sure. She just means well. She's very caring. She sees a colleague in distress and wants to help because she's been spending so much of her time working with him. But her hand lingers. Her fingers stroke me, ever so slightly - a punch to my stomach. She moves her hand, looks away. I'm tense.

Hit the brakes!

Our bodies jolt towards the dashboard and back. "Oh my God Dean did we hit something?" she gasps.

"No! No. But - wasn't there someone there? A kid with a blue turban. Behind that car? About to cross?"

I'm out of breath! She looks over her shoulder. "Hang on." She leaves the car, looks around then sits down again inside, closes the door and shakes her head. "No one there. Must have run off."

I let out an immense sigh, relieved.

"Hey - hey look just park *there*, we're really close." She says.

I park, and my lips mouth 'good evening' but before I say it she's speedily reached over and taken the keys out of the ignition.

"You're not going anywhere until you've had a cup of tea at my place to wake you up. Or maybe some coffee."

I smile. "Ok. It'll have to be quick though." My words are slurred. The stop has shaken me. She locks the car and we walk.

I'm inside. How did I get *here*?

"Right. Now just relax," she says, as her hands unwind my shoulder muscles. "You're so damn tense Dean. This is long overdue. Make sure you tell her."

I will, I will tell her, I will...

What? What will I do? Who will I tell what? I'm tired. So tired... And feeling good, melting, as I'm rocked backwards and forwards by Jennifer. What a great friend, surely, I realise just now, that I have found, as the CD player runs through its last few Billie Holiday tracks.

Blue moon, you saw me standing alone... P.S... I love you.

I don't know what the time is - should I know? I see the dials on my watch but I don't read it -

shouldn't I read it? I breathe deeply and my eyes grow tired in the gloom. She keeps her flat dimly it. It's very dark here. Only a small reading lamp on in the corner.

The warm yellow-amber tinge of the reading lamp fades out to a very real, cold blue which enwraps our surrounds, the blue daylight allowed in by the massive window to our right, and although it's cold here in this blue place I'm warmed by her touch.

Our shadows are long. It's cloudy outside. I can hear soft drops of rain beginning to fall. My eyes close. I seem to be sleeping. And falling, down, into water, a flood, and very soon everywhere inside there's an ocean and I'm reaching out to someone drowning down below – *but who?* - and suddenly I'm wide awake!

I tell her to stop, she does, and we sit there on the sofa in silence as I nervously finish my nth cup of coffee.

"I can't really see properly in this light. I think I need glasses." I say. And I notice that yes I cannot even see my hands – any part of me – clearly, in this dark blue place of hers. Where am I? I wasn't here a minute ago. I was somewhere far away.

"I really should go." I mutter.

She puts her coffee down, and touches my hand, and stares straight into me. Oh my God

Dean, oh my God, what the hell are you doing here? But… where else would I be? Am I not in the right place? I don't know. *I don't know!* Weren't we talking about something? I don't recall what. Inside there's a demon, stirring.

She's on me. Her leg over my lap. She's kissing me. Softly. Softly. Oh my. I push her away to the other side of that immense, tiny sofa. She is startled, hurt and looks away, then down at the floor, then at the empty coffee mug.

When her gaze falls on the wall to my left her eyes widen - she seems to notice something as if seeing it for the first time in all the years she's lived here - and then her eyes come back to me.

And I have not blinked. I watch her, my body throbbing. The moment holds for eternity until finally she stands up, switches off the lamp, slips off her high heels, pads into the kitchen with her naked feet and closes the door behind her.

I'm frozen. I stare forwards, fixed on that door, a dark gateway in the blue nothing where I sit. I wonder whether I should go now. No. I wonder whether I *will*. With this misfired thought the pain starts in my stomach. So many broken wings of butterflies. So many.

Silence. Soft muted sounds come from behind that door millions of miles away in this dark dimly lit flat. It's raining hard outside and suddenly I notice the thing she must have seen here for the first time. A silhouette of the rainstorm's trickles and drops, eddies and currents and its streams and oceans sliding down the immense window, runs along the entire wall on my left.

Beyond that I can't see anything else here but that door, that deathly still portal which I so want to open. Damn these butterflies.

The door opens and she's there, so petite, so pretty, leaning on the kitchen table, looking down through her stylish designer spectacles, looking at her feet, at her beautifully painted toe nails. The eager rain is audible - that, and our breathing, no more. And we're there for what seems like hours, until finally I stand up.

I look down, away from her, and perceive a line before me on the dark ground, at my feet, a thin slender beam of light that does not exist, a thing not to be crossed, a burning fire-imbued line that will scorch me if I move. I focus on remaining on this side. I must stay on this side. This side, damn it.

And I say, quiet but firm, "I'm going now." But I don't move and for a moment someone has reached into my torso and mangled my innards, and the butterflies become winged reptiles inside, and the pain intensifies, a crescendo and then -

I take a step, and I'm free of all the anxiety. Oh God, no - the line is now behind me together with its twisted, gnarled butterflies. My darkest demons, hitherto residing in a place where I could not see them, are pleased. But I move no further.

I stare at her, and she fixes my gaze and mutely, softly, submissively, she undresses, removing her items of clothing, one by one, continuing to undress until she is there, naked and bare, a phantom white image of beauty in the fathomless blue shade of the evening light. The shadows of the water outside are there too, in the kitchen, surreally running down along her wonderful, sensuously poised body.

Suddenly the space keeping us apart surrenders, as our bodies move hurriedly together we pass through mistrust, passion and ecstasy, and at the end a blinding light fires off like a new-born sun in my mind and I feel nothing but life, pure life, and nothing else. No pain. No angst. No death.

III. DROWNING

Chapter 13

The days go by, on and on, and I persevere in my unconscionable affair like a man newly born into fresh sin. The weeks pass, and my sense fills with her scent, her breath, her touch, the sensation of biting her lips, her neck, reveries of erotic pleasures recently experienced, I see her, smell her, taste her.

I lace up my trainers and head off, running early into the hours of coming dawn, down my street past the avenue of evergreens and around the corner to the left where a dog barks at me as I leap over it and continue on my way. I haven't had a run like this in ages.

I breathe deeply. Relish each moment. Each and every impact against the ground.

It's cold, the leaves have almost all fallen, the roads are clogged up with them and as I turn right into another street I see the road sweeper making its way slowly down toward me, humming, growling. I'll be warm soon enough. Then I'll go home and change and get to work and maybe Jen and I can shoot off at lunch break for yet another passionate exploit for the – how many times is it now? I've lost count! I laugh and a postman walking past glances back at me, his silent domain disturbed from a distance.

But first I must return home, and in my house the silence, ever audible, has deepened. I try not to think about it, no, for I feel young, alive, carefree, and my desires keep pulling me back to that moment weeks ago in *her* flat, where it happened, where it began, where my madness took me as I took her, and without compromise I offered myself to my insanity by my undressing, the way she offered herself to me.

I run into the park, and it is getting lighter, slowly. I should be getting warmer. I smile as I recall the revelation she put before me one evening. As I lay next to her small sensual form, she turned to me and things became clearer - how could I have been so wrong?

"Hey," she said. "I don't think we should tell Uncle Henry about this."

I frowned "What? *Uncle* Henry?"

"Didn't he tell you? Sorry, I knew he was keeping it quiet, but I thought he'd have told *you*. He's my mother's brother." She shrugged, and rolled her small shoulders, burrowing further into the cushion of my arm and chest. It made sense, but I laughed.

"Your mother was born a Lewis? That's a relief. I thought you... fancied him."

And she laughed in return, a brief, hollow, echoing laugh.

"Dean, that's a disgusting thought. Blind fool." She teased, and as she stood and closed the curtains, bringing further darkness to us both, I stepped up behind her and claimed her for myself once again.

Now I'm sweating, I can feel my t-shirt sticking to my back, and I'm heating up and it's slightly suffocating, nauseating, and fulfilling all at once. I reach the lake in the park and head over the bridge, then stop in my tracks half way, panting. Panting. Panting, and looking around. I can hear something on the wind. A voice. A murmuring whisper. Something. I glance around me. I see no one. I am alone in the opening rays of the day. I look around. Over the lake. And then behind me, a blast of wind swings down from the skies and the trees here unleash their last leaves and I hold my breath as I am surrounded by them and they swim around me and as I turn away from them they rush past me and I feel them softly hitting me in the back. The ghostly offspring of the trees touch me lightly and I feel them, feel I can see each one, each individual shape, with its own cut, pattern of growth, the place it has lived on its branch, the course of each of its veins, the variations in hue, the very unique feel of each piece of existence, signified by these falling, dying, drying leaves. They rise up into the air, all of them following an invisible path, an arc in the sky, until they move on into the waters before me and lie there, still, dead. I swallow deeply at this vision of an eternally repeating life path, of their rise and fall, season after season, brief, intense bursts of existence, of life, their movement being only one-way, unable to return to their maker. Once created, it is theirs only to bloom, grow and pass away to nowhere, to lie drowning in this pool of water, and I think, who could be content with such a fate, would it be better not to have existed at all? It was as if they never were.

I shiver. I've cooled down.

I begin to run home, slightly perturbed by my frame of mind, and below me my shoe laces untie and I trip and fall, curse, rise, tie up and run on. But I have a curious sensation within, a curious tickle of a thread being pulled.

And now I'm in a meeting with Henry and Geoff and I'm smiling as I remember a night with her. Henry's talking, talking about the 'Good Head' matter and Geoff mutters on for a while about something, and I'm not really focussing just this second but then I realise I *should be* because the last person I want to alert to my filthy liaison is Jen's uncle, who -

"Well? Dean?" Henry's asking me.

"Um... Sorry... Miles away, could you repeat that Henry? I'm sorry." I flounder.

"Can we get your idea on the road?"

"Which one?"

He frowns. "For God's sake Dean, the newspaper articles."

I raise an eyebrow, and, *somewhere*, dim recognition occurs. "Ah, yes... Um... Well, I'll need a week or so to see how I want do this, and I'll have to call a meeting, see what all the departments think, what they want to highlight..."

...she's kissing my neck...

"Are they all falling into line yet?" Michaelson asks,

"What? Oh! Well, there's resistance... but what can I do? I have to lead them. Jones is the worst of the bunch."

"Surely not!" Michaelson laughs, defending his fellow fool.

"Yes. He had a right shot at me in our last meeting, kept asking why he should listen to me, what did I know about teaching PE and-"

"Well don't be too pushy then!" Michaelson interjects, annoying me instantly.

"Will you at least let me finish?"

Geoff snorts, Henry watches us both, closely.

"Thank you." I say, not without a hint of sarcasm, and then I gesture in the air before me, trying to explain the problem. "Jones and a select few think I'm telling them what to do. Dictating to them how to do their jobs. Thing is, Henry, all I'm doing is asking them to set internal targets, and I'm just trying to make sure every department is coming up to a minimum general standard."

"Sounds fair enough," Henry reassures me. "How are things progressing?"

I shrug. "I've been doing my bit. They're getting things done. Albeit slowly. Too many of them avoid the meetings, Henry, and I'm sure Marshall is encouraging them to show me the finger."

"I'll have a tactful word, Dean, don't worry..."

...her softly pleasured moans...

"How is Jennifer? How's she coming?" Henry's question startles me - there's something in his eye - suspicion?

"Yes, yes, she's settling in... The pupils like her, and those who cause her trouble, well, she's short but she keeps them in order. I've been in class with her on occasion. She's good. She keeps them in line. She's good."

"Yes." Henry says, looking me in the eye. I pause for a moment and drop my grin. He closes the meeting and Geoff wanders off humming some tune to himself, forever in his own world. I hang back a moment to ask Henry something, and for a second I wonder why I'm even asking, but it's too late as the words leave my mouth –

"Henry, I'm curious. Why didn't you tell me Jennifer's your niece?"

Henry looks at me but doesn't want to meet my eyes. Curious. "Hey? Oh. She told you? Well. I'm surprised. *She* asked *me* to keep it quiet. The governors knew all along. She just wanted it quiet. You know. Wasn't sure if it would be wise going on about it just at the start – other staff might have made suggestions of nepotism, you know… those kind of reasons. She asked me to keep it quiet… Um…"

He seems embarrassed. I rescue him. "Just wondered. Not important."

"Ah - Ok. Um… Dean, are you sure everything is ok between you two?"

"Yes." I say, alert. "Why wouldn't it be?"

"I mean, if there was anything… anything I needed to know, you'd tell me, wouldn't you Dean?"

"Of course."

"But there's nothing?"

"No." I say, relishing the thought of our bodies joined together and – "No. There's nothing at all…"

I leave as quickly as I can.

106

Chapter 14

Hours later I'm two thirds of the way through my lesson, I am wearing my self-styled, teacher's I-take-no-bullshit-but-am-friendly-too mask, and am focussing on my act but only barely, sensations of a sensual nature hovering behind all five of my senses. I am tense. But for an instant, I glimpse *her* eyes and focus returns.

I speak.

"Ok," I say. "Listen, class. We're going to do a bit of a comprehension exercise." I take my own form group for English, and as they straighten up in their seats, placing their pens down, a few fidget, mutter, yet cease once my gaze is felt.

"You, me, anybody who reads... will interpret what they read. You will have your own idea of what is being said. You might not realise it, but you will have some idea which is your very own and no one else's. Example. Suppose I write 'a tall man wearing a suit walks through the door' and I don't describe him any more than that," I point at one of my pupils. "So what do you see in your mind?"

She shrugs. She's chewing gum. "A man with black hair?"

"Long hair?" I ask.

She squints. "No."

"Why is he wearing a suit?"

She shrugs. "Maybe he's a lawyer."

"Why do you think he's a lawyer?"

"Because lawyers wear suits! So what?"

The other kids smile. She has spunk this one I'll admit. But it's an intelligent cheekiness, which I find endearing.

"Well. What you just did was make a guess – an educated guess – about the man being a lawyer. You inferred that he was a lawyer, because he wears a suit. Others may have inferred something else - who thought he was just another teacher?" Two hands are raised, very timidly, and one of them is Edward's little hand on the far side. Good, they're thinking, individually. "So, the point is, class, that you will have different interpretations. Half of you may have seen a black suit the others a cream one. You all had a different interpretation, even with something as simple as this. So imagine if it had been something a lot more complicated. Your interpretation, the way you 'fill in the gaps', will also be more complicated. You will use what you already know to help fill in the missing parts the author left out – you *infer* something from the writing. Write that word down: to infer. This is important, as it's something you do all the time, but need to be aware of it. It's about reading *between* the lines."

I put the word up on the board and hear a brief flash of scribbles behind me.

The bell goes. They bolt for their bags, all stationery and books away. How do kids pack their stuff so fast?

"Sit!" I shout. "Homework." Groans all round. "I want you to use the man coming into the classroom as the start of a story. Just write a few paragraphs. Think about who he is and what he might want. 500 words. *Now* you can go."

They file out, and at the end of the class, Edward wanders up to me and asks me a question.

"S-Sir?"

"Edward, how can I help?"

"Can I-I write a longer story if I w-w-want to?"

"If you want to, Edward, of course!"

"Will you read it s-Sir?"

"Yes, certainly." I reply, a little taken aback by his eagerness.

"But don't tell anyone, ok s-Sir?"

"Why not?" I frown.

"Th-they'll tease me, Sir. Call me teacher's pet."

"Don't worry about it Edward, your secret's safe with me. Just hand it to me after registration sometime, here's some paper." I hand him several sheets, and he leaves the room, happy, with my eyes on his back. I suddenly recall meeting his mother at a progress evening, recently, a wan woman who had told me that Edward really liked my lessons and looked forward to them very much, and that she could see I was a good man, a good teacher. I thanked her for the compliment, but then she suddenly spoke tearfully, and told me that Edward had never been the same since his father left. That he had been lively and happy a few years ago but had become withdrawn after his father stopped making contact. She said she hadn't seen Edward act as alive in a long time. Mr Sekar's English lessons had started to bring him back to life, she said. It was very touching, if bewildering. I had no idea Edward was dealing with such pressures, his file didn't make any of this apparent. I wondered, briefly, how on earth I had reached him.

Now something disturbs me. Rather curiously I'm not tired. No. Something else is bothering me. I pause and look down at the table in front of me, at the grain, at its cracks and crevices.

In an earlier lesson, I was explaining to a year ten class that books, words, carry purpose and meaning. In so far as I could keep their attention, I challenged them. Pushed them as far as I could.

Told them they had to *think* when reading. Told them it was important to question, to probe, and to continually ask *why* - something an old science tutor once told me, and something I had never forgotten.

Usually, teaching that lesson would have set me alight, on fire! But this time? I felt untied. Loose, as if the tie around my neck was not in reality there. Unconcerned. I had them make some notes, all the while wondering where my sudden stroke of apathy had arisen from, and as the pens fell silent, I floundered, and was forced to check my lesson plan.

I told them to consider what the writer intended them to think or feel, if anything. I asked them to consider the possibility that he may have just wanted to confuse them, and simply suggest things, without having any firm argument. Told them always to question why the writer had presented something in a particular way. What effect he was aiming to create. Perhaps he was trying to brainwash them, maybe he wanted them to disagree with him, maybe he just wanted them to keep an open mind.

I paused. They wrote. I wanted to push my pupils to think for themselves, yet several colleagues had ridiculed me when I had shown them this lesson plan, years ago. Those people, drifting pieces of dead wood that they were, are now thankfully long gone, but their negative attitudes and low aspirations sometimes still reverberate in my ears. No one will get it, leave it, do the minimum; go home to your wife, have more fun, relax! Unbelievable. So many of them just wanted to do the least they could and go home, but I actually cared enough to push my ideas through to the head of English. He was impressed, and asked me to update some of the older teaching schemes that needed seeing to. So began the road to promotion. I don't know what motivated me. I guess I just strongly believed in what I did.

And as I gave this lesson today for the umpteenth time, I already knew I'd lost some of the kids - it's always a case of touch and go. The eyes of two at the back were glazing over into oblivion. They'd need a little more attention. But a couple of them were coming alive - you could see it in their eyes! I had them, even if I'd lost myself.

Even if I'd lost myself...

What *is* the point? Of writing? Reading? Teaching these things? I try to remember what the hell I'm doing here, and as my anxiety grows deeper, heavier, I suddenly recall the words of an author who once touched me, and who once wrote that the novel-writer's job is to explore existence. Not the oceans or space, but existence itself. What we are. As humans. What we were.

What we might be. The future, the past, the possibilities, in the mind and outside it. To go beyond ourselves and enter into another's mind, another's imagination and experience, as explorers, all.

Exploring existence through words. I wonder. Is this right? Isn't it an inherently poor substitute for existence itself?

I breathe deeply and try to relax myself. Now there's a calm coolness to my being, to my heart. I don't understand - suddenly my self has penetrated the closed windows and escaped, and I am left teaching things and I can't figure out why I'm even here, let alone what on earth I'm saying to these poor kids! Curious. Odd. Once I saw it clearly. The next minute my words were meaningless mangled vowels and consonants fluttering up from my belly and out into the world. To explore existence in words. Could that really be the purpose? Is there nothing more? I'm unnerved. I have a feeling which I haven't experienced since I left University in that pivotal fit of frustration more than ten years ago. Doubt. What the hell am I doing?

Suddenly everything in the room looks crooked. Old. Worn out. The plastic chairs, the laminated tables, the cream, patchy, peeling paint on the walls, the musty smell. So I take my keys and my phone and lock the door behind me and leave that room with its cracked tables crooked chairs and meaningfully hollow words, as another desire arises.

I want her.

We went somewhere at lunchtime, some old deserted industrial estate and did what we had to do, her thong dropped around one ankle, her feet against the backs of the front seats, we were cramped, hot and hungry, and I was a little rough with her.

I don't know what came over me, but now that I'm back in my class my room appears straight once more. Un-crooked. No doubt as to why I am here - I chose to be here! I give out a short laugh, but it's an empty one. This is wonderfully strange.

What *am* I doing *here*?

I'm losing my -

Disturbed by the turmoil, I ponder who might be able to help me. But it's not as if I don't already know, I'm just avoiding him, he'll be angry with me, two months now and no contact since I swore at him. No contact. A very rare thing indeed. A wide distance. I shouldn't have been so rude. Maybe I should go and see him soon. Apologise. Maybe.

So I wake up now and I see a ceiling, and I put my arms behind my head and I vaguely recall being with her the night before. Jennifer. I take in a deep breath and I feel intoxicated. Stuck in a careless moment, I'm high, rising through a thick cloud and levitating before a thin, fragile sky.

And then reality bites. This is *my* ceiling, and I hear breathing beside me - *Serena* - just gazing at me with those huge brown dim eyes of her, breathing hard. Suddenly she throws off her side of the blankets and I see her, naked, shivering, cold, and I recoil. She peers at me and I freeze as she looks into the pits in my mind, the depths and the cold abyss. She sees into them as she has always done, and it's as if something suddenly strikes her there, and she quivers, turns her head to one side as if hearing an interesting idea for the first time, and starts to shake, lying there, next to me, as she looks inside, and I realise that this is no dream! I realise this is real. She quivers, trembles in the cold, naked as she always used to lie with me in the past, I see a longing in those eyes and an unspoken desire to kiss me, in her lips. I sit upright and peer over her elongated body, from the tips of her hair to her toe nails, and I see the scars that run up and down her long legs, the stitching, the skin grafts, the battered bare textures there, glowing a deep furious red, from the sting of a new pain, the sting of my eyes on them, of my rejection of her body, a rejection of what I once thought of as beautiful and tasted and loved. Her scars glow the colour of betrayal and anger, abandonment and fear. I back away from the

115

sight, the bed, and it seems my room lengthens until she is far away in my tunnel vision, alone on the bed, her head buried in the crumpled sheets. Her legs! On fire! Mangled in steel! I escape from the room, I run, I flee, I cannot watch her, I cannot see -

And I can't take this any more. I have to see my father. I reach the living room and make the call, and he's surprised to hear from me, and is annoyed, upset at our too long-lasting silence, yet he senses the urgency in my voice, and we arrange to meet as soon as we can.

Days later as I'm driving to him, I realise I've taken a wrong turn somewhere and I curse, turn, and head back the way I came, back to past roads, until I reach a junction and I pause for a moment, unsure of the route to take. The moment lasts only seconds. Then I turn. Continue my journey. Familiarity suggests it is the right way and yet it seems I've never been here before. With my window down there's a Winter scent in the air, wandering into the car - wet wood and the promise of snow soon - and my soul drifts away once more.

Chapter 15

"What the hell?!" Richard screamed as he ran as fast as he could, a dark speck on a white soft plain, and hid behind a tree. There he fell silent, breathing deeply. Moments later the soft crunch of feet on snow alerted him to imminent attack yet it was too late. The snow grenades smashed into him from all sides and he screamed and curled into a ball and then emerged moments later laughing so hard his guts hurt.

"Gotcha!" Dean shouted.

"Yes, I rather think... we... did..." panted Ajeet, sucking on his inhaler.

"Richard you're getting fat. I swear you ran faster last year." Yasmine teased. Richard put on a face of mock misery. And then he shouted: "Get her!" and as Yasmine screeched and ran the three boys hastily pulled together an armoury of lumpy snow and chased after her. Dean's was the first to make contact and she span round and returned one whilst Ajeet's effort struck her side.

Meanwhile, Richard fell over. "Ahh!" he screamed. "My knee!"

"Oh what the hell?" Dean said. "Richard you twat."

"Don't be a meanie, Deany!" Yasmine ran to Richard's side and helped him up, whilst the other two stood, laughing.

"The park is awfully quiet for a day like this," Ajeet commented. "Where is everyone?"

"Who cares!" Dean shouted. "We're here now! And while we are, it's ours! No one else's!" he laughed.

"Hey! The slope!" suggested Yasmine, and then ran and disappeared off the side of the usually green field. Dean followed her, and Ajeet saw him slide down like a ski-less skier, straight into Yasmine.

"Sorry," Dean apologised.

"That's ok," she whispered.

"Come on, Aj…" Richard nudged him away and limp-slid his way down to the bottom, and stood with the other two, waving to Ajeet, encouraging him down.

"Ah well," he muttered, took another puff of his inhaler, stepped over the edge, slipped, fell, spun and slid all the way down backwards on his behind to the waiting trio. He gazed up at them and adjusted his turban back into its correct place.

"Hello." He said.

"You ok?" Dean asked.

"Of course…" he replied, not having moved.

"Right."

They pounded him with snow fire.

And then, Dean was thrown to the ground by a large thing that had stepped up close behind him.

"Pussy!" Arnold laughed from high atop his mountain. Richard limped over to him and stared up rebelliously at the bully.

"You want something, Dick?" Arnold spat, grinning.

Ajeet fell into a panic and crawled away muttering something about death, Richard remained silently standing before this thing twice his size, whilst Dean simply lay and watched.

Yasmine tugged at the beast's arm. "Come on Al-" she pleaded. He looked the three boys in the eye, one at the time, smiled in a pugnacious manner and then turned and left with her. The three rose to their feet and watched the couple leave.

"What a bastard." Richard muttered.

Dean nodded. "She could do so much better…"

Ajeet shot him a quick look. "How much better? Surely not better, Dean, as to mean - you?"

Dean frowned and laughed. "Don't be silly. We're just friends! Just friends! I mean… better as in - a retarded monkey with crutches would be better."

They laughed. And then an insanity gripped Dean. "Guys, he's still close enough for a strike."

Richard grinned broadly. Ajeet whimpered. "Do we have to?" asked Ajeet. "I think you are forgetting that he has a gang."

"Who cares? It's a great idea, damn it." Richard said, distributing snowballs to each of them.

They splattered the couple, and over Yasmine's girlish laughter the curses of Arnold Walters rang out on the wind as he turned and gave them the finger, and yet she managed to *placate him once more as they continued on their walk away from the boys.*

*"Ah well. We do not have to run after all."
Ajeet said, relieved. "Makes a change."*

*"Ahem - Dean, here's your latest gal..."
nudged Richard.*

Dean looked about and noticed a girl with curly blonde hair coming their way, dressed for the cold, she smiled, waved and shouted hello. The two boys left to continue their foolery elsewhere, and although Dean was busy chatting to the young lady, he could not help but glance over her shoulder at the other couple, the beast walking away with the younger beauty on its arm.

But soon, Dean gave up the watch. He landed on his behind in a pile of snow, lay back, and produced an angel. And the girl fell by his side, laughing. And then he lay there and looked up at the sky and saw future joy painted there among the clouds. And for an instant, he felt as if he could see himself from the future, glimpsing back at himself, a happy teenager, lying warm and content in the cold, cold snow, laughing with the glimmer of a tear in his eye.

Chapter 16

"Good of you to finally make time to see me." he says.

I feel the burn of my shame on my face. I *should* have made more time. I haven't seen him for two months. We haven't talked. I was expecting a far icier reception. Harsher. I let him lecture me for a while - to be honest I deserve the ear-bashing. Then he stops, and as he orders the starters – we're in a small restaurant he's fond of – he takes up his wine glass, has a sip and looks me in the eye.

"So, son. What…?" he says.

I blink. "What?"

"There's a reason I haven't seen you in this long. I know it. And there's a reason you wanted to see me tonight."

I chuckle. "How can you tell?"

"I feel it. I'm your father. I just know."

I lean forward and look down at the table cloth. "Dad. What's happening to me?" I ask.

"Now why don't *you* tell *me*."

I nod. "Yes I suppose I should. I haven't told anyone else. And it's starting to get to me… I feel like I'm losing - losing my-"

A pause. Dad waits. Then speaks. "Well son, look at it this way. I'm here for you right now, so tell me what it is, or let's just eat and go. But I don't think you should waste what little time we have together."

"No, you're right." I shake my head. "I shouldn't waste it." I take a deep breath. "Well - you know all about what's happened at the school... everything. You know I'm working hard." I stop for some water. "And nothing's changing at home. I just see her. Lying there. But she won't move. She won't move! Won't utter a word. I don't know what to do for her anymore. She just sits there, blankly, staring at me. I tried. Tried and tried. Everything I do, Dad, it's like a half-finished gesture. Like trying to send someone a gift they never receive. It's eating away at me. My heart. My mind... I thought I'd freed myself of this. Of her. I was wrong. I see her sitting there, mute, all the time." I pause. He's staring at me, wide-eyed.

"Why are you looking at me like that? Why!" I snap, disturbed, sinking inside, so fast, as if I've suddenly seen it all and I realise what it is that he's staring so wildly at me for and my hands begin to sweat, coldly, and I grip the napkin on the table before me, and he asks me, like what? And of course he knows - what is he trying to do, let me down gently? How can that be, considering what he has to say!

"Son… Well… Serena, she… she's-" he flounders and I leap in.

"Dead! Go on, say it Dad! Say it."

"Calm down, son!" he raises his voice, but I continue my rant, not allowing him to interrupt.

"Oh my God… I'm *insane*. I'm seeing a woman in my house who's dead, who died months ago, I'm insane, I'm fucking crazy! She never comes with me anywhere because she's fucking dead!"

I'm shaking now, on the chair, unable to breathe properly, hot, losing control as the thread inside is pulled, and then Dad reaches up and holds my arms firmly! And he speaks to me so sternly, I feel as if I am six years old once more.

"Son. Get a grip! Serena's not *dead*. What on earth is wrong with you?"

I allow myself to shrink in his hands. I crumple, exhausted by these steps forwards and backwards to insanity. I wish I could fathom what held me for that moment. What deep demon got hold of me and tried to declare me mad.

"I… don't know what came over me. I'm sorry." I say, relieved by his few words, his reassurance.

Serena's not dead…

"Don't you remember? All that you've been doing for her?" he asks.

It returns as quickly as it left me. The memories. The truth. Of course she's alive. I remember the therapy sessions I drove her to for months after the event. The few times when Dad and Margaret came to visit us, to visit her, to try and get her to speak, and she just sat there. The Summer weeks in which her parents flew back from Chicago to spend with her. The 'get well' cards from her colleagues, signed by her patients, little children in distress, missing her at the hospital, the flowers, condolences for our loss, addressed to us both. The times that her friends came round to unburden themselves of their gossip, unable to acquire even a smile from her - she was *real* - she *was* still alive - *of course* - what the hell came over me? It was as if I could only now see those patches of silence, between her and I, and all else was damned, lost, gone. And yet, though she was alive, she was a phantom, a ghost, a pale memory of who she had once been, what she once meant to me.

"Listen, calm down, I know you're under a lot of pressure, but this is ridiculous." Dad says.

"Yes. I'm sorry. Of course. I'm being... stupid." I relax.

"Yes, you are! Keep a tight grip on yourself, son. There is a problem, of course. She hasn't uttered a damn word in months, I know. But she's still *alive*. Perhaps you should have forced her to come out tonight."

An empty thought, for if I'd asked her, she'd have ignored me, if I'd have touched her, she'd have shunned me, physically, I'm sure, and in any case she cannot be here to witness our discussion tonight. She can't.

"She never goes with me, anywhere." I shake my head. "She's psychologically housebound. I can't remember how they diagnosed her - her *silence*. I don't recall the right term... But she stopped seeing them anyway - her therapists, one day she just shook her head when I picked up the car keys! I told the therapists - they just said there was nothing they could do. No medicine they could give her. That it was all up to her. She would either come back, or not. I couldn't afford private and we lost our place in the NHS queue."

The starters arrive. Dad sips his soup after cooling each spoonful with a purposive light blow. I eye mine, and, recalling the real reason I had come here this day, the thing that I had to confess, I season it, take small gulps and let it burn my tongue. That feels right for some reason, just now. That I be hurt by my own food. Let it burn me scald me and cause me immense pain.

"How do you feel now?" Dad asks, concerned.

"Better... Sorry. I don't know what just happened. Dad - I just don't understand.

126

Everything got too much a few months ago, round about that time you called. You remember?"

"How could I forget?" he says, dryly. "You were incredibly rude. I was sure I'd raised you better."

I begin to give birth to my confession. "I know, I know. But I did something - with someone - and I'm still doing it. And I don't even know why, I know it's wrong but I just can't stop! I'm losing myself, Dad."

There. The child is arriving, feet first.

Dad stops eating and places his spoon down, looking up at me, and I find it so hard to make my lips move, to bring the words out and to name the demons that have taken hold of me. My pleasure. My pain. But then I don't have to. He's my father. He just *knows*.

"Who is she, Dean?" he asks, softly.

"She's... no one."

"Tell me everything."

I shake my head. Everything? *Everything?* No. No, I can't do that - he's my father. And yet... who else do I have? So I tell him. How it began one night where I was shaken after nearly killing some kid in the road.

Did that actually that happen? Wasn't there a kid with a turban? Wasn't I shaken? Were my demons inventing it all just to take me to her?

I tell him how she massaged me and that that was when it happened, and as I tell him this now, her taste returns to my lips for an instant, causing me to drink some water to wash her sweet salt from me. I feel no shame. This is my father, yet I feel no shame! Peculiar, I tell him, how it was so damn easy to do it. To just see the other side of existence beyond that burning white line, and then go there within the blink of an eye. One moment I was holding myself on the other side of the line in that blue room of hers and the next I was enjoying her flesh. What? How? Why did I do it? And could I not have stopped by now? Did I not want to stop? What was I doing?

"What the hell am I doing Dad!" I whisper my shout, as the main course arrives.

"Son. This is going to be difficult. Either way. I know what this is about."

"You do?" I ask, surprised.

"Dean, don't be silly. You… You know why your mother left me."

I shake my head. The stupid, incomprehensible thing is, I *do* know why she had to go. Why does this seem such a shock? Of course he understands. And yet, it burns me inside to think of this, of what happened between them, of why she had to go.

"I don't want to talk about her... Not with you."

My father shrinks into himself at the comment. He stops eating and looks at me. "After all these years, son, I thought you might have at least begun to think about forgiving me."

"I won't talk about this." I say, and he knows I won't be drawn. That I won't forgive. He goes on, subdued somewhat by the hurt I have just dealt him.

"Well. Regardless. I understand your situation, son. You have to listen to me. Stop it. Before you lose the one you *really* care for. Because that's what it's about, son. No matter how difficult she makes your life, for reasons that aren't even her own, you can't do this to *her*. She is your life companion. She is the one you chose to be with, and she is still with you, albeit hurt, silent, and in pain. You don't know what's going on inside her. How she feels, what she sees, what she saw. She has never told us. You have no idea, and it is hard but *she* is the one you have to be with and exist for. Whatever happens. Even if she is about to leave and she can't tell you. Her pain is your pain. You must make it your pain to heal both of you. What do you feel, Dean?"

That I'm losing something, myself, and that whatever I thought I was is slowly slipping out of the confines of my old shape. I see the outline of my being growing, escaping me, as I try to fill the gaps, the crevices, the huge holes left behind, but they are too great for my animal passions alone to fill, I need and crave *more*. Sometimes we can see it all so clearly inside and just don't have the words... If you could speak what you feel, would you be free?

I straighten up in my seat and try to convey my feelings to my father. "I feel... frayed... unravelled. But I *enjoy* it, Dad, and I can't stop." I look down once more, shame creeping over my body, squeezing me tight, pinning my breath down, I continue.

"But what we do is - cold. So cold. And lonely. It's just my voice inside. I used to hear *her* voice." I notice a young couple whispering into one another ears over Dad's shoulder and my being fills with envy and anger. "For years I heard *her* voice with mine. Serena was strong, soothing, warm. And now? Nothing. I can have this other woman wherever and whenever I damn well want. But it's lonely. Ever since the crash, Serena's voice has fallen away - I don't even remember what she sounds like. I can't hear her anymore. We haven't made love since before the crash."

Perhaps I say it too loud and perhaps I'm embarrassing Dad, but I can't help it, because I feel like tearing out my eyes and setting fire to them and I wish the food would choke me for my lack of self-restraint.

Dad stops eating again and looks at me. "Son. I'll say it one more time. Stop this. Or you will suffer. Unimaginably. I know." I look up at him and I see the pain etched into his wrinkled face.

We eat silently the remainder of the main course.

As desert we order exotic fruits, and as I bite into a watery pink-flavoured fleshy piece of something, I notice the couple again. They must be no more than twenty-one. Young. Free. Happy. *I wish...*

"There's something else, Dad." I say, as our coffee arrives.

"What?"

"I don't know if you'll understand. How you'll react."

"Try me," he says.

"I keep going back."

"What? To where?"

"To that year... I was thirteen."

"Oh," he says, looking down. "Why?"

131

"I don't know. I just see the good things. Like I want to go back." And I let the sentence trail off, and Dad has no answer for me, but he nods, as if to say that I should be consoled, for this is the plight of man, universally, eternally, and it has ever been so. I glance over my shoulder and sense an object move into shadow, something stalking me, watching me, serenely poised out of sight. I know it's there. But I choose not to look. I blink and the sensation is gone.

After dinner I drive home and I resolve that this is it. Whatever I've been doing, enjoying, taking these last two months, I must now reject. I must give back her delicious body to her.

Chapter 17

The next night I'm on top of her again, unable to stop myself, thrusting, touching, feasting, feeling moist and sweating myself out onto this little woman's frame. Why am I doing this? Why can't I stop? She knows where to touch me, she quickens me, I move faster, she won't stop me, she enjoys it, she takes only what she wants, I give out a cry of joyful pain and frustration as I reach the end.

I collapse atop Jennifer and close my eyes and see Serena. Oh God. Am I insane? Am I crazy? Is everything drifting? Where am I? Her flesh should *relieve* me - but what have I done - what is happening to me? I roll off Jennifer Dunley and lie, facing the ceiling, pensive, silent, still.

"What exactly is wrong with her?" she asks.

"Hey? Who?" I snap, my concentrated turmoil disturbed.

"You *know* who, Dean."

I take a deep breath. "My wife? Phew... Well." I pause. I don't even *want* to talk about her. Not to *this* woman. Doesn't feel right. No. And yet. I may as well explain.

"Well... Earlier this year... July... She was involved - she was in an accident. A train crash. You remember the freight express disaster?"

"Yes."

"That freight train that shot up a wrong crossing somewhere or something and - and ended up hitting a local passenger train…" - *for an instant it happens again, the two collide and my world inverts as they rise and fall* - "Serena was on that train."

"Oh."

"I saw it all. From the hillside. I was waiting for her."

"Oh my." Jen whispers.

"But that's not all." I swallow. I promised myself never to think of it. "She - Oh God - She was… pregnant. Carrying our first child. A few months in. And -"

"The baby?"

Another shake of my head conveys our child's fate. "There was no way it could have survived." I pause. Gather my thoughts. "I don't know. I hadn't even wanted it really. But then, when we lost it? I don't know. I felt so… cheated. And she hasn't spoken a word since the crash." I fall silent for a moment. "She wouldn't go to therapy any more. So they gave up. They said she's fine. That it's all in her mind. So no medicine will help. She just has to get up one day, and do it."

"Do what?"

I shrug. "Speak to me."

She watches me for a moment and then turns and places her naked body against mine, with her back to me. "Lie with me. When you're ready again. You know what to do."

How can she be so cold? I'm angered. When I'm ready, I'll take her once more, roughly. And it will be purely for my pleasure. Not hers.

Forgive me for my madness, someone...

Chapter 18

A few days later I'm back home and it's cold. Ella Fitzgerald is singing in our CD player downstairs. Every time they say goodbye... she dies a little. I hum the melody. School has tired me out so completely this week what with this pupil or that pupil being suspended and another one having to get stitches in hospital because of some fight in the corridor.

And that's not all - yesterday saw my plan wheeled into action – my idea about contacting 'interested' media parties in order to promote the school and give us some positive press space – something Henry seemed very keen for me to do, considering our disastrous first few weeks this school year.

Anyway, I wrote to them a few weeks ago, inviting them to spend an hour or so at the school with me one morning. Out of the twenty or so letters I sent out, the response was thin, but of reasonable quality. They came, one TES journalist, and a local radio station editor. There was also a regional evening paper journalist writing an education feature, accompanied by a photographer with a camera hanging heavily from a strap around his neck. Our second encounter with the press in so many months went far more smoothly – I found them interested, focussed, genuinely hoping to find something positive to write about Autumn Lane. They mentioned the 'Good Head' matter but thankfully we were all able to laugh it off together quite quickly. As the late November rain beat down harshly outside, they drifted in and out of the rooms and corridors, and I talked to them about our good class discipline and pointed out Jones's regimented pupils standing neatly before him as he barked about the importance of proper warm ups before exercise and scowled at a child for fidgeting.

They met Henry and discussed things in his office, asked him how he felt about being the acting head, and took some pictures of prefects carrying out chores, walking from class to class. After a quick coffee in the staff room, they decided that enough children had filled their view for one day, thanked me sincerely, and wandered off.

So I relaxed, feeling it had been a job well done, and went in search of Ms Dunley, for once not intent on having any intimate contact with her, rather just wanting to drive out to a local pub for a celebratory lunch. We got into my car, and I talked excitedly, my mind racing with images of the positive review I was sure we would get from the friendly hacks I'd met that morning.

But as we drove up the school drive, I slowed as I noticed the photographer and journalist standing by the main entrance, taking a few shots of the school. I stopped the car by them, lowered the window, and glanced back – the school looked imposing, odd, an artificial cut out standing up before a tumultuous Winter sky, the elegant fountain in the quad utterly mismatched by the grim red school itself. Then I looked back at the two of them and smiled, and flash! Flash again! My eyes! When I recovered, I realised they'd taken shots of me - with Jen in my car. Shit. I frowned and they detected my annoyance, as they explained they had forgotten to photograph me during their visit, and that the pictures would be sold on to the TES as well as being used in the local paper. They thanked me again and left the campus.

I looked at Jen, tensely. She asked me what was wrong. What was wrong! Seeing as she didn't see it herself, I left the matter there. She seemed unconcerned. I, on other hand, was not at all pleased.

I spent the better part of today at school worrying, anxious that the evening paper would be at my door before I'd even reached the house and would carry somewhere within it a picture that would reveal my indiscretion to my mentally tortured wife. I'd told her about the press day I'd arranged, told her that today's paper would carry the article. Of course she merely looked at me, mute, and nodded lightly before closing her eyes once more.

How could I reach her, when she seemed to care so little?

This evening, then, it was with some trepidation that I stepped into the house and wandered into the living room and espied out of the corner of my eye my wife sitting back in an arm chair, a plate of fruit peels on the table before her, and a newspaper, opened out at a two page spread: *'Autumn prepares for Summer inspection'*.

I almost choked and went to the paper without uttering a word to her and scanned the page quickly for photographs and I let out a deep exhalation as my body un-tensed.

The photograph of us in my car revealed nothing. Thankfully! I saw my monochrome smiling face taken unawares by the flash, looking quite photogenic for someone taken by surprise, and beyond my shoulder was the shadow of someone else in the car, someone leaning back, looking sharply in the other direction, gender unspecified as the length of her hair was cut from view. Only I could have said who it was for certain, and most people would have missed her, sitting there, in the passenger seat, hiding. I relaxed. But that did it! I decided I needed to unwind by going for a swim.

Now as I pack my swim shorts into my sports bag, I realise that for some ungodly reason it's been ages since I did this, and I sense how much I need it. As I stand here in my room I catch a glimpse of myself in the mirror, and notice the light highlight a hair or two – my God are they grey? - and then my wife's at the door to the room rubbing her arms and looking at me, silently, her brown eyes pleading. I'm unsure. What does she want? Somewhere inside, for a brief second, I register the fact that she may well have read the article, or at least glanced at it. Maybe she did see something... Or... Maybe it reached her.

I walk toward her, but she side-steps to her left, and hides behind the wall. I frown, and as I get closer to the door, she darts past, without glancing my way, running. What on earth is this! I think, but on instinct I wander briskly after her as she switches lights on and off and she drifts in and out of view, playing hide and seek, like a child, an innocent game that I follow in, as Ella sings ecstatically about a knife called Mack, but I can't get to her – what is this! Am I dreaming? She hasn't been like this since - I follow her, walking patiently at a distance, unwilling to close the gap between us, and as she switches off lights, I turn them back on and laugh at the oddity of it all. It reminds me of the way we used to be, like kids in love, playing in a field. I follow her through the house, an ape swinging through the trees to catch a playmate. I drift through this unreal evening moment as she unelegantly yet lightly appears and disappears like an apparition from my past. I laugh, but soon I grow sick of her madness, of this inanity! I sniff the air and realise dinner's about to burn. I stop and go to the kitchen to switch off the oven, having lost sight of her in our home. I return to our bedroom upstairs.

She follows from some dark place behind me, like an unhappy child, but I'm annoyed by this sudden unexpected game play. Something has reached her, and I should be joyous, but I'm not. This playing around mocks me. She mocks me. Mocks me and our pain. I return to my packed bag, and once more catch a glimpse of myself in the mirror, noticing the light pick out a grey – yes, grey - hair or two, and again my wife's at the door to the room, rubbing her arms, smiling one moment, pleading with her dim brown eyes the next.

...*don't go to her*...

"What?" I snap at her, scowling. No response. She shrinks.

"Oh God. Sweetheart..." Sympathy washes away my cold front. "I'm sorry." I go to her. "I'm just going for a swim. I'll be back in an hour or so. Dinner's in the oven for you. Ok?"

She looks up at me. Silent. I walk past, bag over my shoulder, but something happens. I don't believe it. She touches me. My arm! She moves over to me, puts an arm around me, places her head on my shoulder. She's cold.

But I'm warmed. I feel like laughing. Crying.

We stay for a while, the song changes twice before I finally put my arm around her in return and lift her face with my other hand. I sigh, overwhelmed. I don't know how, but I understand. "You want to come with me."

She smiles, and nods once, like a child on the cusp of speech - her first word.

"Oh my…" I murmur. Has it really been so long?

And as we drive together in the car I look over to her and see a smile on her lips, and everything seems clear, I can feel it. I feel that the car isn't on the road and I'm not really sitting on anything. I feel the nothing that I am, that the steering wheel isn't really here, my hands hold it tight but there's nothing in them, and it's as if the world rushing up and past the windscreen is meaningless, speedy matter, which passes through every piece of me, every strand, fibre, thread. So far away had she gone, I had forgotten the comfort which her presence alone beside me in this car could bring. I feel I am insignificant. Nothing. We're nothing. But content.

But the feeling passes, quick, as quick as those things rushing past us outside, and my mind begins to cloud over once more. Wasn't there someone else? I frown. Was I supposed to see her tonight? I don't remember.

She looks outside at the passing world.

It looks like a train going by.

Chapter 19

As I line myself up at the water's edge I shoot a quick nervous look over to my wife, who smiles from the side. Silently, she watches as I dive. I still have that then, at least, I can still dive with perfection! I remain under the water for a moment, and feel the rush of cold against my skin. I glance around in the blue. As I rise up and break the surface I stop and lean against the poolside and I feel... my ring... our ring... on my finger. Haven't I always worn this? Yes. Yes, I have. I'd forgotten. For a long time. The thing has long been part of my skin. My word. How could I have forgotten our ring?

I smile, and launch myself into the water once more. Hardly anyone here today. The lights inside are dimmed and it's very solitary. I rise up after a few lengths and then decide to do some more under the water. I go down. Down, down, down, and swim along the base of the pool.

I stay there. But air is running out. I look around me and vision fades to a cool blue several feet away beyond which viewing anything is impossible. I rise up to the surface and do some lengths on my back, where I can see the dark infirm night sky far above, through the pool's glass roof, which half reflects the light from inside the complex. No thought in my mind, I turn in the water and push my face in and -

I think I see her, drowning. Down below me in the pool, fathoms and fathoms down, down, she's gone, drowning, away from me, and I can't reach her in time! And I'm about to dive down and try to get to her but then reason holds me back, rationality tells me to look to my right where she sits merely metres away. I smile at her, and calm myself, and look back to the waters before me. What is that down there?

I'm losing my -

I'm back down below, determined to find out what it is I see, but there's nothing here. Of course there's nothing here. She is up there. What am I doing in the water? I should rise again, but instead I stay down below at the centre of the pool a few seconds more. I dive just to touch the grate at the base of the pool. My mind clearing of all thought. Relax, Dean. Nothing can reach you here.

I exhale too much. My vision grows fuzzy and my thought is bent now on returning to the surface, my body is tingling. I need to rise, but – but – my locker key, tied to my wrist – it's caught in the grate at the base of pool! I panic! Only one pocket of breath remains within me and there's a line of light coming toward me, a barrier I mustn't cross, nearing me, my body touches its edge as I lose strength, and cross the line - I breathe.

I kick out violently as the water floods into me! I cough and splutter at the chemical taste, drowning, until I float there smiling, dying.

And I see a light above me, smiling back - amber, blue, grey, white –

IV. AMBER WARMTH

Chapter 20

Black.

Silence.

Cold, black, silence.

Peace.

Lights. Flashes. Noise. My eyes blow open momentarily, the water leaves my lungs, and I see her, she smiles and touches my cheek and I sleep again.

Silence.

Flashes. Roars. I open to the world for a moment and I know this place, and its surgical scent, but I'm out cold once more.

Nothing.

Bursts of certain known sights and sounds and I'm better, says the doctor, I'm free to go, journey home, return.

Innocence...

I let out a large breath and it evaporates before the comforting green glow of the car radio display, and soon my body feels heavy and I sleep once more, and awake, not knowing where I am. There's a moment of nothingness.

I'm nothing. No one. I never was.

I blink. The room is a deep, deep blue, and I'm facing the ceiling and there's a white blanket and the soft sheets comfort me. I close my eyes for a moment longer and there the image is fading of a nurse who's been sat by me and somehow I know it was *her*. I open my eyes, slow.

Everything is so quiet now. Peaceful.

I'm at home.

Quiet.

And then - voices. I sit up in bed, and listen.

My father, and an old woman. Margaret? And someone else.

My heart stops.

I lie for a while. Growing accustomed to the sketchy echoes of a sound I haven't heard in a long, long time. Could it be true? It's windy outside but bright. Blue. Seems an afternoon. I stare at the bare tree outside our window, where the light bounces off the branches.

I'm free...

Footsteps on the landing. "Son? You're awake?" It's my father. He enters, and closes in on me in my blue room. I sigh. "What happened?" I ask, weakly.

"Don't you *remember*, son?" He says, excited at my consciousness.

I consider it for a moment, and the taste of the pool arises in my saliva and lingers like a bee trapped in my mouth, and I see an after-image of a light wavering above me. "The pool... yes."

"You've been delirious for a few days now."

I frown. "I was in hospital?"

"Yes. They told Serena she could bring you home."

"I almost... drowned?"

"Yes. You took in quite a bit of water it seems." he says. "You gave us all quite a scare - to be honest, doctors weren't sure why it effected you the way it did. You had a fever for a few days, slipped in and out of consciousness. Must have been the shock, the stress, or something. But it's good to see you up. How do you feel?"

"I'm fine." I say. "I feel very... clear headed. My eyes hurt. But I'm f-fine."

Dad laughs. "Fine? My son nearly dies and he says he's fine! Only God himself could rattle you Dean. Him, or the Devil."

We sit silently for a moment.

"I… Uh… don't know what happened, Dad."

"How so?"

"Something happened down there - in the pool."

He frowns. "Oh?"

"I don't know." I shake my head. "It's hard to describe. Like I lost it all. For a minute - *everything* just… left me."

My father places his hand on my shoulder. "Try not to think about it. You've been under a great amount of stress."

"Serena…?"

"Is here. Seems your little mishap cracked her shell. Perhaps something good is yet to come out of this. He works in mysterious ways and all that. I'm just glad you're both ok."

The idea has yet to sink in. Solidify. Margaret comes to the doorway, smiles and waves, and I lift and lower my hand lightly in response.

"Well, I better go." Dad says, quietly. "Margaret and I were just on our way out. Won't keep you. Besides there's someone else who you should talk to." He places his hand on mine for a moment and grips it hard with his rough hands, and I look into his wrinkled eyes, and he whispers from the depths, "Take care, son. Remember what we talked about. Get back on your feet and look after your wife and yourself, and don't let the ills of the world hurt you and defeat you. Rise above it. You're going to be fine. Whatever happens, you're both going to be fine." He pats my hand gently and then gets up to leave, placing his scarf over his shoulders. I glance behind him and speak up.

"Margaret. Sorry I can't be much of a host, today..." I say, tired.

She chuckles. "That's ok young man. Just take care now. I've left you some of my home-made soup."

"Margaret, how can I ever repay you?"

She tells me I'm talking nonsense and then takes my father's arm. They leave, pausing downstairs to say goodbye to Serena and I catch another sound of her and my heart beats faster yet sinks simultaneously.

I swallow hard and close my eyes to the blue as the sound of the front door closing and her walking up the stairs softens and disappears. With no knowledge of the time that passes, I sleep...

When my eyes open, I jump with a start. The room looks smaller now. And everything is so - purple - a pale, pastel purple. My eyes hurt. And she's here in this colour, before me, on a seat near the bed. She's watching me, smiling faintly. She strokes my hair with her delicate hand, and the side of my face, and I feel so warm yet hardened inside, and an anger grows.

Why so long, her silence?

"How... are you feeling? Are you hungry? I can get soup." She speaks to me again, and there's an incomprehensibly strong rush of adrenaline. Her voice is unsteady, uncertain as it returns from the dark where she left it lying. I let out a deep breath.

"I'm ok," I mutter and hold back my awful elation. "You're talking again."

"I know..." she smiles, and her eyes, so alive, her round brown glowing eyes, grow vacant for a moment, and something inside me hurts greatly. Something has ended here. A time of insufferable isolation out here in the world. She is coming back to me, and yet, where has she been? Where was she hiding? Why did she have to go? My lips harden. I'm angry.

She shrinks slightly, knowing I am bittersweet. "I'm sorry. Sorry. I was... somewhere. I had to be there alone."

I nod, not completely understanding, seeing the thing in profile only and not wanting to see it face on, because I'm angry. She pauses a moment and then takes my hand and speaks, caressing it with her soft fingers, and she speaks slowly, growing re-accustomed to her more whole self. "I... I didn't *want* to be there. But... didn't know how to come back. I saw you… struggling. Looking after me. Cooking. Cleaning. Working. Everything. And all I could do was watch you. I'm so sorry."

I do not soften. She looks away, pulls her hand away, then walks away and as she disappears from my field of view, whispering her sorrow, I'm overcome by sleep again. For a long time, I sleep a sleep without dreams. And then I awake and remember the last words she spoke, and my lips harden again, and I'm angry, sad, confused, unforgiving. Sorry.

The room seems wider now, more spacious, and my eyes hurt, seeing in a faint red colour reaching for orange. Serena stands before the bed, looking back into our world, and she asks me something. Whether she should just leave me and be quiet. Whether she should go back. Away. Though my teeth are gritted I yearn to hear her, my pleasure my pain, my wound my joy.

Stay…

"Keep talking, please…" I whisper. "Tell me."

She turns slightly, her long brown hair shifting with her. "I saw us both suffer so much… I should have been stronger. Kept it together…" She quivers but holds back. She takes a deep breath, her renewed speech tiring her easily, she whispers now, her voice a delicate thin knife cutting the immense frail silence of our home. "They tried so hard to make me talk! So hard… I gave up because they couldn't... nothing... most they got from me was a 'No' and 'Yes'... and they wanted them the other way round!" She smiles, laughs lightly, quietly.

And as I am here, glancing at the verge of her speech I almost sense its wholeness again, the richness of her voice, the variations in tone, the gestures and facial expressions and the way her hair moves as she laughs, how her eyes smile when her cheeks draw back to reveal her teeth, the way her light laughter reverberates unexpectedly into and out of her spoken thoughts, these things I had thought lost. How long has it been since I heard her laugh? My smile belies my agony, my eyes close and I sleep for a long, long time.

And I dream and in my dream I see a monstrous freight-hauler hurtling towards me -

And I'm awake. Breathe. Slow. Deep. That was just a dream. Just a dream. The room - the colour has changed. Amber. I shiver. She's in front of me. Lying on the bed. Looking at me. Her eyes, deep. I speak, angry, confused.

"I wish I'd been there in the train with you. With our baby. But I wasn't." If I had been there, if we had almost died, all of us, in that breath together, would we have been closer in the aftermath? Or would we both have lived on in silence together all our days? Now we sit mute for quite some time, and she brushes the side of my face, her sweet hand warming me, and I recall once more the hole she left me resting in. "This is... hard to believe." I say, finally, annoyed and overjoyed all at once. "All this time you've been gone. I felt so alone."

"I know. I'm sorry." She pauses, feeling the inadequacy of verbal apologies. "I don't know why - I came with you to the pool... and when you didn't come back up, I screamed out your name – the life guards hadn't even noticed – one of them held me back and I shouted at the other one to get you!" She pauses, looks down. "I was so scared that I'd lost you..."

"You saved me, Serena. Thank you, my love." I stroke her arm.

She smiles. "What happened down there?"

I swallow, my face sets, expressionless. "I don't remember." Oh but I do. She was stroking my hair, somewhere, by the pool? Hospital? At home? I could taste her eyes' saltwater falling on my lips.

And something else. In my panic, a calm desire to breathe in the water and finally just let it all go, let go of life. A permeating light, shining above me, holding me, transfixed.

"They pulled you out of the pool. You were almost gone - they got the water out - you coughed and..." she pauses.

"What?"

"You laughed! And then you cried."

I frown. "I don't remember…"

…but I do…

"Hospital ran some tests. The nurses knew me… recognised you… doctors said you just needed to rest… and not try to down the whole pool next time!" She smiles, laughs.

"I phoned your Dad… and Henry… They didn't even recognise my voice… how long have I been gone?" She seems tired now.

I consider it. "Months… Too long…" I hold her hand, tight, for fear she might go again.

The light is better now, bathing the entire room in a golden hue, a wonderful rich amber glow which I can taste, a think honey-like colour I am immersed in, bathing at peace, here in this place, where I used to be, where I feel alive, together, whole. The light dims slightly and then returns again, embracing us in warmth as I reach over, kiss her, taste her once more. It has been so long. *So long!*

Oh time… what are you? Hours become days, days weeks, weeks months, months years, decades, centuries, an eternity and nothing all at once, existing and not, all at once in my mind.

Slowly I draw her to me, and unclothe her, but as I remove her skirt I see her legs and the pain written there by steel and in her eyes water as I glance up to her.

"Don't be frightened." I say.

"They're so ugly..." she whispers, eyes closed.

I look down to her legs and the scars I've been seeing all these months suddenly mean nothing. They disappear, dissolve, into her beauty, her emerging voice, into her dreams and into those parts of her that I adore, and have always desired, and into the amber glow of the places I love, this fine glow, the glow of the past, of reminiscence. An innocent placid lake of peace stretches out and an image of a raft bearing us both softly across its taught surface appears and I can smell the mountains of this foreign land as the craft carries us around and around in a circle, and I feel the wholeness of this, this circle, this ever-motion, the comforting, gentle repetitive rocking drift of simply *being*, together. I breathe deeply and the image fades to nowhere.

Now I touch her lightly on her legs with my fingertips, tell her I see only her, kiss her where she was hurt by the world around us, and slowly, as she allows me into her existence once more, we make love, tired, exhausted, exhumed.

When I fall asleep, I feel young again.

Young.

Chapter 21

"Dean!" Richard shouted, running up behind his friend.

Dean turned, frowning.

"Dean I need to show you something!"

"Richard, we're late you know."

"Yeah I know but look Dean I have to show you something -"

"Can't it wait?"

"No! Stop! Come with me. It's really important! It's about Yasmine!" And he ran back the way he came.

Dean threw his arms into the air, glanced at his watch, then ran off after him. The two came to a stop by the bike sheds at the back of the school, and Richard motioned Dean to remain silent. Dean did so. Soon, he caught a sucking sound emanating from behind the sheds. He looked over to Richard, eyebrow raised, and mouthed the words: "What the hell?"

Richard gestured to Dean, indicating a hole in the corrugated metal sheds, and Dean peaked through, to witness Arnold kissing a girl, a girl that was not Yasmine. Dean looked up at Richard, unhappy, and mouthed: "Oh my God."

"What are you two doing back here?" a voice probed, loud.

The boys' hearts stopped and they turned to see the school's caretaker staring at them, ominously. "Wait - I know you," he said, pointing. "Richard isn't it? Yes, you're always causing trouble! Get to your lessons boys. And I'll forget about this..."

"Um... ok! Sorry Sir!" Richard replied, his voice coming out as a shout.

Dean glanced nervously at Richard and at the opening in the shed wall, hoping that their voices had not carried over, knowing that they had. The boys ran for their lessons as the caretaker wandered off. But Richard glanced back to the shed at the last minute, and espied that fiend Arnold, beside it, cracking his knuckles, staring straight back.

The boys regretted being late for their lessons - they were held back during break to make up for it. As they went through the day, they politely greeted Yasmine, avoided eye contact with her, and discussed what they had witnessed only with Ajeet. That afternoon they walked the school corridors, oblivious as to their course, talking intensely.

"This is gonna kill her - she doesn't love him or anything, but this is just horrible," said Dean, and Richard nodded in agreement. Ajeet was certain of one thing - that the news be broken by Dean.

"Why me?" Dean asked.

"She's closest to you, Dean." Ajeet explained, and headed off for his final lesson of the day, whilst Richard and Dean turned a corner, and froze.

"Dick!" Arnold shouted, grinning inanely, a small group of his cronies beside him. He lunged forward and pulled Richard over to the wall, and talked into his face. "What the hell were you doing spying on me?" Richard fell silent, yet his face betrayed no fear.

"Arnold, leave him!" Dean shouted.

But Arnold didn't want to, and Arnold pushed Richard repeatedly against the wall, and shouted at him, and finally Richard had had enough. He clenched his fist, and drove it into the huge head of Arnold Walters. Arnold fell back, squared up, and Richard ran for him. But the collision was abruptly prevented by the well-placed arms of the Deputy head, who happened to be passing, and he dragged both of these teenage pit-fighters to the Head's office for disciplining.

Later that day, Dean turned the key and entered his house. Moments before, he had overheard his father shouting at the top of his voice, but as he stepped in, his father fell silent, and walked out of the living room at the back, muttered hello to his son, stepped out of the house, and drove off, his face dark. Dean placed his school bag down and wandered over to the room. He could hear a sound. Crying. He stepped inside and saw his mother curled up on the sofa, with tissues, looking worn and tired, her eyes red.

Dean swallowed. "Hello Mum..." he said. She smiled a little and waved a shaky hand. "Are you ok Mum?"

"Yes Dean... Yes I'm fine Dean..." then she smiled through her tears and laughed a small but deep laugh. "Yes I'm fine. Go and do your homework and then I'll get some food ready."

Dean shrugged, and wandered off to his room upstairs. He considered for a moment what they might have been arguing about. But it soon left *his mind, as he had more important things to worry about.*

Yasmine.

How was he to explain? And why did it bother him so much? Everyone knew this about Arnold, Dean thought. Being the big, strong, arrogant, fifteen year old that he was, he was bound to get the attention of plenty of girls. And yet… the current situation hurt Dean deeply for some reason but he could not see why. He cleared the mess from his desk and opened his folder. Professor Lloyd. Science. Chemistry. Chemistry…

His mind wandered away from his homework and came to rest on a picture of the family that his mother insisted he keep on his desk. The three of them stood there, on some beach somewhere. Dean, a happy nine year old, his father by his side and his mother taking his father's arm, the orange glow of the sun warming them. For a moment, it was as if the breeze itself was captured there in the image, and their hair blew in that breeze even now.

Dean blinked and turned his eyes back to his books. How would he deal with this? Break it to her? He didn't want to hurt her. To his mind it seemed the greatest challenge he would ever face

162

in his life. *For what could be more difficult than this? Hurting a friend with the truth.*

Dean switched his radio on and wondered how on earth it had come to rest on the classical channel. His father, Dean concluded, must have been in there earlier, listening. Dean leaned over to change the frequency but was disturbed by a sound at his window. He turned to face it. And a small stone hit. He moved quickly to the window and opened it, expecting the neighbours' children, and as he prepared to shout –

"Dean!" someone whispered.

He glanced down. "Yasmine?"

"Yeah…"

"What are you doing here?"

"Well, you told me to drop by sometime…"

Dean shrugged, and smiled - how would he explain?

"Go back out the entry, I'll let you in at the front…"

"No! No! Watch…" She took several steps back, placed her glasses in her pocket, and then clambered up a side wall, shuffled over, stood atop the veranda roof by his window, and then she swung round effortlessly and leaped into his

163

room, and returned her glasses to her face. Dean stood aghast. Still.

"What?" she asked, smiling innocently. "I like gymnastics."

"You are insane, *Yasmine."*

"Yep, that's why you love me, Dean."

They laughed, she wandered over to his bed and bounced down onto it, pulled off her trainers and sat cross-legged. "You know, my parents think I'm at some homework group or badminton club or – shit - which one did I tell them I was at?"

Dean laughed. "Would they really be upset? If they knew you were here?"

"Oh yes - you have no idea - disgrace to the family!" she laughed. "Don't you know the score? I thought you were half-Indian…"

"Yes but I don't know that many Indians. My grand-parents died years ago and dad was an only child so..." Dean shrugged. "I have an Indian middle name, did you know that?"

"Oh?" she said.

"Yeah - I never use it though. Ajeet knows more about it. He's not a half-breed like me."

"What is it?" she asked, curious, and Dean told her.

"Oh yeah!" She said. "Of course. It means lion, I think - my Dad taught me a lot about Asian religions. You're right, Ajeet goes on about stuff like that all the damn time, I can't shut him up!"

Dean shrugged. The topic didn't interest him. He was more concerned with his friend, and how he would express himself to her. She looked about his room, and her eyes came to rest on a book lying on his bed. Her eyes widened. "Oh my God! You read Tolkien!"

"Yeah…" Dean muttered; seeming a little embarrassed, he went over to the bed and tried to hide the book.

"What are you doing?" she asked.

"Hey? Putting it away! You'd hate it…"

"What? I've read it! Loved it! Those maps of the world, the strange creatures, swords, sorcery, and a little guy for a hero - I love it - really, I do!"

Dean stood back from her a moment and turned his head to one side as if seeing something for the first time, through a circular portal in his mind which had suddenly crept a *few inches ajar. Then it came back to him. How was he going to tell her?*

Knowing he was at a loss, he leapt into an attempt.

"You, um… you heard about Richard?" Dean asked.

"I heard something. I haven't seen him though. What happened? Was he hurt?"

"Well, no, but he could have been. He can be so bloody stubborn sometimes."

"Why'd he do it? Arnold's twice his size…"

Dean thought about it. "Well. You know Richard. Not too clever but if anyone says anything or does anything against him or his mates, he jumps in, without thinking - that's what happened. He'd finally had enough of Arnold, because… um… Arnold was-"

"What? Picking on you guys? Arnold's an idiot. Richard should have known better and just ignored him. Sometimes I worry about our boy Richard I really do. He tries so hard with his homework but I don't know - he just can't see some things. Anyway, Richard's fantastic, so much fun, I love him to bits, but he can be so stupidly stubborn sometimes. Arnold's an idiot - he could have really hurt him."

Dean laughed, nervously. "Do you even like your boyfriend?"

She smiled. "Yeah... He's alright. I know he's not perfect, but I do like him. But then, you don't know him like I do, Dean. He's had a lot of problems. Where he lives. If I tell you something you promise not to ever say it to anyone?"

"Yeah, of course," Dean muttered.

"Promise." She said, solemnly.

"I promise!"

"Ok. Arnold's Dad used to really beat him when he was a kid. With anything he could put his hands on. I know he's horrible to you guys, but he's just jealous cos you're close to me. He can be really nice when he's on his own. And he's funny in a very, very stupid way. Besides, you..." She looked down, whispered the rest of the sentence, and Dean missed what she said.

Dean shook his head, unable both to fathom her attraction to the bully, whilst acknowledging that this was news indeed about Arnold. Were he so inclined he would tell everyone - there was more than a small amount of humour in the thought of Arnold being beaten. Immediately, Dean sensed guilt forming inside at this cruel cold thought, and decided the fact was best forgotten.

His mind turned back to the task of imparting the sad truth to Yasmine, but just as he was about to speak, his mother called out to him to let him know that his 'tea' was ready, and his tongue tied up inside his mouth.

"I better go." Yasmine said.

"The front door?" Dean suggested.

"No. No. I'll do it my way!" she smiled, pulled on her shoes, removed her glasses, and headed back out the window, onto the veranda, and almost lost her balance as she landed on the ground.

"Bye Dean!" She waved, blew him a small kiss, and ran off, disappearing from view out of the corner of his eye.

As she left, the portal finally opened fully within him, and his hidden feelings greeted him.

Chapter 22

Several days later, Dean found himself at the door of both his science tutor and the drama society organiser, Professor Lloyd. Dean stopped at the door and watched as the professor's hair floated behind him, making strange patterns in the air. The thing seemed to have a life of its own. The tutor was concentrating on marking test papers, muttering to himself as he did. Dean knocked and entered.

"Deany!" The professor shouted. "Good to see you young man, what's wrong?"

"Nothing… can I just sit here for a minute?"

"Of course! I'll just finish marking this…" he scanned down the paper, placing various ticks and crosses, and Dean was able to catch a glimpse of the grade - an 'F'. The tutor cursed. Then he jerked his head up and sideways, smiled at Dean and waited. Dean had arrived intent on asking the professor about one thing in particular, but a new thought escaped his lips.

"Professor? Why do they call you professor? Why don't the other teachers have that name?"

"Always the inquisitive one, yes Dean? Very well… I used to teach at a university you know.

Lecturers who have been at university as long as myself often get the chance of becoming a 'professor'. Just a title, Dean. Just a title. Suggests I know a lot about things. Heh!"

"Why did you come here then Sir?"

"Why? Let's see…" his eyes grew vacant for a moment. "Well… I realised that I didn't want to do it anymore. It seemed to me that being an academic was just about chasing older and older chairs and titles. Waste of time. I was bored of teaching there. When I started teaching here it was a hell of a culture shock, kids were no-where near as bright. But that's precisely why I came here. I wanted to help those kids who would try hard nonetheless. You see Dean, at a school like this you get a couple of gems, like yourself, and Ajeet – he'll go far – and Yasmine… But then you also get the other side, the Arnold Walters - " Dean, guiltily, shamefully amused, envisaged a shoe being thrown at Arnold by his father "- of this world. And then you get the Richards. Those kids who do try their best but for whatever reason of His own God has not blessed them with intellect. That's their first flaw. The second is-" he pointed upwards, and Dean's gaze shot up to the charred lab ceiling, his friend's legacy "-they don't know when to stop. So, they're the ones I wanted to help. I came from a good *university full of very clever and usually very rich students. I got bored of teaching them. They came in clever, they left clever, but with greater arrogance and good jobs secured. I couldn't believe their lack of understanding of other people in other situations – did you know my father was a factory worker? Worked hard to give me an opportunity and most of the people I taught had had privileged, money-laden childhoods and something just started to feel wrong. The work had no meaning anymore. I wanted to help the Richards and Richardesses of the world. That's why I'm here."*

"Ok." Dean swallowed, trying to digest it all.

"I'd like to think I do some good here... Ah, but nevermind all that Dean! Ignore my insufferable smugness! You didn't really come here to ask me about that did you?"

"No…"

"What's wrong then?"

Dean drew in a deep breath, and then explained his predicament to the professor. That he knew something about her boyfriend that would truly hurt Yasmine, yet he was struggling to tell her.

"That's very odd Dean. You have no loyalty to Arnold. Why don't you tell her? Your little group of friends have been together for almost three years now."

"I don't know Sir. There's something stopping me. I just… don't like the idea of her being upset. I want her to be happy. More than anything."

The professor blinked, and then smiled, and said slowly, "Dean. I believe you need to look inside yourself and think about what you're really feeling!"

Dean glanced around inside him like a startled animal picked out by a torch in the dark. "But leaving that aside, she needs to know what's going on, Dean, and it will sound better coming from you than anyone else. Trust me, I know her, she speaks to me sometimes as well you know."

"She does?" said Dean, surprised.

"Yes. And sometimes you have to be prepared to tell people what they don't want to hear. The truth. It can hurt greatly. But in the end, it is best. Sometimes pain is worthwhile. Sometimes it can be good for you. You can't lie your way through life Dean, or hide from truths anymore than you can hide from your shadow. Things *like that can pursue you until you face them and do something about them, or they just consume you slowly from inside. What I'm saying is a little heavy for one so young, but I think you're ready for it, Dean. I think you are. If I were in the situation, I would tell her... but it's up to you of course, it's your life..."*

For a moment, the professor returned to his papers and allowed Dean to consider it. Oddly, Dean thought, he actually understood what his mentor was saying for once. He understood, clearly. Dean stood up.

"I'll tell her." He said, and left.

Chapter 23

A few hours later I'm awake, turning over the words of an old mentor in my mind, annoyed at the fact that I can never recall quickly enough the more immediate lessons I learned in that time.

She's sleeping. Holding me tight. So warm, now, both of us. The first time we've *truly* slept together for... too long. One of my hands is free enough to be resting on my chest and I feel the coldness of the ring, my ring, *our* ring, which once followed her down into the depths in a dream. As I look at her body rise and fall with her breath I realise she needs me, to guide her out of that lost place, just as I need her.

When she finally loosens her embrace I roll slowly out of bed and feel her weight fall away to one side. I reach over to my mobile phone and switch it on. It bleeps. A message. I dial into my voicemail and listen. "It's *me*," she says. "I heard about what happened. Henry told me. I've been *worried*. Call me when you can. Bye now."

I delete the message. Stare at my phone for a good while. Look back to my wife, sleeping. Stare back the phone. An eternity passes by.

I scan down my phone number list and find hers. I stare for a moment. Thinking. Look back to my wife, sleeping. Stare back the phone. Blink.

Then I enter the options menu, select a command, watch the number dissolve, and switch my phone off.

I return to our bed. Whisper to my wife until she is awake, "Serena, Serena."

She looks straight into me. "What is it?" she asks, sounding almost foreign as her voice emerges with every word spoken.

"I need..." I swallow. "I need to tell you something."

At dawn there is a moment between deathly sleep and vibrant consciousness where all things play out silently in a quiet tone of their own. Movements seem slower, lips move but voices go unheard, and even the life in the trees pauses, sensing a solemn moment.

Into this peace-imbued frame runs Serena, half dressed, her silk gown trailing, leading her to trip and fall in the centre of our grassy garden where my eyes register a cry that my ears will not hear.

Silently I follow her, betraying my panic in my loud yet voiceless calls to her, in my slow fall to the ground beside her, and in my rough embrace of the woman who could finish me. I beg for warm forgiveness in our wet grassy garden.

I'm sorry... so sorry...

We sit for a while, as life all around us observes our ragged, fractured selves, our grey forms grasping one another in the unreal thinness of dawn, and I refuse to part, even as she turns and whispers calmly, into my ear, that she doesn't want to talk to me ever again, *ever*.

But I stay, stay, with her, touching, close. I will never let her pull away back into the silent stillness she craves so much. I will never let her go there alone again.

I would rather I had died, in the light of the pool.

Chapter 24

"You look well!" She said.

I went back to work and it was the end of my first day. She was pleased to see me. Ecstatic. She had been worried, she said, that my sexual energies may have been dampened by my brush with death less than seven days hence. My laughter was not so deep. There was something on my mind and she knew it but as soon as we got into my car and I announced our destination a wicked smile came over her face, and she became animated, unbuttoned her blouse slightly to tempt me, opened the window and let her blonde hair flap about in the cold Winter breeze.

At the peak of a hill I know there is a fantastic view of the city and the surrounding countryside and the motorways that wind through the land, encircle our town and then continue in all directions. Here, once, weeks ago, Jennifer and I had parked my car and, laughing, half-clothed, we had taken one another like animals in the open, and I like a fool had forgotten the significance of this place, of what I had seen there.

She talked excitedly about friends she'd seen recently, old university girls she used to study with and some boy she used to date once and a party they'd all arranged and been drunk at. She talked about how the department was doing fine without me that week but was crying out for some attention before the imminent Christmas break. She told me about little Edward, who had been asking after me, hoping I'd be well soon. She talked about her body, and what she wanted me to touch today. She sounded so young.

I smiled. But I was not aroused. I drove us to the peak of that hill.

When the car came to a rest she threw herself onto me and kissed me with energy, whispering that she'd missed my touch and my body, and her hands reached down to my uninterested member and then she stopped and looked at me with her steel eyes.

"You don't want me." She accused.

I didn't respond. I moved her away from me and she sat with her head against the chair, looking at me intently, frowning.

"Get out of the car please." I muttered. "Come with me."

She obeyed the command, no doubt interpreting it as yet another sexual game, she ran to my side and took my arm and stroked it lightly with her fingers, smiling. We stepped up to the edge of a sheer drop, and looked down onto the trees far below and she muttered something about having this strange compulsion to jump. For a moment I identified with this, the desire to jump, to fall, much like my desire to breathe in the water in the pool and just-

...*let go*...

"It's over." I said.

She held my arm tightly and laughed a short nervous laugh. I pulled away and turned to face her. "It's over." I repeated.

"What?"

"You know what I'm saying. This is finished, Jen." I said it softly yet cold, firm.

"But we only just started..."

"It's over."

"Why?!" she asked, angry, upset.

"It's finished. I'm a married man, and-"

"*That* never bothered you before..." she half-smiled and I had an urge to slap her for the sting she'd just administered.

"I was confused."

"No, you knew you wanted me."

"I was vulnerable. Messed up."

"Yeah, yeah... You still *wanted* me Dean... And you still want me now." She teased and reached up on her toes to kiss me, but I moved back.

"No. I don't." I asserted, and her confident front fell, as I noticed her hair being pulled fiercely by the wind, like a hand pulling her over that edge, I could see her falling -

"I don't understand! Why are you doing this?!"

"Serena."

"What about her!"

"She's my wife."

"So?"

"She needs me, she's getting better, she's talking to me again and I-"

"Oh I see. She needs you now. So that's it? You got your kicks elsewhere and what now? She's back? Back from the dead? Are you having sex with her again now? Is that all I was? Just a shag whilst she moped around -"

"Jen, *don't…*" I warn.

"Why? You don't like the truth, do you Dean? She abandoned you-"

"Stop!"

"She couldn't have fucking cared less about you! The bitch!"

I grabbed her arms and she gasped. "Don't you *ever* speak about Serena that way! Do you fucking understand?" I shouted.

The world was red and she was a dark spot on my existence and she was trying to attack Serena and I saw soon what could have happened as I shook her so near to the edge, oh God I knew it would have been so easy just to *push* her! I let her go, she lost her balance, tilted backwards, and crumpled to the ground by my feet.

"Dean you're crazy!" she said, through tears. "You could have killed me!"

Could I have? Inside I was frightened. Of her. Of me. Of what I'd become and of the limitless possibilities of my existence, of the self-drawn boundaries of fragile light on the ground that could be crossed so easily, the desires, the urges, pushing you to the other side.

My God... I could have killed her...

"Why are you *being* this way?" she pleaded. And for a moment I really felt for her. It touched me to see her suffer. But there was no other way. I had to cut her from my life and from here on in it would all have to be professional. It had to be harsh. This had to be swift. Even if I did care. I couldn't watch her. I turned away and walked.

"Get in the car." I ordered over my shoulder.

"No!" she screamed.

"Get in the fucking car! You know it's over."

"No!"

I got into the driver's seat. She sat there, a young, naïve twenty-something who had never understood me and never would. A materialistic sexual being who couldn't touch me inside the way that Serena had done time and time again. No one could touch me like her. No one. This was *finished*.

She rose to her feet and removed her heels and stumbled to the edge of the hill. "I'll jump Dean!" she said. "Dean!" I watched with a blank expression. She wanted emotion. She wanted me to stop her. She stepped closer to the edge. I sat, emotionless, blinking, unconcerned. Yet my heart froze as she teetered on the edge and became unsteady for a moment! And then she regained her balance. And she smiled, laughed nervously, hoping for some sign that it was all a joke.

Then she cried. Moments later she conceded defeat, picked her shoes up and joined me in the car, and I sped the vehicle back down the winding roads that had taken us to that dizzy place and she spent all those lingering moments looking at me, at the side of my face, trying to decipher my secrets, fathom my method, crack my madness and lighten my dark heart.

I betrayed no emotion. I simply switched her existence off, and broke the speed limit in a desire to remove her from my car and my life. I brought it to a halt outside her flat. She looked at me.

"Dean…"

"Yes?"

"Please Dean… we can do this differently…"

"No. We can't. From now on when you see me, it will be business only. Do you understand Jennifer? We were never supposed to do this. It was an accident. A stupid mistake."

I could see the flashes of pain encompassing her with every last insult I threw out, and yet the thing I had done to Serena, the harm I had dealt her, was all that mattered now. I reached over, unlocked her door, pushed it open, and unfastened her seat belt.

"Please Dean… Dean…" she begged, crying. I looked at my watch, hurting her with every exaggerated gesture. But I didn't know how else to do this. Serena deserved me. I owed her so much for my indiscretion. She awaited me and I had to go now.

"I have to go. Get out of the car, Jen." I told her.

"Dean!" she whispered, "I *love* you…"

My heart sank. Oh God. What had I *done*? I reached over and took both her arms and pulled her to me and she saw it as a loving gesture and readied her lips to kiss me, but I stopped her an inch away from me, and whispered in return, into her wet eyes –

"Jennifer. Please go now, and take care."

I pushed her gently hard out of my car and out of my emotions and my life, and pulled the door shut behind her, and started the car, and noticed her fingers gently pressed against the window, reaching impossibly, pathetically, for me.

They trailed off lightly, as I drove away.

Chapter 25

It was springtime and it was raining. The school was silent but for the voices of cleaners and a few late-working teachers. In a classroom on one side of the school a pair of teenagers sat in a darkened room, huddled next to each other.

The girl had been crying - the spent tissues littering the floor told the tale. The boy had his arm around her, her spectacles in one hand, and was rocking her gently.

"I'm sorry Yasmine... I should have told you as soon as I saw them. I waited. I didn't know how to... I took so long to -" he said.

She embraced him in return. "It's ok, Dean."

"I know you liked him." Muttered Dean, but for the life of him he still could not see why she ever had.

"It's ok Dean. Just hold me for a while. Just you. Forget him."

And as the rain continued to fall, they stayed, sitting together like this, close, exhausted, innocent and peaceful, until the staff ushered them out and pointed the way home, in the fading light of day.

V. EMERGING

Chapter 26

The truth shared, Serena took a huge step back into that silent confined place that my near drowning had pulled her from, and I struggled to prevent her from closing the door again, from returning to her silent time. For seven long lingering wet Winter days after ending it on the hillside, Serena was quiet again, but differently so. She remained more active, moving around the house, no longer sinking into our sofas or armchairs or bed.

I was gentle, but determined not to let her go. Not again. After the crash, I had simply pushed her towards therapists, burying the memory of our lost child, my eyes seeing only the ugliness of the scars that criss-crossed her legs. It was a split thing I saw, a tree with fine leaves but torn-up roots, my broken Serena.

But after the pool everything changed. Our closeness to our paper thin frailty had brought us back together. We may have been on the edge together, but we were together all the same.

Yet I was profoundly worried that by confessing my indiscretion with the other woman I had lost her again, that the crisis would now simply recur, that it was for Serena to sink once more, and for me to follow and drown behind her again.

Thankfully, that was not to be.

One night, I made her laugh as we sat rigidly beside one another. Whilst watching some American comedy, I made some unexpected quip I had not intended to voice out loud. She smiled, then laughed, hard, and collapsed into my side. She did not pull away from me as I tentatively put my arm around her.

It was remarkable; like her game of chase through the house on the night I almost died, she just suddenly switched on as she crossed some line inside and came back to me, and my muscles tensed, fearing another disappointment after those agonisingly long, silent, days. But that night, we made love, slowly, quietly, no urgency. A soft expression of our rekindling love and intimacy. The next morning, she shook me awake, smiled, and simply wished me well.

Soon her trust in me returned. Slowly, she emerged more fully from her mute isolation. She began to rise in the morning, wake me, then cook breakfast for us, as she had done in the years before the accident. We began to live once again with familiarities of the past, the replaying of our earlier time together.

We smiled, we laughed, we argued, we made love.

And time, senseless and ruthless traveller that it is, moved on, and for a brief while after the affair, things were difficult and tense at school. Jen would never look me in the eye and she would answer me only with a small 'Yes' or a 'No' and never any more. Thankfully the Christmas break was only a short interval away at the time. Henry Lewis continued to work like a peasant in the fields whilst his all but helpful Deputy Michaelson continued to frustrate me, as I tried to gather in documentation from the various departments in readiness for the inspection. And yet Henry could not, or would not, see the massive mistake that had been made in deputising Michaelson. Meeting after meeting took place concerning Ofsted, in an attempt to iron out kinks and develop strategies to fill in remaining gaps early on, but every instruction I gave out was later in some way contradicted by Michaelson and the whole thing became nigh impossible to orchestrate.

When Christmas break finally arrived it was with a collective sigh of relief that everyone went home to rest. For me, personally, things were improving, life was in motion again, a forward motion I understood and needed. Ms Dunley existed but she had become a ghost, an insubstantial shadow wandering the corridors, in search of an accidental moment which I had left on the floor behind me; somewhere there in those corridors, lay the corpse of my indiscretion.

As the richness returned to Serena's eyes, much was still missing. She talked tentatively of her impending return to work at the start of the new year. She was nervous, apprehensive. Frightened. Her patches were not completely re-sewn, but her voice returned inside me and spoke to me in my silence. Although my indiscretion was forgiven, the shame I felt still burned me deep and the coldness of that time with the other woman still chilled me on days.

Once, we went walking, during that Christmas break, Serena and I, in the park, hand in hand, talking, laughing, joking, recounting old times, how we'd met through a mutual friend at a house party in Cambridge, where she'd just started her nursing career. Somehow, we'd fallen into an argument, and then hated one other with a passion for weeks to come, as our paths continued to cross, and our initial annoyance and attraction continued to disturb us.

But one day I found her crying on one of the many bridges crossing the river Cam. Comforting her on that cold Autumn day, I found that she was missing her family, who had moved to Chicago only months before. We began afresh, apologised for our drunken outbursts at the party, and then went on to become close friends until, a couple of

189

years later, I turned up on her door step having walked through those ancient college-lined streets, soaking in the rain just to see her. I stood there, drenched that night, confused, unsure of my future, confused about my past, missing close people I once knew, now long gone.

They happen on occasion, moments of that kind; pivotal nights, days when many things converge in space and time, and just *happen,* things of sadness, things of beauty. That night I found a direction. That night I fell.

And so it was, years after we had met, after so many things had happened for us, between us, and against us, that we found ourselves walking in the park during the Christmas break, crunching the thickly built layer of snow on the ground. We cut over a white hill where someone else's footprints directed us, and soon came to an open, flat area where a number of empty swings shifted leisurely an inch forwards, and an inch backwards, for their phantom occupants.

Serena spoke fondly, her voice rising and falling with her excitement, her eyes animated, of a place she used to sneak away to in her darker moments when she craved light and grass, a park from her childhood. As she spoke of this, she piled snow a foot high onto a swing and gave this thing a head, and a single lonely stone for an eye, and then pushed the swing until the cyclops fell to the ground with a whoop of joy. She laughed richly at this and at her memories and I thought I could hear the child that she was, cushioned somewhere in that laughter. The thought occurred to me that she was at her core just a child, yet capable of such devastatingly powerful switches to maturity and depth, that I could spend a lifetime observing and discovering who she was.

Nearby a group of boys were throwing snowballs. We regressed for a moment, and fell about in innocence on the ground and covered one another in snow, until an old lady wandered along, wrapped in an immense coat, shaking her head and cursing at us 'youngsters' as her walking stick led her onwards, past us, and away. Feeling spoken-to, we sniggered, and then we walked on, some small amount of dignity remaining, leaving our youth lying laughing loudly in the snow behind us.

It was at the lake that the revelation came. We stood looking out onto partially frozen water. Then she turned to me and, being only a couple of inches shorter than me, she made our cheeks meet in an embrace as she whispered in my ear.

"I have something to tell you Dean-" and the second half of her statement followed thereafter.

"What?" I asked, frowning, unsure of what I'd heard.

"I'm pregnant." She whispered, again, and again, and again, and she laughed lightly, straight through my ears into my soul and back out through the crevices of my own fragmented self.

Chapter 27

New Year's Eve came and went, and 2002 became 2003. As Serena grew, slowly, the school lumbered its way through those tiring Winter months. With the news of Serena's pregnancy, and with her increasing return to strength by my side, work felt not as heavy as it had all those months ago. It was as if a steam roller resting on my body had of its own accord decided to move on. Even with the lateness and solitude of evening overtime, I felt lighter, more able, less alone. Stronger. It occurred to me that that I was returning to the core, to the centre. That my drift was coming to an end, my fragmented pieces floating back into their rightful place. The school year rumbled on.

Although removed from classes on a number of occasions, Layla and Carter somehow continually avoided permanent expulsion in the manner of professional criminals ducking the arm of the law at every turn. Intelligent but scared little Edward walked alone from class to class, now wearing a bright red scarf that made him all the more a target of abuse. Jones's screams echoed down the corridors from the school gym and Ms Dunley's heels beat the ground at a more confident pace as she wandered past me from time to time and gave me a sidelong glance. I worked away at my inspection duties, keeping everyone focussed on the trial to come. Occasionally, the "Good Head" matter returned to haunt us, with the press hovering at the school gates, trying to tease out new scandals, but, thankfully, no one had been as stupid as the old Head and his Deputy. Not even Ms Dunley and I.

Nothing, in essence, had changed at the school. I still worked incredibly hard, running my own department as well as doing all else, and I still stayed late into the evenings every day. But now, it didn't matter, for she was *with* me again.

Dunley, the workload, and all that had been derailed the year before, all of it blended into the background, and it suddenly seemed irrelevant. And yet, even in this state of relative calm, on this uneven plateau I had reached, this uncharted state of recovering mind, of all the things that could have bothered me, I was surprised to find that it was Michaelson.

I was doing more than we had originally agreed when I took on my new duties, and much of my work was being delegated through Michaelson. Work that he should have been doing himself. Yet what annoyed me more was the deaf ear Henry turned to my plight. He called me into his office and announced that the Ofsted inspection date had been set, that they would come towards the end of June, and that preliminary meetings with the inspectors were to be held in a week's time, my attendance, of course, being necessary. I was relieved that we finally had a date to work towards, and since we'd started the ball rolling almost six months previous, the time scale afforded us by this notice period was going to be enough to collate all the documentation, despite the reluctance of other department heads, with relative ease. But the news did not deter me from my own purpose in seeing Henry that day. I managed to corner him in his office for a moment. We stood, raising our voices across his desk.

"What's the issue Dean? I told you it would involve-"

"But Henry, this is clearly something Geoff should be handling. Why on earth am I having to – I have a department to run as well you know."

"Of course I know!" Henry snapped.

"Well speak to Geoff then!"

Henry shook his head. "I might. But it is well within his rights to delegate, so I'm not sure what I can say."

"Come on, I *know* you can do better than that."

"As a matter of fact Dean, maybe I can't, ok? I have things of my own to be getting on with so just stop complaining and get to it!" he snapped again, red in the face.

A silence fell that went on for too long a time, so I relaxed myself, and allowed diplomacy to take over. "I'm sorry Henry."

"Been that kind of year, hasn't it?" He sighed.

"You *know* how it's been for me."

"Yes…" he muttered with sympathy, but I once again had the odd feeling that he knew more about my actions than he was letting on. Perhaps his niece had finally told him everything. Perhaps he was as disappointed in me as I was in him. Perhaps he too sensed the distance that had grown between us since his support for Michaelson grew and my distaste for Jennifer swilled around in my mouth. Perhaps. Perhaps that's what I saw, hiding behind his eyes, behind his spectacles, the look of a man wary of someone he thought he knew. I knew that look. On occasion, I saw it in the mirror.

"Look… Let's just leave it for now, ok Dean? I'll have a word with him after the Easter break. That way, you'll be clear enough to focus on the inspection and not have to concern yourself with any other duties. I've decided that after this year I want us to go back to having two deputies - it seems we need them after all. This cut back approach is too stressful - it's not like you're not doing a good job Dean, but it's not working is it?"

"I don't think so." I admitted, taking a small dent to my professional pride.

"Well, forget the whole thing for now. I know you've been working hard, but like you said the documents should be ready for Ofsted in May, so relax. Once they're off, the inspectors will run their discussion evening with the parents, and you can sit back until the inspection week itself. Dean - I know you've had a lot of... personal upheaval of one form or another. So just, you know, switch off for most of Easter. We'll deal with everything soon enough. After the break I'll personally make sure you can focus on the inspection."

I nodded, grateful, and headed for his door.

"Oh and Dean. I wanted to invite you to something, over Easter. We're having a bit of a dinner event one evening. If the weather holds we're making it a very early barbecue. Otherwise just an indoor thing. Bring Serena! We're dying to see her again. It's been too long."

I instantly warmed to the man again. I smiled, nodded. "Yeah... I will. Call me with the details?"

"Ok."

And just as I stepped out he stopped me again.

"Dean. Just so you know. Jennifer will be there."

Having just accepted the invite, to show reluctance now in any way would have been a blatant indication of guilt.

"Fine." I said, holding my poker face only for a few seconds before leaving him and going back to my teaching, my head pounding instantly.

Chapter 28

And so now as my wife's body takes on the changes of nature, I observe the growth of our second child. Once more, I am to be a father, and I find myself feeling differently than I had a year hence, when we first conceived. Somehow, this time, it seems almost like a tangible reward for our perseverance through the hardness of the year, and yet there are moments where everything appears slightly unreal, my vision tinted by impossibility, I feel as though a veil has been draped over the eyes I see through, and the world does not appear quite right.

Now, as I look out of the window on this crisp April day, I feel the coolness of our wood-panelled floor on my bare feet, I notice buds appearing and sense fully the beginning of Spring. And I try to remember a quotation from one of my favourite books - something about having a familiar feeling about life and its renewal.

No. That doesn't seem quite right. I must look it up sometime.

The house is airy, windows are open, and a cool breeze passes through. I hear Serena's footsteps echoing in the corridors and she stops somewhere and chuckles at a memory or a photograph or something.

And now, I wonder. About the events of the last eight months or so. I wonder how all of that happened, how I allowed myself to go to those places I had never been before, to be seduced by Jennifer, to be taken into *her* cold blue world. I shake my head. How could I have become one of the things I most detest? A liar, a cheat. The barrier is truly so thin between here and there. Between being what you are and should be, and being what you can and will be. It's absurd.

Now I stand here in my house, looking out at the world, at the trees and their odd branches wearily stretching out and twisting amongst one another in a slow dance that lasts centuries.

And I remember something.

Chapter 29

"I just don't think you can do it, Yasmine!" Dean challenged.

"Right then. Watch this." She removed her glasses and put them in her pocket. They were in a park, and the leaves on the trees had re-emerged and greeted the world again. And there was a particular old tree which rose up high into the air, its first branches a good five feet above the ground, thick, strong, and able to support the weight of keen youngsters.

"Watch this," she repeated, took a few steps back and breathed deeply in the chilly Summer daylight. Then she ran, ran toward the tree, her face focussed and concentrating on the task ahead. She ran a few steps up the tree, found a finger hold in some place Dean could not even perceive and a foot hold here and there and scrambled up cat-like, grabbed the branch and swung up into the air, managed to get her leg round the branch and sat there, beaming.

"Ha!" she shouted, laughed, and placed her spectacles on once more.

"How the hell do you do that?!" Dean asked, throwing his arms into the air to indicate his lack of understanding.

"Come on, it's easy. Go on, give it a try."

Dean stepped up to the tree, touched it with his bare hands, and scraped his skin against the scratchy brown bark. "No." he concluded, and slapped Yasmine's dangling legs beside him. "You just want me to get hurt!"

"Don't be such a girl, silly. Ok, if you can't handle it, forget it. We'll never get married then."

A surprised look came over Dean's face and he laughed at the suggestion.

"Married? We're not even going out!"

"Of course not."

"Are you blushing?" Dean smiled.

"No! Shut up! Get your arse up the tree!"

"You'll never do this, Dean." Ajeet's voice from behind suddenly interjected.

Dean turned. "Oh great, what do you two want?"

Ajeet and Richard glanced at one another and grinned. "Nothing. We saw you two over here and thought we'd come see the show. What's happening?" Richard asked.

"He's gonna climb the tree." Yasmine explained.

The boys laughed, and Richard snorted. "Climb?! Dean? He's bollocks at PE!"

"Be nice, Richard." Yasmine said.

"Ok…" Richard said, but then added excitedly, "Dean! Climb a tree?! Yeah right!"

Dean, insulted, gritted his teeth. "I can do it."

Richard laughed again, and Dean shouted, "I can do it!"

"Fiver says you can't."

"Done!" Yasmine answered the wager.

"Oh dear." Ajeet whimpered.

"Right then." Dean stepped back and stretched his legs, and crouched a little, ready to run. Richard laughed.

"Fuck off!" Dean shouted. And ran! But as he approached the tree his concentration lapsed, and as he scrambled up he was unable to get a foot hold and, banging his head on the branch, his body traced a backward arc in the air and he slumped to the ground on his back.

"Fuck." He muttered, humiliated.

Yasmine leapt to his side. "Are you alright, Dean?" she asked, whilst the two boys doubled over in laughter and the leaves on the trees chuckled in the wind.

Chapter 30

As I turn our car into Henry's street, I blink out of the silly scenes I am replaying in my mind, and return them to their pit, their casket buried deep. I make one last attempt to avoid the inevitable, and glance at Serena as I speak.

"You're sure you want to do this? We can cancel you know, I -"

"Dean. Don't worry. I'm ready. I have to come out more."

"You *know* what I'm talking about." Why does she have to make me say it? I feel my guilt enough.

She reaches a hand to me and strokes my hair. "I'll be fine. It'll all be ok."

I bring the car to a halt and take a deep breath. I step outside, go round to her and with Serena on my arm, walk to the door, and chime the bell. Someone answers.

"Elizabeth," I say, warmly. "It's been too long."

"Yes it has Dean, I ought to spank you!" Henry's cheeky, incorrigible wife of twenty seven years smiles, and then turns to my own wife, tilts her head to one side and holds out her arms for an embrace. "Serena... how *are* you? You're looking wonderful."

"I'm looking pregnant, Elizabeth!" Serena laughs.

"That's what I said - wonderful. Come on in, Henry's in the back. The boys have some friends watching football in the lounge. We've been banished to the garden, as we're old and therefore not allowed to even put our heads round the side and so much as say hello to the friends of our bright young twenty-somethings. Children! Fortunately the weather's holding out. Not bad for April in England is it? So, we decided, a barbecue it is. Go on through Dean, I want to have a woman-to-woman with Serena..."

Serena slaps my behind. "Go on boy, get out." She commands.

"Yes ma'am!" I salute, take a look at them both laughing together and momentarily espy the motherly compassion in Elizabeth's eyes, and remember my own mother's face for a brief flicker of a moment. Then she is gone, the thought recedes. I look at them walking away, Elizabeth with one hand on Serena's shoulder, the two women seemingly as close as Henry and I.

I find my way to the back of the house, wander past the lounge and hear youthful cheers and whoops of joy at what I presume is a goal well-scored. I wander through the kitchen and out through the patio door into the weak Spring sun and the sound of a hissing, sizzling barbecue greets me. To my left in the corner I catch a view of Henry through a huge pale of smoke, concentrating, focussing, on his cooking, cursing. I glance around, a fox, watching for a hound. No Jennifer. Yet. Thankfully.

There's a group of Henry's friends, who look familiar, loitering close by, beer glasses in hand, chatting and admiring Elizabeth's rock pond, where the gold fish swim aimlessly. A rather fat man with a huge beard, seated at the garden table, laughs loud at something his wife is whispering into his ear, and simultaneously drops his drink and laughs all the harder for it. If I didn't know better I'd swear it was Brian Blessed. There's a CD player playing some toe-tapping jazz music and it's all so incredibly relaxing. I wasn't sure what to expect. I wonder though, was this really such a great –

"Dean!" Henry shouts, beaming at me from behind the smoke. I wander over.

"Henry I'm sure there's not supposed to be so much smoke."

He frowns. "You think so? Hmm. Ah well. Nevermind. Help yourself to a beer. There's punch and wine over there too." He points them out.

"You thinking of getting a licence?"

Henry grins. "Help yourself, first round of - burgers? Yes they are - burgers will be up soon. No wait, that one's a sausage."

Unsure of whether to laugh and feel welcome, or to flee the mysterious and unidentifiable cooking meats, I help myself to some beer, introduce myself to the fat man who hasn't yet stopped laughing - in fact he's been laughing so hard he's now crying, poor man - and wander back behind Henry's smoke screen.

"How's the Easter break been for you Henry?" I ask.

"Fine. Very nice, in fact. The boys are back from university for a while, so it's good to see them. I'm not going into work this week. Things will be stressful enough when Ofsted nears. For now, I just want to rest a little! How about yourself? Not been thinking about work, I hope."

"No, no. I haven't really. Caught up on an immense backlog of marking but aside from that I've been resting. And I've been… Ok. Actually it's all been good, this break. The worst lies behind us, I think. Serena and I have been - well, there're no words for it really. We're doing ok for once."

"Good." He says, but he seems distant. I swallow and decide to try to explain something.

"Henry, sometimes, you know, sometimes things, things get to you. You think you understand yourself. You think you know where you are in life. Then you do something. So different. I don't know. You, you lose yourself, I guess. And then - "

"Shit." Henry curses, and I see a sausage do a flip up into the air and land several feet away. The fat man bursts into laughter.

"What happened?" I ask.

"God damn these things! How can they be so slippery?"

"Henry, what have you done to them? I've never seen anything like it."

"I know. Exactly!"

With Henry clearly preoccupied, I drop my weighty attempt at conversation and help him. As I'm placing a sausage onto some fried onions in a soft powdery bread roll, he says "Jen will be here soon - she's been held up," and my sausage also decides to commit suicide and slides with some speed off the onions and skids down my cream trousers and onto the floor. Cue uncontrollable laughter from fat man – I've forgotten his name – and me and Henry both join in this time. I stare down at my stained clothing in disgust, laughing despite it all.

"It's the fecking onions!" Henry shouts. "We're putting them on the bottom! No wonder!"

We soon line up our all too large, slippery fried onions on the top of our snacks. With the change of strategy comes a wave of non-slip burgers and hotdogs ready to eat and soon there's a line of hungry guests wading into the food whilst I somehow end up wearing an apron and turning burgers!

Jazz music swings on in the background and Henry's next to me with his beer and we're chatting about Miles Davis and laughing and joking and then suddenly he clears his throat loudly and the next thing I see is Jen throwing her arms around her uncle and giving him a kiss. Then she withdraws and looks at me and smiles a small smile and I can feel Henry's eyes darting from one to the other – *does he know or doesn't he?* – and the moment is tense, awkward, lasting only seconds, before I recover.

"Jennifer," I say, leaning over and kissing her cheek quickly. "How are you?"

"Um… I'm ok. I'm fine." She says.

"Henry's decided I need a change of profession." I joke, pointing out my apron, and the three of us chuckle, artificially.

"Where are the boys, uncle?" she asks.

"Lounge - football - didn't you see them when you came through-?"

But she's already turned and is heading off in the other direction, and she throws some explanation over her shoulder as she enters the house.

Suddenly I'm trying my damned best to focus on the sizzling burger in front of me. On the mottled texture of the heating flesh and on the parallel lines formed by the mesh and on the spitting and the glowing coal beneath, and I'm trying *not* to think about the fact that Serena is also in that house and that Jen will imminently run into her. And I'm shivering slightly.

"You alright Dean?" Henry asks, and I feel his stare.

"Yes, I'm fine."

He smiles and laughs. "Look like you've just seen a ghost."

Doesn't he know? Doesn't he know about my insane time, my indiscretion, my flaw, my fault, my most painful error?

I breathe a deep, deep breath and try to forget, but *they* will meet in moments, it's inevitable, I turn the burgers.

"You know I only married him because he was good in the kitchen." Someone laughs, my head turns quickly and it's Serena, walking toward us, smiling, on Elizabeth's arm.

211

"Serena!" Henry says, full of joy, and he wanders over to embrace her. She seems surprised by the love my colleague and his wife shower on her. They think she's wonderful, they have always, and seeing her now after almost a year they seem to have sincerely missed her. Henry asks her how she's been feeling and about work.

"It's going well, Henry. I was lucky they held the post back for me so long - and all this time, I've been sitting around doing nothing, lazy girl that I am!" She laughs a little at her own self-mockery, her way of dealing, as the three of them come close to the grill.

She looks at me a moment, and maybe it's the fire or smoke or metallic smell of the mesh that does it, but her eyes seem to glaze over, and she speaks of something unexpected, as if in a trance, as if the wordflow cannot be stopped. Somehow her whisper carries itself through the gaps of the sizzling food before me, and Henry and Elizabeth listen, intently.

"I had… an aisle seat. To my left three ladies were talking about work, and before me an old man sat with his hands together as if in prayer. He seemed to be elsewhere, somewhere, sometime. Occasionally he'd come out of it. Glance up at me, smile, chuckle lightly then close his eyes and go away again for a moment. A few seats further down a little girl licked a lollipop and rocked left and right with the movement of the train and joked and bickered with her kid brother. And I touched my belly, where our baby rested, growing. For a moment, I understood. It was all so clear. I was so content. Happy." She paused momentarily, and then became animated.

"Then it happened. All of us in the carriage, we were thrown across it, first to its rear, and then to the side. The sound was - *unbearable, so loud* - God crying at us in anger for something we'd done wrong but we didn't understand what it could have been! A second later it came, the thing, the train, like His hand, it crushed us, smashed our carriage… I huddled in a corner, bleeding, feeling my baby dying within me, and around me all I could see was blood, and fire, and twitching hands and feet, and hear cries. Everyone dying. I was the only one who - I was the *only* one to survive in that carriage. Why me? Why."

We stood, shaken, and of course, no answers suggested themselves. For the first time since the event itself I felt I could begin to understand what had happened to her. She came out of her trance and smiled, and the melee of guests behind us, oblivious to the importance of her speech, whirled around the garden, laughing, joking, ignorantly blissful, unaware of all our frailty. Only Elizabeth dared ask her that which I had been unable to understand myself, these long months. "Darling Serena, why didn't you talk about this before?"

"What would I have said, Elizabeth?" She smiles. "In the face of all that, there seemed nothing to say. You know, it's very difficult, being pregnant again. The crash threw me out of my - my life. Took our child. And I surrendered to it. I gave in to the thing. Life had beaten me... Turn those burgers honey." She points out my duties, and I act quickly to prevent them burning. She takes a sip of water, her eyes focussed on the ground before her feet. "Sometimes you find yourself at a barrier, between doing one thing and another. Speaking or not speaking. The line is so thin. You can go from one side to the other just like that, not know why you're there or how you got there, and then struggle to find your way back to where you came from. To emerge from it all. To return. But you *can* come back. It's as easy as going there. I went when my baby died... But I came back. That night at the pool. I came back for Dean. He needed me." She smiles.

I let the batch of burgers burn on the grill. In her words I hear the expression of my inner most thoughts, my sensations of lines and boundaries crossed, her voice giving shape to my maddening thoughts. Elizabeth once more puts a gentle hand on Serena's shoulder, and my wife smiles as we stand there with a saxophone solo floating softly into the air around us. Then focus returns and I finish off cooking the final round of meat, cobble together a few dishes of these fattening snacks,

214

pass some plates around the garden then hold one for Henry, Elizabeth, Serena and I.

"Feels so strange to be pregnant again. You know, I was so scared about going back to work in January." Serena says, and Elizabeth nods in understanding.

"Seeing the kids in the ward - it was hard! Made me wonder what I was doing there. Why I'd decided on nursing sick children. I spent the first week or so wishing I'd stayed at home. But then this one baby - she kept crying all the time - no one could handle her. Then one day I was the only one around. And I took her in my arms and looked into her bright little eyes, rocked her gently and whispered to her. I don't know what happened. I spoke to her and she giggled happily and since then she's been peaceful. It was like -" she laughs "…a sign."

The audience is quiet, admiring her strength. There's a moment of contemplative silence whilst we all return to some time when we were all ourselves pained yet brave inside.

Such a long time ago…

And then it passes. "Excuse me, I need the bathroom." Serena laughs and rushes away.

We watch her disappear into the house, and suddenly I tense up again for I realise who she will meet there. "She's a mystery that one, Dean,"

Henry mutters. "But you did so well to find her. Take good care of her." I nod and before I can reply he says. "Dean, I just remembered I have something for you."

He leads me from the lawn into his house, and into his ground floor study, a room full of books and folders and papers all piled up precariously on shelves and he reaches over to his desk and sits on its surface, passing me an envelope. I open it and take out a hand-written note. I read it, frowning, curious.

I shake my head. He watches me, intrigued.

I stare at the note, reading it over and over. I hardly believe my eyes.

"How do you know him, Henry?"

He shrugs. "I don't. He gives talks on various teaching matters at conferences and the like. Something you get to attend as a head teacher. He saw an article about our school in the paper."

I raise an eyebrow.

"Don't worry! It was one of the better ones. The ones you arranged for us. He found me at the end of a conference. Said he admired the way we'd handled the affair. Said he'd be very much interested in speaking to you some time. That was it, he didn't explain anything else. I asked him to come along tonight, told him you'd be here, but he said he couldn't make it. He lives about an hour away by car." Again Henry shrugs, and leads me out of the room and into the hall.

There's a wave of emotion that rushes up inside me. I would very much like to see him, even if just briefly. I slip the note into my back pocket, and jolt as Ms Dunley's laughter wanders round from the lounge, but then its gone and we're back outside and the guests are laughing and joking and the music continues to have its mood-lightening effect. I smile as we return to our wives and as I put an arm round Serena I notice her eyes harden as she looks over my shoulder and I realise what she must see there.

Slowly following her gaze, my heart pounds intensely, and as I turn to face the imperfect shadow of my past the silence hurts my ear drums. I look briefly into Jen's eyes and see the pain shimmering there and then her steel grey spheres solidify as I make the introduction.

"Jennifer - meet my wife, Serena. Serena, this is - this is Henry's niece, and my colleague, Jennifer." I say, quietly.

Serena reaches out a hand and they shake. "I've heard a lot about you," my wife says.

"Likewise," the shorter woman replies.

Stillness.

They look one another up and down whilst Elizabeth and Henry – *does he know or not for fuck's*

217

sake?! - speak of something to one side, and when Jennifer turns and heads off for some food, Serena whispers into my ear, her lip quivering slightly.

"She's beautiful, Dean."

And in that one simple sentence she sums up all the pain, the unspoken hidden pain that I know she carries inside, caused by my crossing of the line, that ridiculously thin, narrow stretch of existential nothing which lead me to Jennifer's body. For a brief second, the guilt is overwhelming, and I want to die, to end, here, now.

Serena… finish me…

Then the boys come out of the house and we greet Henry's sons and their friends, and the group of familiar strangers mixes in with us as we chat and joke and lightly speak of many things. I notice Jennifer out of the corner of my eye, on the arm of a young man, and she feels my gaze and glances back but looks away hurriedly. In another time, another life, perhaps we could have been. But not in this one.

And so as more people arrive the groups move on and the circle of people travels round and around to the continuing jazz soundtrack, and as the light of day has all but disappeared and the breeze is picking up Henry switches on the garden lights and a cheer goes up amongst the thirty-strong crowd. And the groups move on. Until we find ourselves standing with the fat man, Elizabeth, Henry and a very quiet Jennifer who drifts in and out of the edge of my vision.

Then Serena screams lightly and clutches her growing belly. "Oh my..." she says, and wobbles slightly. And I'm by her, so is Elizabeth and we hold her steady, asking if she's ok, and lead her to a chair. We give her some water and she looks vacant and we ask her once again if she is ok. She lifts her t-shirt, takes my hand and places it on her belly.

I smile.

"It's kicking!" she says.

"Oh please may I?" the fat man with the beard asks, delighted by the news. He comes over, and places one huge hand near to mine. "How positively remarkable!" he booms and then he looks at Serena and his eyes wrinkle up and his mouth falls open, letting his laughter burst forth to announce to the world that he is happy.

Serena takes one look at this ridiculous rotund jolly person before us, smiles at me and joins in, "I've never felt this before!" she says, through her rich laughter. And he dances around the garden, a drunken fat man embarrassing his wife, his guffaws rising into the air with the thin wisps of remaining barbecue smoke, as she speaks quietly about the sensation.

219

And as I listen to her voice, I realise I have been blessed by her forgiveness, as if I had never in fact done those things that I had, as if they had never been, those filthy enjoyments of flesh in flesh. Who are you Serena, that you can return from nowhere to reign me in from my chaos, my madness, my desires, who are you to be able to do what you do. You hold me as if I were no more than a small amount of water poured into your cupped hands, fearful of the separation of your fingers. Were I to slip through them, you would never gather me again, I would splash against the hard jagged surfaces below us by your feet and evaporate with the first flickerings of the rising sun.

I glance over to Jen and she manages a half smile.

I turn back to Serena and as night falls I see in her eyes tears.

Oh my…

Chapter 31

The crowded queue of school children moved slowly through the fish and chip shop, and Yasmine stood to one side finishing off her greasy potato lunch. Some little boy in the line smiled at her and she smiled back, and was about to say hello when her arm was suddenly grabbed hard and she was jolted out of the door, the wrappings falling to the ground behind her.

"Arnold! That hurts!" she protested, as he dragged her to the side and pushed her against the wall, took both her arms and shook her repeatedly.

"Why won't you talk to me?" the beast demanded.

"Why'd you think? Just leave me alone!"

"No! Look, that girl was nothing, ok. You're the one I want... I - I love you!" and he tried to kiss her. She resisted. "You make me sick Arnold! Leave me alone."

"You're the only one who understands. You have to come back to me!"

"No I don't, maybe I have someone else!"

"Like who – who would – ?" Then an age-old suspicion surfaced. "It's that pussy, isn't it? Dean."

"Maybe. Anyone would be better than you, you're a fucking-"

And he raised his hand as if to hit her and she saw it and screamed and suddenly Arnold was pulled back and thrown against the wall and a very red-faced Dean was shouting into his face and Arnold was actually taken aback by his shorter assailant.

"Keep your hands off her you bastard!"

"Yeah? You twat! Pushing me around. Was that supposed to hurt?" Arnold shouted.

"No, but this will -" and Dean smacked him in the jaw.

And the world paused as Yasmine looked on in silent shock, shaken, stunned. Dean backed off, breathing hard. Arnold moved his massive frame from the wall and felt his jaw, thinking. A large crowd had gathered, and people were muttering the names of the two fighters, Dean Sekar and Arnold Walters. Arnold, embarrassed by his apparent defeat, looked Dean in the eye, muttered yet another death threat, and walked off in anger, alone, bitter, cold.

Dean turned to Yasmine. "Are you ok?"

She embraced him.

Chapter 32

In the cottage where my father lives there is a round wooden table that sits in his dining area, and it bears four large candles which provide the light for evening meals. As we sit, laughing, enjoying conversation as we have done on so many occasions in the past, I look over Margaret's shoulder and catch Serena's reflection in the window. She smiles at mine. And the fires of the candles flicker and play on the wicks and their reflections do a counterpoint dance as classical music crackles on the radio.

"Delicious, Margaret, thank you." I say, breathing my words out slowly as I'm full and the thick sweet aftertaste of pudding lingers. I take hold of my plate and Dad stops me.

"Nevermind son, it's not important. I'll sort them out later."

"Not like you to be untidy, father." I tease.

"When I'm happy, I'm untidy."

"Margaret, what's the secret to this whole cooking thing? I can't even fry an egg properly." Serena jokes.

"Now child, I know you can! As for the secret? My secret you mean?"

"Yes."

"I intend to take it to the grave with me," she says, tapping her nose.

And as we sip our coffees we find topics of conversation and when the candles begin to burn too low, we shift and melt into the comfort of the living room. Dad gets a fire – a real fire! – going and I lean next to Serena on the sofa and listen to Margaret and Dad bickering about preference of radio station - 'Radio Three' or 'Classic FM'. I don't pay much attention, just sit and laugh at the nonsensical play-fighting of our seniors. I flick through a book on Dad's table. A dictionary of quotes. I find the 'age' category, and grin as I read *'for they say an old man is twice a child.'* Shakespeare. Hamlet. My father, twice a child. I laugh a little at the thought. I flick through the book and stop at a random page.

'All the things one has forgotten scream for help in dreams.' Canetti. I close the book.

Later my father's there, Baileys in one hand and gesturing with the other as we try to decipher the elaborate charade that he is enacting.

Film. Three words. First word. One syllable. Rhymes with red. He lies on the floor, still. "Dead!" Margaret screams.

Second word - Dad stands and pretends he is reading something out - something - an announcement? A scroll? A book, a poem? Poem! Poet! Plural?

"Poets!" Serena shouts.

Last word - first syllable. Dad takes off his sock and waves it in the air. Sock! Sock?! Ah – on the tip of my tongue, oh shit, yes, um –

"Dead Poet's Society!" I shout with a whoop of joy, and down my whisky in delight and let it burn my throat and everyone's laughing as I hear the classical music playing I shoot a quick look to my wife and everything in the room –

...slows down...

...and I see her turn, slowly, as if she can't move any faster, and for an instant the world slows to a pause, a moment frozen in time, as her face comes into view, her brown eyes meet mine, and her hair, her long hair, loosens itself from her shoulder and rolls down her front and rests there as if it is asleep. And all the while the light from the fire, the warm, amber glow of the fire caresses her and I wonder whether this is it. When you contain this feeling of being so complete, so content, is this it? The time at which you should go? Is this where there's nothing left to say and if there's nothing left to say is this where everything should end? Where everything balances - you don't need to be here anymore, you don't need to exist, you can go, you can go, you can let yourself go. Is this when you should go? I feel I could die now. Here. Life, take me at my most content. It's

226

all so clear. This is how she must have felt just before the trains smashed together...

...*she smiles*...

"Dean?" she asks, concerned, for I have not stopped staring at her.

"Hmm?"

"Are you ok, oh love of my life, my love?" she teases.

"Yes. Yes. I'm fine." I smile.

A little while later, however, I am far from fine. The radio has been switched off, and Dad has, in his infinite wisdom, decided that a private viewing of the Baby Dean Photo gallery is in order, and I am subjected to the 'oohing' and 'aahing' of two grown women and an ageing old man. I'm suffocating! But smiling, despite myself.

"Such a happy little boy!" Margaret smiles, as we flick through picture and picture of me, mostly alone, playing with something or other. Sitting in a grassy field. On a swing. Slapping a friend. Perched on a car bonnet in my nappies! Trying to eat a huge rubber ball. As we near the end of the album the adoration begins to die a little, as the boy has aged and taken on a less innocent appearance. And then, one page from last, a photo falls from the pages, and floats of its own accord to the centre of the room. Silence.

Everyone pauses. We can all see it. Pause, world, pause. Mute.

Finally the crackling of the fire becomes too loud, and my father steps over to the centre of the room and sits down cross-legged on the floor, and takes up the picture in his right hand, and he stares at it for a long, goodly while. And I know what he sees. A moment in time. Frozen. A perfect moment in his hands, which heralds a time gone by, a moment frozen, a moment past, and I'm not sure what the picture is, but as the smile appears on my dear old father's lips, I crouch down next to him and ask him if he is alright. And I see it. The family in the picture. The three of us stood there, on some beach somewhere. Me, a happy nine year old, my father by my side and my mother taking Dad's arm, the orange glow of the sun warming us, and, for an untrue second, it's as if the breeze itself is captured here in this image, and our hair blows in that breeze even now.

I shake my head and turn my eyes back to my father. It's been a while since we saw this shot. He looks up, slightly choked, and speaks.

"She looks so happy. And beautiful. Doesn't she, Dean?"

"Yes Dad. Of course. Come on."

And there the evening ended. Margaret returned to her neighbouring cottage and Serena and I lay down for the night on the opened-up sofa bed. For a moment, my father sat on the stairs, and kept his eyes on us lying together. We switched the radio on again and the orchestral music continued to play very low as the fire died. We covered ourselves in a blanket and Dad stayed there, staring, at our stillness.

"You alright Dad?" I asked.

"Yes. Yes. I'm fine." He smiled and then he left us, alone.

Chapter 33

That evening after school, Dean and Yasmine found themselves at the tree once more, where the brightness of the day gave the leaves a surreal green glow that widened their eyes. She ran round the tree a couple of times and returned to Dean.

"Hey - I really appreciated what you did for me today."

"What?" Dean asked.

"Arnold - he could have hurt you."

"I don't care. He tried to hit you."

"But he's really big and he could have really-"

"I don't care Yasmine. Who does he think he is? Bastard. I'm not going to just let him throw you about like that. No guy should ever do that to a girl. He cheated then he tried to hit you?! Bastard! Fucking Bastard!" Dean flared up in a fluorescent shade of red, and kicked a stone on the ground.

Yasmine did another circuit of the tree. "You're so sweet!" She said, and ran round once more but this time caught him with a light kiss on his cheek as she sped past. His face reddened further. "Maybe we will get married…"

"Um -"

"Relax Dean, it's a joke!"

"Oh…" he muttered. "Um - but don't you think, I mean -"

"Hey? Sorry Dean speak up I can't hear you!" Yasmine shouted, from the other end of the tree.

"I said! Um… do you think… I mean we…"

"What?"

"Um, you know… we could… you and me…" his tongue failed him, he looked to the ground.

"Really Dean, you gotta speak up! I'm in a race here!" she laughed as she darted past once more.

"Would you stop that!"

"What?"

"That running thing."

"Why?!"

"Because -" Dean floundered once more.

"Because what Dean?"

"Because I'm trying to ask you out, stupid!" he said, and immediately looked to the ground in shame.

She stopped, ten feet away, and stared at him.

"What?"

"You heard me. I want… I think you should… I hate this, why can't I just say it? Um -"

"You want to be… my boyfriend?"

"Yes!" he said, embarrassed, afraid more than he had ever been that he was about to be rejected. But as he was looking down, he could not see her smile. Silence.

She stepped up to him, slowly, and his heart tried to escape from his body, and flee behind him, as it beat the rhythm of the running man. She lifted his head with her finger, a gesture so unusually beyond their age that Dean felt he was living in a cinema scene of old. It was at that exact point, that exact moment, that she entered his memory forever, and he realised what he felt. With the tide of emotion within, his tongue tied further, and he tried to speak.

"Well… would you be… be my girlfriend?" he asked.

She brought him close to her. And kissed his forehead. What is this girl, Dean wondered, what is she? What will she mean to me? And the silent moment then seemed to freeze for Dean and he stood there, an eternity, waiting for an answer.

"Maybe..." she whispered, smiled, pushed him to the ground, giggled and ran around the tree again, and Dean laughed as he fell to the ground, to the soft green lawn by that immense wise old tree, for a second time in so many days.

Chapter 34

I cry out silently as I hit the ground. I've rolled off the bed! Why?

Was there something? There was a dream... and I see it now, still fading behind my eyelids. She lay there, between the twisted metals and plastics and fabrics of the broken trains, as she gave birth, silent, no screams, calm, silent, sad, as if she knew the answer already, knew what awaited her. The child slowly emerged from Serena of its own accord, and it arrived. And surely this would have been a deep golden moment of joy for us, the beginning of a new life, a new family. Genesis!

But our baby simply slumped to the debris-littered tracks like a bag of lifeless sand. I touched its fleshy cheeks, in desperation, with some vague sense of hope, yet it was cool, breathless. I turned away from the scene; rolled off the bed.

I lie here now. Awake. The cottage has ceased to be warm. I stare up at the cracks in the ceiling. I wonder what I would do if our second child emerged, without the breath of life. I wonder. Which lines would be left to cross then, Dean? What would remain to be done...

As I rise up onto my feet I see her, my Serena, innocent, wonderfully swelling with child, yet the room is dark and her skin appears as stone and I

234

pause before I lie down next to her and sleep again. I take in the colour of her face before I close my eyes, and I inhale deeply her fragrance. Before me now she lies here, breathing, her eyes rolling within, following the plot of her dreams. She lives. Yet her hue resembles the dead baby in my dream.

Cold.

Blue.

VI. THE PAPER THIN SKY

Chapter 35

Late June. The inspection is merely a week away. At some unnoticed point – I had so much else going on in my life that truthfully I was past caring – the department heads grudgingly fell into line and simply did all that I asked, which wasn't a great deal in the first place. So, three weeks ago, amidst a flurry of last minute activity, the documentation was sent off to the chief inspector. It was done. Henry was pleased, I was pleased, and both of us were exhausted.

I yawn and lock my classroom door as a crowd of pupils wanders past and out for their lunch break. I need a coffee before my meeting with Henry and Geoff. It's incredibly empty, this corridor, when everyone has left the building. It feels quite... Lonely. I hear a sound behind me and I turn and walk left round the corner to the exit, only to be confronted by *that* couple, kissing.

"Layla, Carter, get out - it's lunch break." I say, tired.

"Sir! Hello. How *are* you?" Layla asks, rolling her words out slowly. She sounds - and looks - drunk, high.

"I'm fine Layla. Now come on, both of you…" I yawn.

"Aw, poor Sir. You've been working too hard." Her wicked smile emerges. If she didn't have all those facial rings she might even be attractive. How does she get away with them anyway? They're not uniform.

"Not hard enough obviously. I see the two of you still don't know how to behave."

"What you mean, Sir?!" Carter asks and then falls silent again, in behind his mistress.

"How many suspensions so far this year? And you've been spending a lot of time watching fights lately…"

"So what, Sir? That don't mean anything, everyone watches, they're good fights!" Layla says, looking a little rattled. "What are you tryin' to say?!"

I smile. "You know exactly what I mean Layla. Funny how you two always seem to be nearby when they start. And when they finish. What are you playing at this time?"

She brings on her 'innocent' expression. "Like I said Sir, don't know what you're talking about. But it'd be a shame if there was a fight next week during the inspection wouldn't it? Still - would show 'em what really goes on at this place. It'd be like that time those teachers got caught with their pants down on tape, havin' -"

"That's enough. Go outside." I say, alert once more.

Her goddamn kiss is blown my way once more. Behind me I hear the sound of heels on floor, and I oddly sense that someone is eating crisps nearby. "Oops," Layla mutters, and once again I'm struck by the idea that she may be intoxicated. "Better go. Your girlfriend will get jealous." Carter chuckles as she leads him out by the hand.

I frown. My g-?

"Hello Dean."

"Oh. Hi, Jen." Did Layla know about me and Jennifer? God. I hope not. I sincerely hope not. The moment is quiet. Icy. No smiles.

"How are you, Jen?" I ask, politely. "Classes ok?"

"Yeah, not bad. Ready for inspection?"

"As ready as we can be I think."

"Good. Who was the girl? One of your mistresses?"

"What?" I snap, annoyed by the exchange with the two pupils.

"You know," she continues, "apparently loads of little girls fancy you. Don't worry. *I'm* not one of them. Not any more."

I flounder. Turn red.

"I'm joking!" She says, managing a half smile, but on the other half of her face I see pain washing around deep in her eye.

I chuckle nervously, then hold the door open for her as she leaves the building. Seems an age ago since we had our - our involvement. Our accident. I try to get her out of my mind as she walks away from me, her figure as short, fine and alluring as always, and I hear a noise, something crunching behind me, and I turn.

"Edward?" I ask. "What are you doing inside?"

"Um…" he says, munching on a crisp and swallowing hard. "S-Sir, can I talk to you?"

"Of course."

The boy pauses for a long minute and shifts from one foot to the other, uncomfortably. I'm just about to hurry him up when he speaks. "Did you read my s-stories s-s-Sir?"

"Um – which ones Edward? You've left me with so many!"

He shrugs. "The ones I gave you last w-week?"

"I haven't had a chance to read those… but I tell you what, I did like the set you gave me before

239

Easter. Well done with those, Edward, you're quite talented." The boy smiles, pleased, and I would like to discuss it further but, "I have to go now, I have a meeting to get to and -"

"Sir! Sir-" he pauses, glances around, ensuring no spies are hovering. "There's gonna b-be trouble, s-Sir."

"What do you mean?"

He glances around, and whispers. "I heard them s-Sir. I was right here, they didn't know. Those two. Layla and her b-boyfriend. They said there would be a f-fight. A riot."

"Really. Where? When?"

"Next week sometime. W-when the inspectors come."

Layla's words resurface in my mind. It would be a shame if, during the inspection… My eyes narrow. Suddenly I'm gripped by apprehension. Could they really be planning…?

"Edward, this is serious stuff, you better not be making it up." I assert.

He looks a little hurt. "Why w-would I Sir? I'm only s-saying it 'cos they d-don't know I heard them. I just w-want to help."

I breathe deeply, looking into his tender eyes to find the quiver of a lie but I see only the unshakeable glare of truthfulness and innocent sincerity staring back at me. So I thank him for his information, promise him confidentiality. Would that couple really - would they *plan* to ruin the inspection? God knows. I shouldn't give them the benefit of the doubt though. I head off at speed for my meeting with Henry and Geoff. They need to know.

Chapter 36

My eyes have bags under them, and my lids are heavy. I've forgotten my coffee.

Since April, things have been hectic, my year eleven pupils have sat their exams and are now resting at home, and my focus is on the inspection, which is the subject of the meeting. Michaelson mutters on about some wonderful thing that Jones has done to whip up enthusiasm in the P.E. department, and about how Jones is right about inspections and inspectors – how could they possibly judge a school based on a few days worth of observation?

I shrug the question off, more concerned with practicalities than academic critique. At some point Henry asks me how I feel about the departments' readiness for inspection. After having checked and re-checked certain school-wide standards with them, I tell him, they appear ready enough for a decent performance.

I'm about to mention Layla but Michaelson launches into a harangue about parents' evenings and insists that Henry consider dropping the appointment system next year, on the basis that it is a waste of time. What is more likely is that booking appointments involves too much of an incredible effort for Geoff to bother any more. Nevertheless he rants and goes on and on, and it is only towards the end of the meeting that I finally have a chance to bring up my concerns. "Henry, Geoff. I think we need to give serious consideration to something."

Geoff's ears perk up. Henry frowns. "What's the problem, Dean?"

"Layla and Carter. I think they're up to something."

"Like what?" Geoff asks.

I shoot him a quick look. "I think they're going to try to start another of these racial gang fights next week. To wreck the inspection. And I think it would be a big one."

"Surely not!" Geoff scoffs. "They're a little bit troublesome at times - that Layla's a little outspoken - and they've been disciplined - by me, I might add - so much that I can't imagine even those two would dare to start any trouble next week! I don't think kicking off riots is their style, anyway. They're just kids Dean. Not organised crime bosses."

"Well, we've never been able to catch them at it. But I think they're planning something big to ruin the inspection."

"I'd have to agree with Geoff, Dean. They're troublesome, and by no means my favourite pupils, but - well, this is a school, fights happen, inspectors know that. So I think you're overreacting... What makes you so sure anyway?" Henry asks.

"One of my form pupils overheard them talking about starting a 'riot'. You don't know them like I do Henry. Neither do you, Geoff." I try to explain. "Carter looks very intelligent and sheepish. But he's not. On his own he's actually pleasant. But coupled with Layla? Well, it's a volatile combination. She is definitely in the driving seat, he's her muscle, her thug, and she is incredibly sharp."

"Huh! Her grades wouldn't suggest that!" Geoff laughs.

"It's not about grades, Geoff, intelligence is more than that. No, she's a strange one. She makes it look as though she's just a random playground bully, but occasionally she shows flashes of designed, calculated malice and a desire for disruption. She rebels in and out of class but she's a little more shrewd and manipulative than others. On the contrary, she is *exactly* like an organised crime boss." I realise this is sounding more and more surreal and peculiar by the minute. I begin to wish I'd not brought it up.

"You're telling us that they have some kind of agenda to bring down the schooling system? That's ludicrous Dean. Simply absurd." Geoff laughs.

Henry's eyes dart from his Deputy to me, as I try to assert myself once more. "No, not exactly. But they do have certain anti-authoritarian ideas and opinions. She definitely does anyway."

"What kind of ideas? Why do you think that?" Henry asks.

"The things she says to me. About people having a right to know what happens in this school. Like the stuff with the Head and our old Deputy."

"Look Dean, they've been suspended a few times already, and they've had their final warning, so I don't think -"

"I'm also fairly sure they've had a hand in instigating some of the fights on campus recently. That's probably what they're planning next week. Sorry, but I think we should have permanently excluded them by now."

Henry frowns. "But Geoff spoke to them. We had no way of showing them to be involved. How could we kick them out for a simple suspicion? It's not like someone came forward to tell us."

"Well I don't know, but -" I pause and prepare to say it. "We should seriously consider having them out of the way for the inspection."

"Are you *serious* Dean?" says Henry, wide-eyed.

"Yes."

"Do you realise what you're asking?"

"Yes." I nod.

"This can't happen Dean. It's craziness. We can't just suspend them or boot them out without solid grounds of them doing *something*-"

"What about the fights?" I say.

"What about them?" Geoff asks.

"They're there, every time, Layla and Carter, watching from the sidelines."

"Well so is half the school Dean but that doesn't mean they orchestrated it! They were spoken to! By me!" Geoff insists.

"Geoff, look. It's odd and peculiar, I know. But this is not beyond them, they've already been suspended five times this year, they clearly don't care about that! And I know Layla. She's up to something. She's even dropping hints to me herself. She said it would be a great shame if something were to happen, one of those fights, during the inspection. And someone overheard her planning -"

Geoff laughs and shakes his head. "Who on earth 'overheard' her, Dean? One of her little 'enemies'? It's probably just someone with a grudge, stirring things up. You're going on about them as if they were the bloody Mafia. Grow up Dean, I mean, really!"

I wish I could strangle this fat, useless, warbling fool! The way he always laughs things off, but when *he* has a bee in his bonnet the whole bloody world must lend its ear. I glance over Henry's shoulder and espy a small black monkey moving along a branch, laughing at me, grinning and belittling me. I blink. The stray cat leaps down from the tree.

Henry broods for a moment. Geoff guffaws to himself at random moments, like a car that won't start. I try not to show my irritation. Then Henry leans forward, shuffles the papers on his desk, and speaks. "Dean. Thanks for bringing this to me but... No. There's nothing we can do. I can't *fabricate* reasons to have them thrown out! Not that I'm even entertaining the idea, but if we did it, and they're as crafty as you suggest, where would they go? Straight away? The press most likely. And we've been in enough shit with *them* this year. Just keep a close eye on them. The next time is their last time, and they know it. That's the best we can do."

My heart sinks. They'll be the death of us. I admit defeat. "Ok. But make sure you both remember what I said here today."

They smile together and there's a second where I'm not entirely sure which one is which. The sensation passes, they assure me they will remember, and then I leave the office.

247

Embarrassed. And far in the back of my mind I'm beginning to lose interest. I'm tiring of all these… struggles. These fights.

Chapter 37

The boy awoke to the sound of raised voices. Rising up out of his bed he noticed the coldness of the house and the darkness. He drew the curtains and squinted in the light of the sun and felt peculiarly weightless. For a moment, he drifted, and the memory of Yasmine leaping into his room floated past his eyes, and dissolved just as quickly before the perfect still sky.

Then the voices grew louder, sending a burst of anxiety through his being. He left his room in a hurry and ran down the stairs, into the living room where his suited father stood, holding his mother by her arms, shaking her as he shouted. Dean did not catch the words immediately, but he had a vague notion of what was being said.

The boy faltered, but uttered a plea. "Mum? Dad…?"

But as his father shook her, he shouted, and Dean's voice was drowned. "They meant nothing to me! How many times do I have to tell you that they're nothing, absolutely nothing! I lo-"

"Dad!"

Dean's father spun round, and his rage crumpled as a shaking embarrassment took its place. Red-faced, he darted past his son and left the house, shouting over his shoulder that they had meant nothing, that he loved her and no one else, that he was sorry. And that if she was going to torture him like this everyday, then she should just leave and never come back, or perhaps that he should! The door slammed behind him. Dean went to his mother's side, but as she fell back onto the sofa she cried and told him to leave her alone, to prepare for school, have his breakfast, and leave.

Dean, tired of their endless, senseless, needless fighting, left her and went instead to brush his teeth and think of happier things. He would see Yasmine for a few hours today. He was content with this. He was sick to death of his parents' arguments, since they had been raging for many years.

He tried to put them out of his mind as he ate breakfast alongside his mother, quietly, knowing that only a visit to his mentor and friend Professor Lloyd would help him ease his worries now. After a while, his mother spoke.

"I'm going away for a while, son." she said.

He nodded, and from nowhere it occurred to him that even after her tears, she was beautiful. He smiled, inwardly, and did not notice her watching him closely.

As he stepped to the front door, his mother came up behind him and turned him around, looked into his eyes and embraced him for a long, lingering moment. Embarrassed, he tried to escape. But she held him there. A goodly while. Smiling, the short woman kissed his brow, and said goodbye and told him to take care, and that she would see him soon. She held him, tight.

Tight.

Bewildered, but relieved to be out of her grip, the boy left the house and glanced over his shoulder on his way to school, and the moment became engraved on his memory for all time, that image of his mother, sad yet calm and oddly content, smiling, waving.

Chapter 38

I glance out of the window and then back down to the pages and read out the quote to myself.

'And so with the sunshine and the great bursts of leaves growing on the trees, just as things grow in fast movies, I had that familiar conviction that life was beginning over again with the Summer.'

There's a moment of connection and I feel it, the sensation of life beginning anew. I sigh. I haven't read this in years, a book about a deluded man, struggling to repeat the past. I remember the poetry of the novel, the beauty of the words, the whispers of the characters, the author's quiet, haunting voice.

Serena blows on a container in her hands and coughs as the dust billows into the air and comes to rest around her bare feet on the wooden floor behind me. I close the book, an old, second-hand, hardback edition of Fitzgerald's Gatsby, and place it back along with an array of tomes that rest on bookshelves scattered about our home.

Then I sit on the floor and lean into a massive crowd of cushions up against the wall of our living room. The floor is warmed by the sun streaming through the window opposite me on this restful morning, and as I sit watching Serena's beautiful figure assemble an old music stand by the coffee table, I see the dust dancing downwards in the paths of light before me. She smiles as she opens the case.

"It's been so long, Dean." She murmurs. "Years."

Her old flute. Before the accident, of course, I often caught her turning her head to one side and muttering something about playing it again one day, sometime soon, when an empty moment arose. But she never did.

She opens the case and touches her belly. "They say playing music to a growing baby is good for it," she says. I smile. Perhaps it is.

She takes out the small components of the instrument and connects it all together, its edges and curves catching the light and blinding my eyes. She unfolds an old yellowed sheet of music and places it on the stand, and she smiles as she puts the pipe to her lips, and then frowns, concentrating. I chuckle as uneven distorted notes float out.

"Shut up!" she chides. "*You* can't play *anything*."

"Sorry my love. You're right, I'm rubbish. But - it's so nice to see you doing this. How long has it been? It's strange, funny."

She narrows one eye to display her disapproval of my teasing her. And then she straightens her back and brings it to her lips again, and this time, the notes seem clearer, more confident, the flute's voice returning.

I do not feel any desire to laugh this time. She plays and the scene is familiar to me. Something she did for me once many years ago when we had first met. She played to me. The same piece of music. Some variation, of her own, on 'the lord is my shepherd'.

It's wonderful. Not perfect by any means, the notes still flutter and emerge in an unusual, shaky manner but they are, nonetheless, beautiful, and the music begins to feel whole once more. I let my head fall softly back onto the pillows as her breath through the flute charms me. I fall into a light semi-sleep. Beyond the music I hear the sound of her voice. I see her playing with her hair by the fire in my father's cottage. Happiness. Contentment.

Serena stops playing, I fall asleep, and the phone rings.

She reaches for it and speaks, her voice calling me back from my half-death. It's my father. She chats to him for a few moments and then hands the phone over to me. I take it.

"Everything ok, son?"

"Yes, Dad. Just resting. Calm before the storm. The inspection's about to kick off."

"Ah, well…"

"Is everything alright with you?"

"Yes. I was just hoping -"

"What?"

"Oh, that I might see you soon. Sometime this coming week?"

"Oh. Dad, I'm sorry but I can't spare any time. Straight after Ofsted though, I'll come up? How's that? See you then?"

"Yes, ok." He seems happy, rested, content.

"Everything ok, Dad?"

"Yes. Everything's fine."

"Well, I'll see you soon then?"

"Yes. Goodbye, son."

He puts the phone down on me and in between the dialling tone ringing out to tell me that the call is dead, and the handset being replaced, I forget the conversation.

I return my head to the pillow and sleep, as Serena plays once more.

Chapter 39

Later that day, a small troupe of clouds gathered to cast a shadow over the school grounds, as Richard rolled to recover the ball, smiled as he half lay there, and then jumped up onto his feet and shouted, "Nice one, Ajeet! You came close."

Ajeet, breathless, took a suck of his inhaler. "Really? Really?"

"Really! Now it's Yasmine's turn."

Yasmine patted Ajeet on the shoulder and turned to face the makeshift goals comprised of the boys' coats. "Where's Dean? I thought we were all getting together for lunch?" She asked, as she effortlessly put one past Richard.

"How can you be so good at this sport, Yasmine?" Ajeet asked, in awe.

She shrugged, as Richard spoke. "Dean's gone to see the Prof. He wasn't too happy about something. Um… His parents I think. Fighting? Don't know." He had barely passed the ball back to the girl when she struck it and sent it flying past him once more. She laughed. He scowled.

As Ajeet received the ball from Richard, he stepped up to take a shot and noticed a shadow fall over the soiled whiteness of the ball. He turned and paled as he saw Arnold hankering after Yasmine. The brute had taken her by the arm and shifted her to one side and she stood there with an irritated expression as the boy flexed his muscles in his school shirt, muttering words falling on deaf ears. Richard, unhappy at the arrival of the bully, stared quietly at the scene, whilst Ajeet gave a nervous shrug of his shoulders, sent the ball flying way past Richard, and danced in celebration.

Caught up in this moment of triumph he turned and smiled at Yasmine - who was almost in tears as Arnold shook her by her arms. Shaking, the anger building up inside him, Ajeet found bravery amidst his fear of pain, and told Arnold to leave the girl alone. Arnold, enraged at her refusal to listen, turned his head and with one swipe of his immense arm swung out and sent Ajeet to ground, his turban rolling off, his embarrassment complete.

As Richard returned with the ball he saw the beast making a mockery of his friends. He saw Yasmine's upset expression as she was shaken by Arnold. When he looked down he saw a tearful, humiliated, bare-headed Ajeet on the ground, his top-knot being laughed at by others in the school's playing fields.

Rage grew within him. He stepped up silently and resolutely to the child gangster and breathed deeply as he looked up several inches into Arnold's eyes and formed a fist and Arnold, releasing Yasmine, whispered menacingly, "Do one, or fuck off. Dick."

Richard swung, but his arm was caught by Arnold, who punched the would-be hero in the stomach. Falling back slightly, Richard regained his senses, and saw that a huge crowd had formed almost instantly, shouting and chanting "Fight! Fight!"

Feeling all the frustrations of the year arise at once, all his failures in his homework and his tests and his upset at his constantly inferior grades to his three more gifted friends, he pressed these feelings into a tight ball of rage and ran at this thing, Arnold, the bastard who had tormented him from the first day Richard had arrived at the school to this very moment years later, and he determined he would finish this fight right now.

And it continued unhindered, as Ajeet looked on in shock and Yasmine cried for the pain that was being inflicted on her friend Richard. Bleeding, Richard fell to the floor and screamed out in anger and pain. Arnold, himself bruised, stepped up behind Richard and smiled at the crowd to indicate his victory. He kicked Richard's shoulder, and the smaller boy rolled on his back in pain. The crowd cheered! And Arnold turned his back to the boy.

Yasmine tried to help him to his feet but Richard, frustrated, angrily pushed her away, and the crowd fell silent as they saw him stumble the few feet between them and strike Arnold on the back. Surprised, the beast fell and growled.

"That's enough!" a teacher shouted as he made his way through the pupils. "Stop that!"

But no one had anticipated Richard's strength or courage. And they were too late to stop him from lifting Arnold by the scruff of his shirt, and slamming him head-first into the wall of the school gym. Arnold crumpled. A final cheer went up from the school children.

As the two enemies were dragged away, Ajeet fixed his turban, Yasmine walked in pursuit of the entourage of staff holding the two boys, and Richard relaxed, relieved, safe in the knowledge that it was finished. He had finally done it.

Arnold Walters never bothered them again.

Chapter 40

"I'm impressed with the way you handled that, Mr Sekar." She says.

Friday afternoon, lunch break, the last inspection day. So far so good. I've just been observed during my year ten lesson and I'm fairly relaxed about the whole thing. And yet I am anxious to see that my efforts as inspection co-ordinator actually yielded results. Now, as she stands here, a bespectacled, late thirty-something, blonde inspector-ess, charged with monitoring the English department, I lose the thread of the conversation. I'm shocked, for one thing, that she's even talking to me. Usually, they just come in, watch for a while, and disappear, mutely.

"I'm sorry? Handled what?"

"The lesson. It's not an easy book from their perspective. The character may be young but he's wise beyond his years and some of his attitudes are too cynical for most school children to catch on to. But you handled it really well. They responded, and really seemed to enjoy it." She pauses. "That's incredibly encouraging."

I shrug "Sometimes you really have to fight for their attention. There's no denying that. They're thinking about some soap they watch or the latest blockbuster movie. If you pick something dull to read you lose them on page one. I try to select books I really have a strong feeling for myself. If I don't like it, why should they? I try to let my enthusiasm for the text carry itself over to them."

"I'm sure." She smiles, and I seize up inside as I'm reminded of Ms Dunley. "I observed some of the special needs literacy teaching yesterday. You have a very thorough approach here, very well co-ordinated. And class discipline is good - the kids seem unusually focussed! The response we had from parents was largely positive, a couple of gripes but nothing major."

"You sound surprised."

She chuckles. "Oh no, not exactly. I must admit after last year's news reports I had my... preconceptions... about this place and what went on here. I was expecting a mad-house. I haven't spoken to the inspectors who visited this place last time round, but I've done my research. Some class discipline issues were noted six years ago, and the report says that some of the staff were, to be frank, pulling off laughable, skin-of-their-teeth performances. But the school seems to have fixed that. I also dug up the TES feature you helped put together. It made interesting reading. To be honest I was sceptical about your achievements here. I was expecting things to have declined since the last inspection. But I find myself having to put my pre-judgements to one side."

"That's incredibly encouraging." I mimic.

"Touche." She smiles.

"Forgive me if this seems a bit of an odd thing to say, but I thought inspectors weren't supposed to speak to us after observations?"

"I'm a little unorthodox."

There's an uncomfortable silence. I don't really know what to say. I'm still surprised she wants to talk at all. They held interviews with me and the other heads of department earlier this week and she was there. Mine went ok, I thought, but perhaps she wasn't convinced by my performance -

I glance over her shoulder out of the window and my heart beats erratically. There's a large crowd of pupils gathering by the temporary block, and at the fast pace they're going that can only mean one thing.

She notices and turns. "Trouble?" she asks.

"Could be. Stay here I'll deal with it." I reach for my phone and as I hurtle out of the school building I notice the inspector following me. I put a call through to reception and ask them to get Henry out here. If this is what I think it is, then I want him to catch them at it once and for all, and throw them out!

The younger, smaller ones at the back of the crowd see me coming, they whiten and run, and I think I see Edward looking on from some place, and the crowd is huge - at least five-hundred strong - three quarters of the school must be here, and the inspector's hot on my heels. Shit! What the hell is she doing? She's not supposed to get involved. God, please let this be dealt with simply.

I manage to push my way through and as I'm nearing the front of the crowd suddenly I'm surrounded by upper school kids, some of whom are larger and bulkier than me - and there's one hell of a situation going on. I notice I'm walking through a white-only crowd. And over to my right it's the Asian and black kids, divided by race.

Glancing over shoulders, I see one of the larger Indian lads squaring up against a skin-headed white boy and there's some intense language shooting back and forth. I scan the area. None of the would-be fighters have noticed me yet. Good. I push to the front in earnest and before I get there I overhear what they're saying.

The deep-voiced Asian states his case. "What you been sayin', innit, is shit about my mother being a prosti-"

"Stupid Paki! I ain't said nothin'!" the nasal skinhead replies.

"Well, thas not what *she* said…"

"Man, whoever she is, she's fuckin' you right over!" and the crowd laughs, as the skinhead shakes his hand at the slow, dim-witted Asian, who, embarrassed, frowns and then throws a comment out to someone a few feet away. "You fucking white bitch! What the fuck you stirring for?"

And he heads over to… Layla Larter.

And, sure enough, Carter steps up. "Get back," he mutters, and if I know Carter, it'll all be over for my Asian friend very soon if *he* starts. I'm a second or two away – almost there - and I'm at the front now and as I step forward the inspector follows me. Shit I wish she'd stay back! The crowd pauses as they realise it's me, and I speak up. "Ok, show's over everyone, get back where you were. You boys come with me."

"I ain't goin' with you Sir!" the Asian shouts. "This white bitch is stirring trouble, innit, I'm gonna sort her out…"

"Yeah?" Carter says, removing his glasses and placing them in his pocket. "Try it."

"Come on Carter just step back we'll all go and sort this out and - " I plead.

"Fucking Nigger!" the Asian screams and that's it - Carter's gone - the fists are flying faster than I can see and the skinhead laughs and bolts whilst the crowd cheers and gives them room to fight and all I can hear is the sound of Carter's immense fists beating this guy's head into the ground as I bring my arms between them I hear the inspector telling them to stop! Carter loses it and swings for me and I duck -

And she's hit - the inspector is sent reeling back and to the ground and now by God, I am fucking pissed off! I grab Carter's built arm and twist it round his back, swipe his legs, put him on the ground and place my knee on his back, and push the Asian back with my free arm and - thank God! - Henry arrives with Michaelson and they take hold of the other fighter. And it's over. The racial gangs disperse as the leaders are dragged away. I release Carter to another teacher and I help the inspector up on her feet.

Somehow I sense a gaze and I turn to see Edward, who nods at me. I nod back in appreciation of his tip off, and he walks away as I watch him, a ragged, tired youngster with growing confidence and great, hidden dreams, an immense bright red scarf still dangling from his neck despite it being the height of Summer. His life could take him anywhere, I think, in a fleeting moment. I stand for a second, watching and wishing him well, and then his form becomes anonymous in the crowd.

She's cut on her forehead. My heart sinks as I lead her away to the nurse's room. As we are received I explain what happened, she is treated, and my heart buries itself further. All our hard work - damn those two!

"There you go," the nurse finishes cleaning up the wound. "Don't worry, no need for stitches. Could have been a lot worse though. Carter wears a sovereign ring on his *other* hand."

She wanders off. I sigh. The inspector looks a little shook up. Her suit – and mine for that matter – is soiled. I go over to her and apologise. "I'm so sorry." I shake my head.

"What for?" she smiles, weakly.

"All this! This stupid school. Those stupid kids."

"It happens, Mr Sekar. I do teach as well, you know."

"That doesn't make me feel any better about this. I'm sorry."

She chuckles. "Don't worry, Mr Sekar. I shouldn't have got so close, but I wanted to help - truth be told it's against my instructions to close in on a situation like that. I should have just observed from afar. It's my own fault. Not yours. Don't worry. My boss will hear it the way I just said it."

I relax a little, as she goes on. "Besides, we've seen some good things. A lot of positive stuff.

Fights happen. Maybe corridor and playground discipline is something you need to work on at Autumn Lane but you shouldn't doubt yourselves so much. You don't give the school enough credit." I'm a little taken aback by how well she's taking all this.

"Don't worry, Mr Sekar, there will be no firing squad." She reassures me, and my laughter deflates my ensuing depression, and for a moment she chuckles with me, and then straightens up. "Well, I better go. Still have more to do before we leave this afternoon. You can relax once I'm gone!" she says, and yet I already feel so at ease.

"Thanks again, Mr Sekar." She shakes my hand. "Henry was right. Not sure what this place would do without you."

Henry said that to her? I'm professionally flattered. She looks me in the eye as she says it and there's not a hint of any ulterior motive at all. This isn't Jennifer Dunley, I remind myself. I smile, and we leave the nurse's room together. As the inspector heads off to the staff room I notice someone in my periphery vision. It's Layla, sitting, alone, outside Henry's office. His shouts are audible. God help whoever's in there. She sees me.

"Hey Sir," she says, sullen, her facial piercings sagging.

"Hey Sir? *Hey Sir?* Do you and Carter realise you're both finished here? That you're out?"

"Well then…" she mutters quietly. "I'll *miss* you."

I shake my head, give up with her, and walk off in the opposite direction. But just before I turn the corner I glance back and see her for one last time in my life. She blows me that damn kiss of hers. And I wonder if I'll miss her too.

Lunch is over, the school is again throbbing with little ones and their noise is unbearable as my head is pounding beyond belief. Serena was up all night eating jar after jar of pickled gherkins. Poor thing. What a craving! To top it all, the weight is taking its toll on her, her scarred legs aching more than ever.

I feel myself relaxing. The ant-like crawl over the school of the eleven inspectors is coming to an end. The fight happened, but was stopped in time before a full scale riot began. As I walk to my classroom I wander past an open window and the smell of the cut grass and the pollen in the air and warmth of the sun on my suited body takes me away to another time and place.

Chapter 41

Late after school, that evening, Dean walked home with his three friends in the sunlight, and he put his hand on Richard's shoulder.

Richard winced. "That's the one he kicked, Dean."

"Oh, sorry!" Dean apologised to his bruised and battered friend.

"How long do you think you will be suspended for?" Ajeet asked.

"I don't care! It was worth it... I just couldn't stand seeing him fuck us about all the time. First me, then Dean, and then today when he threw you down and pushed Yasmine around, that fucking did it!" Richard smiled.

"I think Arnold came out worse." Yasmine said.

"Of course he did! Bastard. Didn't know exactly how tough our little Richard was, did he?" said Dean.

"Oh and some girls were asking if you were ok, Rich." Yasmine teased.

Richard laughed. "Good! Well, this is our road. Come on Ajeet."

"What? Yes. Ok." The Indian boy agreed. "See you on Monday guys. For more fun and games, yes?"

"Richard – thanks for everything." Yasmine said, kissing him on his cheek. "When you get back from suspension, we'll go over that chemistry stuff you hate so much, yeah?"

"Ah yeah, whatever, I'm crap at science. I'll never be as smart as you guys and I don't care either. But thanks anyway. Have a good weekend you two. I know I will." He laughed, and he wandered off down the street with the tall, spindly, hard of breathing Ajeet in tow. Dean looked after them for a while, as their colourful forms shrunk and turned another corner, leaving the grey road empty and lonely behind them.

"What a day." Dean breathed a deep sigh.

"Are you ok?" Yasmine asked.

"I guess so." Dean shrugged. "Mum and Dad had a huge row. Mum said she was going away for a few days. To my aunt's place I guess. That's where she usually goes."

They walked on in silence. Dean shifted the bag on his back slightly, and kicked a tin can that lay on the street before him. He reflected on something deep inside for a moment, then turned to Yasmine and smiled. "So, you think Arnold will be back anytime soon?"

"No," she replied, shaking her head. "I know one thing about him for sure. When he's this embarrassed, he never comes back!"

"Good. But - would you ever be his girlfriend again?"

"Are you kidding?!"

"Look I -" Dean paused. "I mean, we -"

"What Dean?" Yasmine asked, smiling.

"Um - Hmmm. How can I say this? Oh God what's wrong with me!"

"I don't know."

"Um…"

"You better hurry up Dean, this is my street, don't want Dad to see me with you, he'll go insane," and she put on a heavy Indian accent, "Oh God no bloody boys Yasmine!"

"Well look, look! Stop. Stop. Wait. One minute." He held her arms and stopped her moving. She laughed a little.

"Um… Yasmine look - I just want to know - what we talked about in the park the other day."

"Yes?"

"Are you-? Well are we-? Look - will you be my girlfriend? There you go. I've asked you. And I can't believe it."

"Hmm. Well. What about all those other girls you were spending time in the park with this year? Huh? What about all of them?"

Dean's face fell as the unexpected question hit him. He opened his mouth as if to say something, to make sense of the jumbled up creatures residing in his gut and in his mind that led him to her, but trying to explain his new found emotions seemed impossible. He was telling his closest girl friend that he adored her and wanted to be the one who held her hand. "Um - ah... Look, that was different. I'm just - I don't know! I just know I like you. I realised I liked you a few months ago. I don't even speak to the others anymore. I've forgotten them. I like you, Yasmine. So much."

She stood, silent. Looking down.

"So, how about it Yasmine? Will you-?"

Then she looked up quickly into his eyes and smiled and laughed, and leaned forward into this terrified young man's personal space and whispered to him, "Yes," and she kissed him *briefly on the lips, and ran away home, glancing over her shoulder and smiling as she did.*

Dean, dumbstruck, felt the silence of the world upon him. It was only when she vanished into her front door, hundreds of feet away, that he was able to walk on, elated, lighter than he had ever felt before. He travelled home in his new found happiness, oblivious to the future and the unknown joy and pain written above him in the paper thin sky.

Chapter 42

School's out. The inspectors left half an hour ago. I'm relieved. I sit in the staff room, sipping a cup of tea, alone, off to one side, not wishing to talk, no craving for conversation, as members of staff move in and out of the room, allowing themselves room to breathe, having been observed at some point during this longest of weeks.

Someone lingers by the notice boards, taking notes from a display about Exams, or Unions, or Attendance, I can't tell which. Another teacher posts a set of leaflets in crammed pigeon-holes, empties out the contents of her locker, and then leaves the room in a hurry. Ms Dunley walks in, looking visibly exhausted, catches a look of me, then looks away, then looks back and smiles, and then flees to the comfort of the coffee, sugar and tea jars lining the kitchenette.

I let the hot tea scold me.

A hand places itself on my shoulder, and then removes itself, someone wanders across and seats himself heavily to my right, a large stocky man, bald, smiling, reluctantly. Marshall Jones. What the hell does *he* want?

"Dean." He voices, low.

"Marshall. Can I help you?"

"No. Just wanted to-" he pauses.

"What?"

"-say well done."

My tea scolds me a second time. What's he talking about? "What for?" I ask, expressionless.

He shrugs. "You know. The fight. I heard they were about to go for it and you stopped it."

"Oh *that.*" I acknowledge, uncomfortable at his attention.

"The inspector – was she hurt?"

"No not really. A little bit shaken. She was very good about it. If you don't mind Marshall, I'd rather be alone."

"Did you dig in?" Marshall whispers, conspiratorially, and leans forward, one hand on my knee. "You know what a little bastard he can be. He would have deserved it."

"What are you talking about?" I ask, annoyed.

"You know. That black kid. Carter. You had him pinned to the floor." He pauses, smirks. "You had your knee in his back. Did you dig in? Really make him *feel* it?"

"What? Of course I bloody didn't! What the hell-?" I'm raising my voice, enraged by the suggestion.

"Steady on, mate! Carter had it coming to him."

"Do you even like kids? Why the hell do you *do* this job?" I demand, angry, loud.

He shrugs. "It's a living. Don't be so hysterical, Dean. Most of us can't stand them. You know that."

"That's bullshit."

"You know I'm right."

"You arrogant-! Don't you dare make suggestions about *me* pushing kids around - *you* bully them about as much as you can, because it's the only place anyone will ever do as you say."

Far in the distance, Jennifer drops her teaspoon, and a number of snack-munching colleagues glance up, and then look away, seeing me red. Marshall Jones, the stocky bald bully that he is, sits there, aghast, my short tirade unexpected, but long overdue, and I slam my mug of tea down, and walk away from him.

"Dean, don't you turn your back on me, I-"

"I've nothing more to say to you." I say, quietly, and stride out of the staff room, all tutors' eyes on me as I go. Did I dig into Carter's back? Idiot.

I stand by the stairs outside the room and catch my breath. I look at my watch – 4:08pm. I'm due in a meeting, and I'm late. I compose myself, let the flush dissipate from my cheeks, and head for the Head's office. Outside, I pause once more, try to put the argument out of my mind but it has upset me, left a bitter taste like stale almonds in my mouth. I knock, enter, and stand there, Henry sitting behind his desk, Geoff standing to my right.

"Dean?" Henry says. "Come in."

Geoff stands and manages what looks to me like a half smile. I return the gesture, unsure of what they're about to say. I'm a little tense. Henry speaks.

"Some of the inspectors popped in to have a word before they left, and most seemed very positive about us. Their boss said there's room for improvement, but was convinced we'd come on a long way since our last action plan. Oh, and the English monitor praised you specifically, Dean, said you handled the - the situation out there, very well. So congratulations, Dean. All said off the record of course, but - it looks like we're going to be a success."

"Thank you." I say, relaxing.

"Also, Geoff wanted to raise something." Henry tells me, looking uncomfortable.

"Oh?" I ask.

"Dean," Mr Michaelson begins, pauses, clears his throat. "I'm sorry to say it but - I think you were a little rough out there. With Carter."

"What?!" I say, my pre-existing anger at Jones's contrary remarks about Carter returns in a flash as my heart beat quickens.

"You didn't have to throw him to the ground! His parents will call and we'll be in trouble wi -"

"Geoff, shut up." I snap. Finally, I've had enough of this man. "I wouldn't have done it if it wasn't necessary, what do you take me for? He's a dangerous kid. He's huge. He knocked the inspector down for fuck's sake! You weren't there. But then, you rarely are when you're needed. Idiot."

This enrages him, and Geoff launches into a melodramatic speech, shouting on about how he's been 'wiping my arse' all year. Complete rubbish, I tell him, it's more the other way round. Henry rolls his eyes heavenwards and tells me to calm down, that this is a good day for us and why ruin it? I loosen my tie. I'm so damn angry!

I notice my phone ringing - Dad's number. I let it ring out and stop. Geoff keeps speaking, his lecture annoying me more and more, and then the bloody phone goes again and I'm shouting and I'm angry so I take the phone and smash it to the ground where the ringer dies abruptly and the thing lies smashed, useless, broken, dead. They stop speaking.

I swallow, a sour aftertaste washing down my throat, and now the last place I want to be is here.

I feel cheated, upset. I pull off a successful inspection performance, and Geoff can only give me grief.

"I've had enough of this for one day." I say, quietly, and then I leave. I drift out of the office, cut Henry off mid-sentence, wander out through reception and through the main entrance and, purpose unsure but with resolve, I walk across the quad, scaring off a solitary magpie, the water spray from the fountain catching me lightly on my right arm. I turn the corner and make my way to my car, wandering past a pile of broken chairs and disused filing cabinets awaiting disposal.

"Dean?" Henry calls out, following not far behind, as I close the car door.

"I've had enough Henry. I'm off. Sorry." I drive past Henry without another word or glance and head out of the school, calm, but quick.

I reach for the phone in my pocket to return Dad's call and to tell him that I'm coming to see him and then remember that the thing has fallen apart back in the office. As I drive past my neighbourhood I consider picking Serena up from home but then realise she's at the hospital on the evening shift. I speed past my house and get myself on to the motorway and not long after my car rolls on to the winding long lanes to his cottage.

I slow the car to a halt as I notice people outside his home. People in uniform. I see Margaret with her hand on her mouth, looking on, and she notices my car and comes straight over in a hurry and I step out in a rush, asking her what's wrong. But she doesn't know. And as I see them wheel Dad into the ambulance I wonder what on earth could be wrong but I'm confident in the paramedic's abilities. I step over to one of them and ask him what the problem is.

He asks who I am and when I explain, he calmly tells me things are fine, as his colleague quickly closes the ambulance door behind him. He tells me I should simply follow along in the car behind them. And Margaret looks at me tearfully and I ask her if she wants to come along but she simply says her grandchildren are here and that she tried to call me from Dad's cottage but couldn't get through. The two phone calls... I tell her Dad will be fine and a tear appears on her cheek and she tells me to go after the ambulance as it drives away.

I follow it. They're going to the hospital, and they're not in any particular rush, no sirens, so Dad must be absolutely fine. I relax and drive. I should have gone in the ambulance with them, I realise, but then drop the thought. I'd have been in the way. They're probably busy telling him to calm down, relax. He hates medics of any kind. I wonder what could have happened?

When we arrive at the hospital they speed him off through an entrance and ask me to speak to the receptionists who will bring me to him soon enough. I don't get to see him but I see his arm lying weakly by his side on the stretcher. I realise where I am and ask one of the nurses to page my wife and ask her to meet me. Moments later, Serena arrives from her ward with our baby resting inside her, and asks what the problem is.

"I don't know," I explain. "They just brought Dad in. He looked quite weak but I think he's ok. They said everything would be ok... Receptionist wouldn't tell me where he'd been taken though. She said the doctor would be with us soon."

"They're probably just checking him out." She says but I can tell something seems odd to her. She wanders over to reception to explain why she's had to come off her ward and they nod in acknowledgement and look at her and explain something to her slowly – I can't hear them – but a moment later she comes over to me. "Come on Dean," she whispers, her eyes like stone. "They told me where to go."

I nod, and she takes my arm and we walk down a long, silent, lonely corridor which seems to stretch out for miles and miles and is split into sections by high arches, each arch reaching me silently and moving past into the space behind me, each disappearing segment marking the passing of a few long seconds. We sit in a small waiting room where a television sparkles quietly in one corner and I notice the wallpaper, a dull but pleasant floral type and I feel the ruggedness of NHS carpet on the soles of my feet and I see the water jug and focus on the tight surface of the liquid within, and I hold my wife's arm and feel goose pimples, and there's a man in front of me saying something but I'm not registering the comment, I'm noticing the rest of the world too much.

He keeps telling us that he is sorry.

That my father has passed away.

That Dad was at home when Margaret came round and saw him collapse.

That they came straight away, the ambulance crew, and tried all they could to help him, to save him, but, moments later his heart gave out, and he was gone.

It was just over an hour ago. I glance at my watch – 5:08pm. It was only one hour ago. An hour ago he was at home when Margaret came round and saw him collapse. An hour ago. The two phone calls...

My lips ask in shock where they have taken him and the doctor leads us there, a quiet, silent, forbidden place. I go in alone and draw back his blanket.

"Dad?" I call out, softly, a number of times to wake him up, but the word pushes out to him and returns to me alone, finding no warmth of response within him, the senseless tide goes out, and comes back in to me. I look at his face. So calm. So peaceful. His wrinkles, receding, his eyes and mouth sinking, pulled down by ruthless gravity.

For a moment, I hold his cold heavy hand and lean over and embrace his cooling body, and I kiss his cheek, and feel it with my hands, and kiss his brow, and touch his closed eyes with my fingertips.

Then I leave the room, and, as if a child again, I fall outside to my knees and Serena holds me on the corridor floor as I push into her, foetal, and cry with my head against the heart of our unborn.

VII. THE ASHES OF TIME

Chapter 43

Late August is upon us, and the sky has been pulled to pieces and stands, fragmented, levitating above me. Behind its cracks I glimpse fearful nothing. My heart lies low and heavy, I sit looking out to the trees from my window at home. I listen, quietly, to the softness of the wind and the notes of a slow uplifting piano piece gently echo around the living room behind me.

I take sips from a glass of milk, and take another bite of my red apple and watch a finch speed past and join its mate on the branch of a tree, and the sounds of Summer still abound. I hear footsteps behind me and I know it's Serena, out of sight but nearby, carrying our child massively from room to room, looking for me, seeking to comfort me, soothe me. "I know you're there," I whisper.

"Good." She replies, stepping up close to me. "God, I feel heavy!" she moans, as I feel her belly press against my back, and I imagine I hear our baby's heart throbbing softly, telling me to rest, to sleep and not dream any more bad dreams. I have a sudden urge to slip away forever in the night, in my next breath.

I feel her fingers on my shoulder as she rubs my back and I place my head against the window frame and let her gently rock me until the music stops. I want to disappear, to dissolve into her being, as if I was never here. When the piano piece fades, there is a prolonged silence as we breathe and sway together like the trees beyond the portal before us.

"Gone over a month now." I mutter. "Still can't believe it. Makes no sense."

"No sweetheart, it doesn't." She agrees, and then a thought occurs to me. I pause, to frame my thoughts before I speak, but the essence of everything on my mind, all that I wish for but cannot have, finally reduces itself to some small and few words.

"There's no way back." I say, and I feel her eyes going away, to a place she sees inside, from where her truths emerge. Her hair tickles my neck as she gives a little shake of her head.

No, there's no way back. No way back, to the crowded room where you first laid eyes on her, to the childhood dream of the snow fight, to the blue room where you now wished you hadn't taken her, to the phone call full of harsh, unintended words, to the moment they said goodbye but you missed the intent in their eye, to the hour you neglected them, the hour before they died.

And yet sometimes, she says to me, we do go back, within ourselves, and perhaps see something we hadn't seen before, and learn something of ourselves. Sometimes, she says, she remembers whole days, weeks of her life, people she misses, things she did, joyful things and some things sad - she laughs briefly at something remembered, prompted suddenly by some smell or taste un-sensed in a while.

Accepting the sad yet joyful transience of life, she says, can guide you in whatever time is left to come. There is a placid deep truth in her insight. There has always been. We sit quietly for a moment.

"Did you find the letter?" she whispers.

"No! I looked in all my trousers and jackets. Nothing!"

"Did you call Henry? Maybe it's at his place?"

"He said he'd look. I'm meeting him for coffee tomorrow."

"Ok."

Then my mind is consumed by an anxiety, because Dad's gone. How can so much happen in just one year? My mind wanders past familiar images and feelings, of pummelled trains seen from a hill top and of lights fading, of butterflies in my stomach, of odd blue places and a drowning glimpse of a brilliant light in the pool and the warmth of emerging from these things. The feeling, long sought for, of an innocence regained, contentment, whilst dining in my father's cottage, watching the fire burn. Then the loss, and now -

Emptiness.

I feel my delicacy. My fragmentation. I need *time*. To pull back. It took the near-death experience in the pool to make me realise what I was teetering on the brink of, and Serena had returned to save me. But he will not come back. He's gone.

"Dean. Let's get out of here. Let's go tonight. We'll spend some time at the cottage. You'll feel closer to him there. He loved that place. We'll get a fire going."

"Yes. Yes." I whisper, the idea a certainty in seconds.

I chuckle lightly. The fire. Somehow even in our darkest time, I knew we'd return there, to that cottage, to that fire he would light there. Serena asks if I'm ok.

"Yes, I am. We'll go and light a fire." I assure her. But as I sit at the window hoping for brighter days, I mutter a request to the world. "I need time."

She takes my hand, twists my arm round and places it on herself. I feel our child moving, and I pull her to me, and she says, "Take all the time you need, Dean. We'll be here."

I hold her close, and a brief flicker before my dry eyes, a blue image, of my father's motionless figure in his coffin, his eyes and mouth sunk deep, soulless, empty, startles me.

I remember his smoke rising out of the crematorium.

And then I remember another moment from long ago, a moment long repressed, emerging from the ashes of time.

Chapter 44

The boy stood, thirteen years old, soon to be fourteen, and shifted uncomfortably in his first black suit, and loosened his black tie, for it was suffocating him. Young Dean breathed deeply as groups of mourners wandered past him, their eyes full of pity for the poor boy. One by one his young friends also passed, unable to look him in the eye, leaving him shrouded alone in his loss of innocence.

His father placed his hand on Dean's shoulder, the boy looked back across a sea of headstones and his gaze followed the brick structure of the chimney up to its peak. Merely weeks ago he had been happy. Joyful. Content. Innocent. Now he stood, silent, dry of tears, watching her smoke rise peacefully up into the frail sky, up into the clouds, reducing her to nothing but ash and remnants of bone.

It was a Summer's day, but the sun was masked behind the clouds and Dean's father walked away, to allow the boy a moment to say goodbye alone. But the thought of uttering yet another farewell did not occur to Dean. As he stood there in his suit, he bathed in the small *rays of amber warmth that reached him through the holes in those cold blue clouds and smoke.*

For a moment, he smiled, and felt as if he was not there.

Chapter 45

I wander through the busy square, past the street performers and homeless magazine sellers, past the town hall and the fountains and those locally infamous stone animals that people meet one another by and I walk into the café, a small, independent, atmospheric little place. I espy Henry, reading the paper through his spectacles, ordering another drink. He sees me, and the waitress leaves to prepare his chosen coffee.

"Dean!" he says. "Come, sit. Order one of these," he indicates on the menu. "It's a South American blend. Very nice. Unpronounceable. But nice."

I smile and shrug as I sit myself down over the table from him. "Good to see you, Henry."

Henry folds the paper, waves the waitress over, orders a second beverage, then removes his specs and for a moment, yes, I see it, a slight resemblance to my former mistress, his sister's daughter. "I was beginning to worry," he says, wiping his glasses. "Since end of term I've hardly heard a word from you."

"I've been resting, Henry." I say, quiet, lacking energy.

"You know you could have taken those last two weeks off if you needed to. In fact, I still think you should have."

"For what, Henry? What could I have done, moping at home. It was better to be in class, finishing what I'd started. Dad's lawyer was dealing with everything that needed doing. And I don't like - unresolved things. Behind me. Who would have finished my teaching?"

"We'd have managed."

The coffees arrive. I stare at the steam rising over mine and my eyes hover up with it to meet Henry's gaze. "Henry. Henry -" I shake my head, and make my announcement. "I can't do it any more."

"What?"

"The job. Teaching. English. The school. I can't."

Henry looks surprised. "I see."

"I want to hand in my notice and start a hand-over process. I can't do this anymore."

Henry shakes his head. "Well, what will you do?"

"I don't know. I don't know. I'm just so tired."

Henry sighs. "Dean. I've said it many times but, look, quite frankly, we can't do without you. Your kind of calibre is hard to come by. The kids like you. Even Geoff admires you but he won't admit it. Jen speaks highly of you -"

"Really? Jennifer?" I say, and immediately bite my tongue.

"Yes, of course! I saw her a few days ago. She sends her regards. Said she was worried about you. She said she was very glad to have worked with you last year."

I smile inwardly. Despite all that had happened, she really said those things?

"I mean, why wouldn't she? What reason could she have not to like you?" Henry says in a flat voice, but I catch something in his tone, see something in his eyes – *does he know or doesn't he?* – yet I look away and let the moment pass.

"*And-*" he goes on. "Ofsted. We received the report a few days ago."

"Oh?"

"Yes, and we did well. There were no 'unsatisfactory' ratings this time, thank God, but they did have a bit of a go about poor discipline *out* of class. That was expected. We're putting our action plan together now. But what I wanted to say is, our success this year, Dean, as far as I'm concerned, it's very much down to you and your role this year in management. You did very well. You came through for me at a hard time and I appreciated it immensely. I didn't always show it. But I meant to. Thank you - and sorry."

"You did a pretty good job yourself, Henry." I compliment, sincerely grateful for his words of praise and his apology. He smiles, modestly ignoring me. There's a silent moment, and then he continues.

"Oh, and I didn't get a chance to explain, but it turned out you were right."

"Oh? About what?"

"Layla and Carter. They were stirring up trouble that day and they admitted it, and Christ, she even let it slip that it was *they* who'd been instigating the other fights! You were right about them. Geoff and I were wrong, and I couldn't believe *how* wrong." A wave of relief washes through me, the gratifying feeling of vindication.

"We've pushed for permanent exclusion. Unfortunately they might appeal but it's up to the governors." He shrugs. "And look, I've been stuck with that bumbling idiot, Michaelson, for a whole year, and 'acting' Deputy has never been a more apt description. He felt like a complete tit for not nailing Layla and Carter when he'd grilled them the first time! The pillock."

"I thought you liked him?" I say, surprised.

Henry shakes his head. "Dean. Dean. You're my most gifted pupil yet you have so much to learn. A lot of politics went on at the school last year. I had no choice but to take him on as acting Deputy. There was no one else. We've been advertising for a year but worthwhile candidates have only now come forward. Geoff can't find his own arse to wipe it, let alone help run the school, but that's what I was stuck with. I had no choice. But things are different now. Things will change."

I laugh at this, despite all my pain. His true view of Geoff is a welcome revelation after all the time I spent thinking he was going blind. Every now and again I'm forced to re-assess this older gentleman, a most shrewd friend and mentor.

Henry's voice softens. "You've had a long, hard year, Dean. Serena being hurt in the train crash, losing the baby. You nearly drowned, for God's sake. And still you went far above and beyond the call of duty at work, and on a day when you should have been out celebrating your success instead of fending off Geoff, you lost your father."

I listen to the summary of the year and sense the unreality of it. It's as if it belongs more to a film script or in the pages of some novel, and yet, it doesn't. No. No, it doesn't, because all this was *real* it really happened this way in this insane, crazy, senseless, bewildering way. It is here, real, true. This is life. Senseless things happen. Senselessness reigns, and exiles you to a life of crossing lines, lines you think define you, limit you, and shelter you.

Henry continues. "Just don't make any rash decisions. It's undoubtedly been the most difficult time of your life, this last year. But you have an excellent career Dean, that you've worked very hard for. Don't throw it all away. These are the times when we need to hold on tight to the good things that we already have. They help shape us. If we lose what defines us, we lose ourselves. I think, deep down, you understand what I am saying."

I'm warmed by the speech – damn him for being so charismatic – and I'm reminded of another mentor of old. But in a moment the pain rushes up within me and I think of the idea of facing another year toiling at that school in those tattered corridors where not even the paint wants to remain on the walls and in that room with its bent chairs and crooked tables, the old worn equipment and my own desk with its cracks and crevices where I sought my refuge, and I ask: do I have any impact? Do I make a difference? Do I really want to stay there, a broken piece of chalk, on the floor before the blackboard?

"I think my mind's made up, Henry. This is it."

He retreats, sips his coffee, calls the waitress over and orders some carrot cake. "Well. If you do decide to change career, or maybe even just change school – I'm sure you'd be snapped up by the private sector like *that* - I'll always be on hand, however I can help. Your reference will be excellent. Just think about it carefully, ok?"

Silence. The cake arrives, Henry takes a bite. I change the subject. "Henry. I - I'm in pain." I say. Slowly. He stops eating.

"I know, my friend, and I'm sorry."

"It's something - I don't know if — I mean words just don't fit its entirety." But I try to explain, explain how it feels, this smashing of hopes held about the future, the tearing up of my designs. Explain that life this year, determined to teach me a lesson, caned into me the fact that it was not going to be the way I wanted it to be. How, when I realised this awful truth, my heart just emptied out from the bottom, because if I could have seen who or what it was that ruled our lives, I could have made some plea, I could have tried to stop them, made a stand, or died doing so. But it can't be seen. It's impenetrable. It stares at you as you float drowning in a pool but you cannot touch it. It's there, but it's not. Your heart caves in on itself and a hole forms in the bottom, and everything, *everything,* simply empties out into your gut, and that is where your life-will sits, waiting, for you to move on, to figure out a way of facing what may happen next, and perhaps you do find acceptance, but even this will not shelter you from the things still to hurt you. In the interim, you can only wait, alone, for the thing to happen, for the monsoon to come.

"I'm tired." I tell him. "I don't know how to help myself. It just sits there. A massive gaping hole. I can forget it for a moment when I'm distracted by something. By Serena. By her playing the flute." I can hear it in my mind, her clear breath playing that same, child-like melody, time and again, but it does not soothe me now. I look down. "Those two weeks at the end of term seemed easier. I had something to focus on. Something to finish. But when we *did* finish, I felt so exhausted. Couldn't celebrate like everyone else. Just wanted to curl up and sleep. Forever." I drift inside and float up to my place of nothing in the pool where the thing, the bright brilliant light, glances back at me in curiosity. "You never met my father, did you?" I ask. Henry shakes his head. I look up once more and smile. "You would have liked him. You would have got on with each other."

My mind wanders to the imaginary scene of their meeting, the mutual respect they would have had for one another, and the immediate warmth that would have arisen, through their shared bond: Dean. Then I remember my purpose. "Did you find the note, Henry? I'm sure I put it in my pocket at your barbeque. I must have dropped it. Did you find it?" I plead.

"No." Henry shakes his head. I'm disappointed. Sunk. But then he goes on. "I couldn't find it, and Elizabeth was worried she'd thrown it away whilst cleaning. But then Jen came round, and I just mentioned the thing in passing, and guess what? She says she vaguely recalls picking up a letter of some sort in the house, that she was going to give it to me but that for some reason she got sidetracked, put it in her bag, and forgot about it. Actually-" he pauses, glances at his watch. "She should be here soon."

"What?"

"Did I forget to tell you? She's on her way. She said she'd try and meet us here, to drop the note off on her way to her boyfriend's place."

"There's a boyfriend?"

"Yes – they met a little while before the barbeque I think. In fact, he was there. Didn't she introduce you?"

"No… No." I vaguely recall her holding on to someone's arm.

He shrugs, but there's this odd glint of understanding in his eyes. Maybe one day I'll just *ask* him how much he knows. Whether he knows the truth. Maybe one day. But not today. No, not today.

We sit in silence for a moment, and then he mentions something, delicately, unsure of whether he ought to. Something unresolved. "So have you spoken to your mother?"

I blink. "Excuse me?"

"I take it you contacted her. She came to the funeral?"

I pause. Realise something. "No, no."

"My word. I knew you two were estranged, but I never thought that things were so bad, I mean, well -" he leaves it hanging.

I look at him, squint, as if I've forgotten something. "Henry, how much have I told you about what happened to her? My mother?"

He shrugs. "You said she left when you were a teenager. That's it. Why?"

"She did leave." I consider her and where she went. How far she went. "She... She left a long time ago." I mutter.

"I know. But, that's all I know. You never told me where she went, whether you heard from her again. I'm sorry - I just presumed she would be at the funeral. I'm sorry I couldn't be there."

I smile at the absurdity. "I didn't see her. But maybe she was there."

Henry raises an eyebrow. "You really aren't on speaking terms, are you?"

I laugh, quietly, a little. It's not his fault. I never have explained.

He looks confused. "Where did she go? If you don't mind me asking…"

I begin to explain. He looks shocked, surprised, almost chokes on a piece of cake, and then he looks down, respectful, mindful. Finally, after such a long time, I have revealed a pain I thought I had mastered, a corpse I had buried. Where she went. Where she felt she had to go. How far away from all things.

"When did that happen?"

"A long time ago. I was thirteen."

"In all this time, Dean, you've never mentioned it." He says, gently.

"I know. I know. I never talk about her, to anyone. I don't know why. And yet, she's always in my thoughts. In the back of my mind. Hovering over me inside. That… moment she said goodbye. It's always there. I sense it but I block it out. Sometimes - sometimes I live out that whole year inside, time and again, I see it, feel it, like I belong there."

A reel of golden images shoots through my mind, the whole year in an instant, in a camera flash, the games, the play, the trials, the bully, the friends - her unexpected passing as unforeseen as a train crash, her lingering goodbye embrace.

There's a prolonged silence, then Henry speaks. "What happened? I mean, why-?"

"She left my father. He wasn't a very good husband to her. She had issues, which he couldn't cope with. Instead of helping her through her problems, he - he had affairs." I glance at him quickly, aware of the guilt of my own mirror indiscretion, my accident with his niece. He doesn't respond. "Dad regretted everything. Deeply. When she found out, it only compounded her problems, and after a couple more years, she left. But she'd always been quite weak. Physically. Emotionally. It's funny. I didn't really know any of the detail until my Dad told me after she'd died, when he felt I was old enough to hear it."

I look into the past, grow distant. "I remember the evening Dad broke the news to me. Seated me down. Looked as though he'd aged twenty years since sunrise."

Yes. I remember, it felt as if the numerous heavy pages of his life had been turned en masse, going from youth at page 18 to old age at 80. "I remember the way he touched my hand. The way he looked at me. His deep breathing. It was like I already knew what my father was going to tell me. That there had been some terrible, terrible news and that she had taken her life. I remember shaking my head and screaming, and running and running until he caught up with me and I fell to my knees next to her empty shoes."

There's a long silence. He doesn't ask how she did it, and for his silence on this I am grateful.

"I can't believe you haven't spoken about this before." Henry says, moved. "How did you cope?"

I shrug. "I don't talk about her."

Once, only once, I explained my pain to Serena, long ago, on a night when, senseless and lost inside, water drenching me thoroughly, I found myself standing before her house in Cambridge, her laughing at my sodden appearance, me, pleading entry and a chance to dry off. "I went back to school. But things felt so different. Blank. Empty. There was a girlfriend." I smile softly as I recall Yasmine. "But I couldn't laugh with her anymore. I couldn't laugh with anyone. My friends just looked like fools to me. Who didn't *see* anything, who didn't *understand* a thing. I just... fell silent. It took a long, long time to come out of that. By the time I recovered, I had already started university and my old friends had left me. They were too young to understand, and I didn't even give them a chance, I just stopped playing, stopped caring, about them and about their games. All I did in my last couple of years at school was study. Study hard. I couldn't have cared less about anything else."

"Must have been tough. Losing her so young."

I agree that it was, and then I remember. Remember how, for a long, long time I still saw, felt and smelt her, wandering the suddenly-quietened rooms of my father's home. Some days I could not contain my anger or my hurt. I would stop whatever it was I was doing, breakdown, shout at her to come home. Sometimes my father would put his arm around me. Sometimes I was alone. And then other times, eerie times, I felt her hand, her gone hand, staying me. Once, in a breeze-swept park, I swayed, backwards and forwards, on a swing, and felt her touch me lightly on my back and push me, stop me, hold me, push me. I had never told her I loved her or how much she meant to me. I never understood. When I was a child, all I did was want. All I did was cry, and whinge until my mother placated me with all the things I desired, yet when she lay there, her pain before me clear to my eye, what could I do for her in return. Nothing. Not a solitary thing did I give her in return for her gift to me. My life. I missed her. Thought of her all the time, and how she felt against my arms that morning before she left, the smell of dried tears and perfume. And for a time, a long, long time, she stayed there, her soul, in that house with us, and we felt her, there, in those sofas and armchairs where she'd been lying, living, and in that kitchen where she had cooked. Sometimes, in the night, my eyes would fall wide open, and I would feel her looking over me from the edge of my bed, and I could feel something else, something greater than everything, watching us both, and yet the absurdity of these feelings overwhelmed me, and I began to think I should bury these things, bury her ashes deep, deep within me, within time. Time. Time moved on, and I studied and passed my exams and left, left school and my friends behind me without saying goodbye and then one day something happened. I came home from college one night and felt her slip away. She wasn't there anymore. Her presence just fell away from the house. One moment she was there, the next, not. What could I possibly say in the face of all of those experiences? I fell silent. I wouldn't talk about her. Not even to Dad. No matter how close we would become in life, I vowed that I would never forgive my father for what he had taken from me. Even now, in the wake of his death, I could not forgive him. How could I? How could anyone. And yet... I loved him so much.

Henry chews his cake and meditates. "So, how does *he* fit into all of this then? That chap?"

"Who? Oh... He was the one friend, I suppose, who understood. He helped me through it. As chance would have it, he stumbles back into my life now." I shrug. "What I really need is time... But I don't think I have it. The baby."

He nods. "I do understand. I've lost people over the years. Family. Friends. It *will* take time, Dean. But have faith -" an image of a light shimmering above me as I drown shoots before my eyes then is gone "- in yourself if nothing greater. It will help you stay healthy."

He finishes his cake and coffee and then opens his mouth as if to speak but instead he looks over my shoulder and he smiles and calls out. "Jen, we're over here."

I turn and see her petite figure dressed casually for a Summer's day and I notice her maroon toe nails through her flip-flops, and she looks radiant. She smiles and embraces her uncle, and then comes over to me and as I rise to greet her she embraces me and asks me how I am. I'm surprised by her warmth.

"I'm not too bad, Jen."

"We need another chair," she mutters, glancing around, but Henry takes his jacket.

"Have mine, Jen, I have a doctor's appointment. Here-" he leaves some money on the table. "My treat for both of you. Dean," he says, placing a hand on my shoulder. "Remember what I said. About the school and everything else. We'll talk again soon, ok? Come round for dinner with Serena when you've got a moment. Before term starts. Get as much rest as you can. You deserve it. You've earned it." He smiles, and suddenly he is my father, standing before me in another guise. Ms Dunley waves to him, and then he's gone.

And we're alone. It's been a long time since we were seated so, just the two of us. She removes her glasses, a lock of hair falls and caresses the side of her long pretty face where her grey eyes watch me and she looks up at mine but glances away and back again as she speaks.

"How have you been?"

"Coping." I say. Quietly but not coldly. I don't have the energy to remain so guarded this day. "I'll be ok." I say, and offer a small smile.

She calls the waitress over and orders a tea for herself and another coffee for me.

"I thought you were a coffee girl?" I tease.

"I'm trying to cut down. Too much coffee and I'm anybody's!" She laughs.

I wonder why she said that.

The drinks arrive, I gulp down half my coffee straight away and let it burn me - I should be burned when I'm with her. I watch her pouring milk slowly into her tea and over her shoulder a little baby whoops with joy as it receives it's bottle from its father. There's something in the laughter of the child, something pulling me up from my deep dark pit. Something beautiful, innocent.

"Ah," she says. "Before I forget, here's that letter Henry told me about." A wash of relief passes through me as I'm reunited with the missive. I place it in my jacket pocket, ensuring it is zipped up this time.

"Thank you Jen, I really needed this."

"I'm curious, though. What is it?"

"Just some details of an old friend. He met Henry at some conference and realised that he worked with me. From the press articles and everything. Anyway, he gave Henry his contact details. Just an old friend. I'd really like to see him again."

"Ok." There's silence as she tries her tea, thinks about it, then adds some sugar.

"So," I try to find something to say. "Who's the boyfriend?"

"Boy-? Oh... *Him...* No one really. I'm just seeing him. I wouldn't really call him my boyfriend."

"I see."

"He's nothing, really. Not really anything at all. I don't feel for him, like-" There's a long pause, then she mutters, quickly. "Like I did for you."

"I see." I repeat. I'm uncomfortable and only the pleased soft mumbling sounds of the baby behind her seem to be able to soothe me, to calm me.

She stirs another sugar into her tea. "Always had a sweet tooth."

"So did my father! Those damn cakes he wouldn't stop eating..."

"You ok?" she asks. She stops stirring and then reaches out a hand and holds mine, gently.

"I miss him."

"Oh... Did you get in touch with your mother?"

"No, no, she left a long time ago. We don't speak. At all." I say, quickly.

"Oh... A shame. Look, I know we've had our... differences. In the past. But I'm still here for you, Dean. I'm still here. If you need me. I'm *here*. For you."

I can't respond. But maybe we *can* be friends, Jennifer and I. She's a lot warmer than I remember her, but - *if I open my mouth now I might break down.* Get a grip Dean! You haven't cried since the day he died and you will not cry now, not with her.

There's a long silence and I notice her watching me, as if deciding something. Then she stands and moves her chair from opposite me round to my side, and sits there and touches my knee and looks into my eyes. "I - I still feel - I still - I'm here..." she says, "for *you*."

I can smell her. She closes in on me and I don't know where she's going, so I back off, and then I see it. I see it, the line on the table in front of me, the line, the line so well-defined and sharp, yet burning brightly, on fire, a line I must not cross. But I can *smell* her and her hands are on the side of my face and I can almost taste her perfume, and the room around us has paled and slowed into a cold blue shade that I know too well, I've been here before.

Please... Stop...

"No..." I plead, but now I feel her gentle lips, and we've kissed.

"No." I stop, physically push her back, back behind the line before me, and someone momentarily glances up from their newspaper a few tables away and then glances back down, uninterested. "You're confused. Stay away. Get back, please." I say, as the line fades before me.

She's upset, but she whispers. "Why? Why can't I touch you? We've touched before! I'm not confused. I just care for you."

"Then why are you doing this to me now, when you know how much I'm hurting? We finished this craziness, Jennifer. I was a mess, things were

really bad at home and you took advantage of me-
"

"I wasn't always on top you know."

Silence. Then I speak. "She needs me. I need her."

"You needed *me* once." She continues to speak in a whisper.

"It was a mistake, and I'm sorry."

"I meant nothing?"

"Don't do this Jennifer... Not now of all times." I beg. "I can't-"

"I meant nothing. I held you when she wouldn't even utter a word and yet -"

"For Christ's sake she nearly died in that crash! She had a problem!"

"What about me?"

There's another, long audible silence and inside I wonder for a moment why silences are the things that have ruled my life for so long, why the mute tongue is the one which burns me again and again and again.

"I... I... I'm still in love with you, Dean."

Oh God, what have I done? What did I do to deserve her love? I try to talk gently to her. "Stop this Jennifer. It's over. It's been over for a long time."

I sit there and watch her for some minutes, my cup in my hand, whilst the waitress floats from table to table and the baby giggles inanely. Then she looks up and something hardens inside those grey eyes of her, and she speaks, louder.

"You're just scared-"

"Of what?" I ask, temper flaring as I reach for my jacket and stand to leave, taking one last sip from my coffee. She swallows. Unsure of whether to say it. And then she does.

"That you want me more than that - that *cripple!*"

I see red, occasionally. That's when the world goes silent and there's nothing, no sound, no anything, just an explosion of rage inside. I slam the cup down. I curse but regain my composure and once more she is before me, this pretty little woman, frozen, seated, looking away, fearful. She is shaking here in this cold blue café, with her cup of milky tea, this woman who I once had an accident with. I notice the look of pain on her face, and I'm angry but the child's confused cooing softens my heart. I go round to her and kneel down in front of her and the man with the newspaper glances over again, frowns, and looks back at his paper. I speak.

"Don't you understand, Jennifer? *I can't.* It was a mistake. Even if I felt something, I should not have. I'm *married.* Serena needs me. And I need

312

her too, more than ever." I rub her hand gently as she weeps lightly, her mascara running. "Forgive me. I'm sorry, Jennifer. Forget me. Treat me like I never existed. As if I never was. I never was."

Then I turn, slowly, and leave.

Chapter 46

We're in the cottage, in my father's living room, and we have a fire going. We haven't been back here since the day of the funeral, and we're here now because I don't feel as groundless here. As unravelled. It's a quiet, lazy Summer's evening. We've just eaten dinner and we're settling down for a quiet night with some soothing orchestral music around us, low, low in the background. As we lounge on the sofa, I lean against her pregnant body, watching our fire, silent mostly, uttering the odd word on occasion.

"Henry thinks I should stay at the school." I say.

"So do I."

"You do?"

"Yes. They need you."

Silence. Moments pass, and the logs begin to whither in the fire.

"I called him, by the way." I say.

"Henry?"

"No, no, not Henry. My old friend."

"Oh! So, he'll see you?"

"In a couple of days. On results day in fact."

"Shouldn't you be with your pupils at the school?"

I shake my head. "It doesn't matter Serena."

"They'll probably miss you."

Again I shake my head. "Can't be everywhere. Henry knows, he'll call me with the results in the morning."

"So does he live far away?"

"Well, an hour or so, driving." Then something occurs to me. "Don't stay here alone, Serena. It's almost due and I don't want you to be alone."

"Well, what should I do then Dean?"

We hear a knocking on the door, the sound of youthful laughter and an elderly lady's voice. I frown, but then I realise it's Margaret, telling someone to quieten down. I leave Serena and go to the door.

"Good evening, Dean," she greets me, carrying a tray into the cottage whilst a small boy waddles slowly, unsure of himself, into the room and another, more adventurous type runs screaming towards the fire.

"Hey! Be careful son!" I shout to the older one – must be about five – and he stops dead in his tracks, looks up at me and sticks his tongue out. I laugh.

"Young man!" Margaret scolds, placing the tray down. "Sean, don't be so rude to uncle Dean!" The boy looks crestfallen, for a moment, and then begins some form of break dance on the floor in front of the fire. Meanwhile, the younger one, who must be only two years old, points and laughs at the odd little performance. Then the smaller one stops laughing and simply looks up at me, sweetly, waiting for an instruction.

"Ah, so *that's* Sean!" I say, realising these two are the youngest grandchildren she always speaks of. "And this little one, he must be Allen. Hello, Allen." I put my hand out to him, and he takes it and I feel the delicacy of the shake and tell him he's a perfect little gentleman. Then I stick my tongue out at him. He laughs, and flees to a corner of the room where his brother Sean continues to spin round until he's so dizzy he crumples to the earth. Then he proceeds to drag his head along the floor, making the sounds of a vacuum cleaner. My God. What a lunatic child.

"They're wonderful, Margaret! Why have we never met them before?" Serena laughs, throwing a cushion gently at Sean, who throws it back twice as hard.

Margaret shrugs. "No idea. Timing was never quite right I suppose. Little Allen over there's amazingly well behaved. Never wants. If you need something off him you just make a face as if you're about to cry and he will give you whatever it is. The other one? Well. Bless him. He's an idiot." She removes the cloth from the tray to reveal yet another selection of cakes, and my mouth waters.

"Margaret, we're forever in your debt." I say.

"You always say that, and, young man, it's nonsense, every time! It's just a few snacks to help keep your strength up. How are you both?"

I pause, sensing the pain welling up in my gut. Yet the inane giggling of little Allen seems to keep it at bay. His laughter does not push the pain down, but seems to act as a counterbalance. I frown. "I'm ok. We're ok."

Margaret brings the tray of cakes to rest on the living room table and sits in the arm chair. I return to my wife and she places her arm around me, and speaks. "We thought it would be nice to come and stay here. Feels closer to him somehow. Like he's still with us."

Margaret nods. "Certainly, I understand. He loved this place. And he loved you both very much." We pause for a minute as Sean manages to flip himself up into the air and land awkwardly. Seconds later he's up again and poor little Allen is just watching him with his tongue sticking out. I nod in understanding of their horseplay. Then Margaret speaks again. "You know, it occurred to me that you might want to consider moving here, to the cottage."

Before I can reply, Serena's there. "I'd been thinking that as well, but we haven't talked about it."

I speak. "It never occurred to me, but..." there's a certain beauty in the idea, I think.

We take a moment to let it sink in, and then Margaret speaks again. "It must be due soon, Serena my love, how much time?"

"Gosh - sometime next week if I've got the timing right. Oh, and that reminds me, Dean's going to be away for the day on Thursday – would you mind if I spent the day with you Margaret?"

"Why I'd be delighted! But I can, of course, come over here if you want me to."

"Would you Margaret?" I ask. "I don't want her to be alone."

"Isn't he sweet dear?" The old lady praises. "And just think, he's all yours!"

For a moment I'm overcome by yet another deep sinking feeling as I remember my indiscretion and the forced kiss at the blue café which I found myself telling Serena about only a few days ago. She took it rather well. And then demanded that I never spend any time with *that woman* alone ever again. I humbly apologised for the matter, and again for the whole damn thing. Then I tried my best to forget about it.

Sean wanders past, having just dragged a blanket out from an open cupboard and draped the thing over his head, he makes strange ghost-like sounds whilst Allen stumbles onward obediently behind him, gripping the tail end of the blanket in his tiny fists. He's singing. Then suddenly Allen runs to Serena and gently hugs her fully-grown belly, and I'm rendered speechless. He places his head to one side and closes his eyes in contentment, giggling, sensing his own kind resting within. His eyes suddenly open with a pop and he runs away in shock - the baby kicked. I see Serena's face in profile, her gorgeous round cheeks squeezed up by her smile, her nose wrinkled by her laugh, her eyes wide and full of light. I look to the boys and -

- and the world slows to a crawl as the fire highlights the great bulbous eyes of the youngster, Allen, before me and he smiles yet he seems to be looking right into my soul, as if seeing or perceiving for a moment my deepest desire to be just as free, as innocent, and happy as a child.

"Dean? Are you ok?" Serena asks.

I remain silent, smiling at the boy, our eyes fixed together. I shiver back into consciousness as Serena touches me. "I'm fine" I mutter, but I can see my father seated on the stairs over her shoulder, watching us, silent, expressionless. She takes my hand, yet I am resolute: my eyes will remain dry, I will not cry.

Margaret comes over and gently rubs my shoulder. "Be strong, Dean. We talked about many things, your father and I. We were almost like brother and sister these few years I knew him. He was very proud of you. Very proud of your strength. It inspired him you know. Not only now, but many years ago. You kept him going. When your mother died, it was you who kept him alive and sane Dean." I glance up at her, and for a moment I see my mother as she *could* have been. She continues. "You were and are his son, Dean, and he lived only to see you be happy. That was all that he allowed for himself. That and this home, which I know he would have wanted you to keep as your own. I know he was proud, so very proud, of you *and* your wife, and he spoke of you both so well. Never said anything ill. And he passed away knowing that you would both be alright, knowing that another child was on the way. Those last few days, I'd never seen him so happy. Content. Calm. I miss him too. He was... like a true brother to me. Be strong, young man."

I have no words to offer her in return. She smiles a little and then walks to the door, gathering up her two little ones en route. But just as she is stepping out, Allen, the smaller of the two, runs back up to me and smiles and puts his arms out to me, and how can I not react? How can I not laugh at this, or not be happy? I give him a small hug and somehow the turmoil inside ceases for a brief eternity. I look up and beam at my wife and at Margaret. I let him go. They leave.

As the fire dies down later in the evening the image of a child holding on to me in this quiet little cottage with my wife watching us comes to me and I fall asleep, smoothly, content.

Chapter 47

The boy sat, a thirteen year old, soon to be fourteen, and shifted uncomfortably in his school uniform, and loosened his tie, for it was suffocating him. The lesson over, young Dean breathed deeply as groups of pupils wandered past him, their eyes avoiding his existence.

His friends, Richard and Ajeet, walked past, as did his girlfriend Yasmine, unable to look him in the eye, leaving him alone in that cold ugly school science lab. Dean sat, eyes downcast, at the back of the room as his mentor and teacher tidied away his equipment at the front of the laboratory, his mane of white hair following him about in a slow dance behind his head.

After a moment, Professor Lloyd looked up to the boy and perceived a timeless river flowing across the outpouring gap between them in this room, a distance that it would take decades to cross. Soon he came and placed his hand on Dean's shoulder, and the boy looked up and smiled weakly. Merely weeks ago he had been happy. Joyful. Content. Innocent. Now he sat, silent.

"Hmm…" the professor began, a little unsure, as his ever-moving hair came to rest on his shoulders. "Well done, Dean, on your return to school. I wasn't expecting you back so soon." He paused and Dean did not reply. "Make sure you come and talk to me. Regularly. This -" he gently waves his arm in the air and speaks, slowly. "What has happened. It is like - like losing your final innocence. It will take a long time to understand. It will take time to come to terms with. I am pleased you came back to the school. Listen. You must hold on, Dean, to the things you still have, your father, your friends, your girlfriend, because you have lost immensely. If you can hold on to these things you can retain a sense of purpose. Hold on to it Dean, all of it, everything. Life is full of pain, confusion. But it is full of happiness too and you will feel it again one day. You may even feel innocent again, once day. Don't let go. I can help you stay on course with all your studies, but… everything else is in your hands. You know you can talk to me, any time. Any time you need to. Just come and find me. Anytime at all."

Dean thanked the professor, and left the room, recalling how, many months ago, he and his friends had run down this same corridor for fear of being caught by the Professor after attempting to destroy his lab, and he laughed lightly. But *then the pain returned to him, and he hardened inside and pushed the memory of happiness into a deep pit, as if he were about to bury his old life, his friends and his girlfriend and their foolish laughter, and begin anew.*

He would forget everything. He would not speak of his mother and the burning, smoking, red-glowing embers inside him. He resolved that these things were not for discussion. Yet in doing so, the young boy failed to realise that he delayed his inner peace indefinitely, and that it would be a long, long time, before he even began to understand what had happened to him in this joyful agonising year in his youth. So he disappeared, resolute, silent, around a corridor, and emerged –

- twenty years later, there I was again, at his door, and I noticed a strange beauty to the parity of my life, to this repetition. It felt as if I had returned to rectify something, to bring together an open end from a long time ago, when he had tried to explain the way forward, what to do, what to hold on to. But I just buried it all, the anger and frustration, fury and incomprehension. I shunned his advice, but were it not for his support, his friendship, I would have been finished. So there I was again. Parked outside his home. I knew he would be waiting for me inside. I glanced at my rear view mirror and then quickly looked again, and on my right temple I saw some newly arrived residents huddled together there, thin grey strands of hair, appearing like old men on a park bench sitting, lonely in the cold.

As I stepped up to the door, it opened, and I stopped. An old man, hunched, his strands of hair still long, but thinning, wandering behind him like slivers of smoke, supporting himself heavily on a wooden cane in his right hand, ambled out and lifted his head up to get a view of me, his wrinkles veiling features I had once known so well. My word, he looked so small, so... fragile. Had it really been so long?

"Dean Sekar?" he said, his voice deeper than I recalled, broken, tired - I barely recognised him when I phoned. The mania in his tone had died down, yet he still jerked his head from side to side, as sharply as his now frail neck allowed. "About time. You're late for class young man!" we broke out into a brief laughter and I was warmed by the sight of my old friend, my mentor, my teacher. One breath ago I had been clinging to some childhood romance, looking forward, and the next I was thrashing about in mid-life turmoil, and here before me walked my future. Time looked on at what it had wrought, and it had bent his body, dulled his thought.

Our afternoon began, as we caught up on life events, he told me the story of how he had spent the next ten years since I left the school as its Deputy and then Headmaster of another school, and that how, in the last five years or so, in his retirement, he had been advising the government on education policy, hence his presence at various conferences.

Soon he came to ask me about my last twenty years and I described, briefly, my passage through the best university the land had to offer and how I'd soon grown tired of academia. I told him about Serena, about her laughter, her love of all things that reminded her of childhood, her playing of the flute, her caring for me, her unfathomable way of striking me so deeply, and the way she knew me so well. How, after marrying her, life had been very settled, happy, enjoyable, up until that fateful day of the train crash, where my child was lost, my wife silenced.

I spoke frankly, freely, and at speed, as I knew we had short time and I needed to speak of so many other things: my mistress Jennifer, Serena's ailment, and the experience of drowning in the pool. I told him of the school inspection, the news of the good results we'd achieved – Henry had called me only that morning to let me know.

I mentioned my father's passing.

I told him how the events of the year were prompting me to end my time in teaching. I told him of how my pride was beginning to die. He sat, leaning both his hands atop his cane, and brooded for a moment. Then he spoke. "Do you remember what I called this, Dean? Facing death?"

"You said-" I remembered! "You said it was like the loss of - the loss of your final innocence. The last innocence..."

"You have an excellent memory, young man. I believe I said something like that, yes. I also said that it was possible to regain some of that innocence in your life."

I looked to my feet. "But I don't understand. I don't know. Professor, how can I ever feel 'innocent' again? How can I possibly?"

"You came through this before, Dean, and you did very well."

"But not as well as I *should* have. I should have listened to you instead of shutting my friends out. I let them all go. I lost them all and had to start again. Instead I should have held on tightly to *everything*. You know I - I never spoke of her after those few weeks when she died, and, I wonder why I haven't talked about her, all these years. Some people believe she just left us, my father and I, when I was a kid, and I've never set them straight on this, I just let them believe it. And I never talk about the child Serena and I lost last year.

"It's almost like… I have never accepted either thing. I act as though she never died. Just left. I act as though Serena never miscarried. Just that she was never pregnant. I lie to myself. Now my father's gone the lying must end, and I feel weak, old, older than I am, greyer than I am. Life is so much more intense now than it was the first time, so much more complex."

A beam of light from the window finds its route directly to my eyes and I blink and let the sensation, the afterimage, fade.

I was drowning…

"We all acquire grey hair, Dean, it's just a matter of time. It's a sign of having lived a little. Back then, for someone who was thirteen there wasn't much else anyone could ask of you but to continue at school the best you could. And you did. Be proud of that. I know I am. I know your father was."

"Pride! I'm forgetting how to be proud." And yet something does touch me. I do feel something. Some sense of achievement. But, would she have been proud of me?

"You're forgetting how to be proud? Well, you mustn't allow yourself to feel like that. That way madness, depression and ultimately an untimely death lie before you. Quitting your school, running from the things that you should be proud of, is going to speed you on your way." He said, severe. And I thought - what should I hold on to? This time, I wanted to face the pain, in its entirety, but how would I do that without being consumed by it?

"You don't think I should leave the school? Stop teaching?" I asked, becoming unsure of myself more, and more, as everyone disagreed with me.

"My God man, no!" he swung his cane around. "When the tabloids got hold of Autumn Lane, I had no idea you worked there. I just marvelled at the stupidity of the teachers involved. But then I read the feature in the TES that *you* arranged, and remembered you instantly. There's only one Dean Sekar, I thought. Such a unique name you have. I spoke to the Headmaster, a Mister Lewis? He praised you. And after what you've told me about the inspection, well, you'd be a blithering idiot to leave the profession!" he laughed, but I felt quite hurt. "Dean, Dean, you're forgetting why you are there! Don't you enjoy it?"

"Yes." I said. "Definitely. It has its down points, and on the whole I like teaching, but-"

"Ah! Be quiet. There is *more* to the matter. Listen. Teaching has never been a thing you do solely for yourself. There are your pupils to consider, are there not? Somewhere at your school, regardless of how many idiot thugs attend, there will be someone, some pupil who lacks confidence but wants to try to get somewhere-" a vision of little Edward shoots past my eyes, his bright red scarf flying out behind him "-and that pupil is relying on some tutor to make a connection with him. To encourage him to step out of his shell and to develop. He's waiting for *you* Dean, and the few like you left in our schools. He needs you." I'd never thought of it this way. I noted wryly, that, coupled with the gravitas of his old age, Professor Lloyd was more persuasive than ever.

"But it's up to you, of course. Do as you wish," he stated, crisply.

"You haven't changed. I still can't argue with you."

He smiled at the compliment. "No, not much has changed with me. I still only know what I feel. That is all anyone can ever hope to know. That is our condition." We both paused.

"What do you feel, Sir?"

His eyes went blank as he glanced at his truth from afar. "Simply - that there are moments when it clears. The confusion. It leaves you. And you're content. You understand. It's as if your body is lifted from the earth. Elevated. You're there. But you're not. You feel as if you never were. Nothing matters. You are content. You accept both the joy and pain."

I knew what he was describing. "It was like that, in the pool. I was so content, calm, ready to let go of all things. But they stopped me, saved me. I cried when I came to. I cried because they had taken me away from there. That place, where I felt peace. And I remember laughing. It was so absurd. Senseless. Everything. I don't know what happened to me down there but I remember seeing a brilliant bright light..."

Why had I laughed and cried? The two things seemed so far in reason yet this last year there were times when the line, the thin burning line, was all that had separated one thing, one form of existence, from another, and I kept crossing it, stepping so lightly and easily from one blasted side to another - wife to mistress, calm to rage, joy to pain, life to death, laughter to tears.

The professor took a moment to consider it. "I have known others who came close to death in life. Some of them describe it as being the most humbling, fearful, awful, yet content experience they ever have. Some psychoanalysts believe that when a person loses someone, a parent, a child, a partner, it awakens in them a deep subconscious death wish - an urge to follow those they lost. You've probably been feeling these things on some lower level for many, many years, since your mother died. Maybe you need to explore these issues a little deeper. Who knows what happened to you in the pool? Who knows what these things are or what they mean? I don't know. I am sorry. We must all find our own meanings in life, Dean." He paused and I took a sip of tea.

"What have you found to be your meaning?" I asked, a little disappointed. But then, could I still really expect him to have all the answers? Had I really believed that he would have?

"Well." He smiled, laughed. "I realised that for *me*, the point to all this-" he waved his arm at the room around him, at existence itself. "-is to *be*. Whether the world brings you joy or is burdening your back ceaselessly, all that matters is that you *live* and *be* and keep moving, trying to make or be something more for yourself, and not just existing in some static form, hiding inside, from yourself, from the greater things you could be.

"You know, my wife died, long ago. I have suffered and am also in pain, my daughters see me sometimes but other than that I live alone, yet I'm content now. I intend to remain busy with my work until my time is completely up. I accept painful things and choose still to *live* life, to fight for every last breath, because I have also seen the other side. All that has gone before me, the happiness and sadness, *both* have brought me to my place of calm, now. Contentment. Some of my innocence has been regained, if you like. Now it may take a long time for you to feel happy again, Dean, but *you* hold the key to the healing of your own wounds. You must learn to accept the feeling of senselessness, Dean, and forge on, regardless. Life is full of suffering, Dean. Acceptance, and moving on, are the key to its ending."

There was a deep silence in the room as the elderly gentleman poured me another cup of tea. The end of this conversation seemed to have been reached, and an eerie sense of calm came over me, as if these last few lessons I had come to learn from my old master were the most sacred of all.

Consciously inside I tried to shift myself so that I might observe the pain without burying it – simply to be mindful of it but not to be controlled by it - was this what he meant by acceptance? I allowed myself to continue exploring this new found sensation, on some other level inside, as I asked the Professor a question. "I don't mean to be rude, Professor, but how do you manage? With conferences and the like I mean? You seem -"

"Older? Weaker? Tired-er?" he chuckled. "Watch. Do you remember how we put on a play the year before your mother passed away?" I nodded, he continued. "Well, I learned a great deal about acting when I was younger, you know. I have always loved science but I would get all dry and emotionless unless I did something creative, so watch."

Then suddenly he walked up right in front of me, placed the cane to one side and straightened up, his hunch almost disappearing completely but not quite, he levelled his hair with his hands and then held them together before him and began to speak in a stronger voice, one which I remembered, one which echoed to me through the decades as his wrinkles seemed to evaporate, and his body expand to the fill much of the outline of his former self that I could still perceive as a hazy aura around him.

He began to speak a prepared speech from a conference, but I wasn't listening to the words. It was remarkable - he seemed twenty years younger! Suddenly I was a thirteen year old boy again and this man, my mentor, towered over me and I fit neatly into his shadow and he hadn't aged a day. Then, he stopped. The illusion complete, the towering mentor relaxed, and he disappeared back into the wrinkled older man that was the Professor Lloyd of now. I sat in awe. For a moment I thought I'd returned...

As he shrank he checked his watch and gracefully retrieved his cane. "Oh goodness is that the time? I'll have to say goodbye soon Dean, I have another engagement, but first, come along, I have something which will cheer you up - make you feel young, as you *should* feel."

We moved into another room, a study of sorts, where the light from outside forced itself past the shaking leaves on the trees and created a bright display of movement and shadows on the far wall. The professor went to a number of bookcases along one side of the room and ran his finger along a vast number of large leather spines, and finally selected one, excitedly. I frowned and then I realised what it was. An album of photographs.

He sat on a leather studded armchair and ushered me to sit beside him on a smaller chair, and I remarked that we would forever be teacher and pupil, he and I. He laughed at this, and then suddenly opened the book and began to flick through, and images of pupils, some that I remembered, some not, flew past my eyes, stars of plays and talent shows and other such spectacles arranged by Professor Lloyd, many years ago.

Then he opened up a page, and told me that there were only four photographs he had, but I didn't care if there were no more as I didn't have any at all and I had forgotten that he had ever taken them. I was returned for a moment, to a place where I was once truly innocent.

I looked at each photo in turn. Me, on stage delivering some line to the audience. Then one of the falling set and my attempts to rectify it whilst appeasing the watchers by throwing a one-liner over my shoulder, keeping my cool as the crisis of the moment tested my reserve.

Then a photo of the cast… ghosts… faces… faces I had not seen in a long time. All of us together, on the final night of the performance. But the last picture touched me deepest. A picture taken just before I had performed that night, before I had even changed into my costume.

"My God." I muttered.

The professor smiled, and left the book open on the desk. "I must go soon Dean, but I have one last thing for you." He hunched over his desk, opened his diary, took a piece of paper and copied out what appeared to be an address and phone number, then he folded this and placed it in an envelope and handed it to me. He glanced up at me through his old, old blue eyes and smiled. "You should get in touch with her."

"Who?" I frowned.

"Why, Yasmine, of course."

I laughed. "Yasmine?"

"Every other year or so, she writes to me. I have about fifteen letters from her. She's married now you know. Settled in London. You should go and see her. She asks about you in some of her letters. Wonders what became of you. Until now, I had nothing to tell her. Go and see her, Dean. Reclaim your friendship. Sometimes, we don't lose things outright. We merely put them aside, unresolved, loose and untied, until we're ready to return to them. Ready to face them again."

I couldn't believe it. Two unfinished strands in time came together and seemed to tie. I would go and see her. Take my wife. Meet her husband. Yasmine, my friend of old, who once made me so happy with her leaping and climbing among the trees of the park. For those few days when her and I were together, I had been so happy.

I glanced down at the photo one last time. Four close, caring, friends stood together, laughing, their arms around one another's shoulders. Ajeet, a frail thin boy who's breathing had never cleared; Richard, the small but strong teenager who never did get the hang of chemistry; young Dean, a confident happy child who knew nothing of pain; and, finally, Yasmine, a pretty bespectacled young girl who was the first I had ever felt love for. My friends.

The warm, perfect moment lay frozen in time before me.

And a short while later I was at his door, shaking his hand, thanking him for seeing me, and I thought my father would have looked thus had he made it to seventy four. The sensation of missing my father returned momentarily yet I also had an odd feeling, a revelation, that I had already begun to observe this vast emptiness from further away, from a shifted place at the edge of acceptance.

"Is this really it, Professor?" I asked finally, on my old mentor's doorstep. I hoped not to hear the answer which I already knew would come.

"How so?"

"Everything. The senselessness of it." I looked out through his open door, focussing on the roots of the tree beside his home. They held on, old, twisted, dug-in, clinging dearly to the earth, from where the smell of the soil rose.

"Yes. I'm afraid so. It always has been. It always will be. Acceptance is the key, Dean."

"I'm scared that I can't accept."

"Well, you must seek your own answers now Dean, and find your own meaning. I have no more to teach you my friend, nothing you don't already know. Just don't hide. Don't run away."

He finished our encounter there. I placed Yasmine's details in my jacket pocket and zipped it up, and he ushered me out of his home, waved and then shut the door behind me.

And it felt as if our story had ended, as if our connection belonged to a past we had now finally understood, a chapter we had finally finished writing.

As I walked toward the car, my new phone began to buzz and push past my meditations. I took the call. Moments later, I was back on the

338

motorway, speeding to return home, as the caller had been Margaret, calling to inform me that they'd gone into the hospital, that Serena was having the baby!

Oh God - I had meant to *be* there but it didn't matter, so long as they were ok, both of them, *both* of them! Mother and child! She was having our baby! I pushed down the pedal, the road ahead clear.

"My God..." I muttered.

I was going to be a father…

epilogue

RETURNING

I arrive at the hospital an hour later but there's no one at the desk to buzz us into the delivery suite. I'm pacing up and down the corridor as Margaret tries to reassure me but I'm nervous, on the edge of my life, I've been waiting here a whole five minutes now.

And I don't trust it - I don't trust life.

"Don't worry," Margaret says. "She'll be fine."

"I wish I believed that."

"Relax, Dean. Don't worry. She'll be fine. They'll *both* be fine."

Both of them.

I'm going to be a father.

I pace up and down the dim blue-lit corridor for an eternal minute and the world slows as my heart punches at me and I'm sweating as I notice a doctor approaching the locked doors from inside the suite. He pushes the release button, opens the door with a frown, and I brace myself for bad news.

And then he smiles. He smiles!

"Mr Sekar?" He asks and I nod.

"Congratulations!" He says, shaking my hand, and as we walk, he tells me I now have a healthy baby girl and that my wife is resting comfortably.

I can't believe it.

He opens the door to Serena's room and I glance about and notice a nurse cleaning up. She finishes and leaves and then my wife sees me, tearfully smiling, and I go to her and hold her hand and I see the small, wrapped being in her arms.

"Oh Dean - look at her, she's *beautiful…*" Serena whispers to me. I kiss Serena's forehead and Margaret comes to her side as I lift the child from her arms.

I look at her, the tiny, weightless, miraculous being that is she, and the doctor opens the room blinds and leaves, allowing the amber sunlight in to me, to us. I place my finger against her hand and she grasps it instinctively with her delicate little digits and I laugh, startled.

As she opens her brilliant brown pearl-like eyes I look in and see myself there and I brim with emotion, for as she sees me for the first time somehow I feel she perceives the vast pain inside me and as I place her gently moving tiny form on my shoulder her existence simply seems to fill that painful emptiness within me, closing the painful gap. And yet she's such a tiny, small thing, my little girl. I rock her gently in my arms.

Since my father slept his final sleep that day, I have not cried, but have moved on in silent agony. Even at his funeral my composure held true. But now I cannot hold myself anymore. I cry and laugh all at once, my body shaking. My wife and my neighbour both look on, unsure what to do for me, but soon it subsides as my precious little girl rests her head against me and sleeps, she sleeps, my child, my meaning, my return.

My return to innocence.

Mother... Father...

***

One warm night, our little girl fell asleep, lying between us, but I was restless, and could not sleep with her small wriggling form next to me. I stumbled out of the bed and went to the open window to be alone with the stars and the dark and the breeze.

I sat at my father's desk, bleary eyed, moving unidentified objects aside in the shadows, and lit a candle. I recalled a moment at the hospital, as I stood there on the day she was born. The light from outside had almost faded completely, but then it returned, stronger, and streamed into the hospital chamber undaunted by me and my dying furies.

Sometimes the light would do this to me, it would catch me standing unawares, and everything would be clear, like it was when I floated free, in water, and it's as if I never was, as if my whole existence had been a nothing and that I was obliterated in those rays, for all eternity, tasting something and nothing behind the thinness of it all, the frailty of us, our being. I stood, rocking her, and the amber warmth ran a cold blue shiver down my spine as I turned my back on all those senseless questions that I would never be able to answer. I was so peaceful. Calm. Content.

I returned my gaze to the desk. I looked out of the window. Leaves in the dark spoke to me, comforting me with their cool yet warming whispers in the twilight. I took up my father's old fountain pen and felt the small etches of his engraved name on its cold, solid metal side, a gift to him from my mother, decades old. I wrote my name on some paper, slowly, allowing the ink to flow in and dry. It was as if I had no power over it, as if I felt compelled to write.

I stopped, glanced back at the bed and saw my wife, curled in the dark, a thin outline of shadow, lying like the child that had once been inside her, the little girl she now slept beside.

I wrote, slowly, letting the ink flow, for I could not stop it.

'When foetal lie I,
Return I to my mother.
There am I safe, warm.'

Reading in the unsteady candlelight, I turned my head slightly as recognition of the form came to me. I smiled, and penned the title 'Haiku to Mother' above it, with a thick, bold, underline stroke. I paused. And then, further below on the page, I wrote four more words, just as true:

'I forgive you, Dad.'

Then I went and joined my wife and baby, and we slept deeply together like children, innocent, oblivious, and at peace, as the candle was blown out by the breeze.

Printed in Great Britain
by Amazon